T0196204

Written Education Induced Schizophrenia

Volume XVI

BY: TODD ANDREW ROHRER

iUniverse, Inc.
New York   Bloomington

Written Education Induced Schizophrenia
Volume XVI

iUniverse books may be ordered through booksellers or by contacting:

iUniverse
1663 Liberty Drive
Bloomington, IN 47403
www.iuniverse.com
1-800-Authors (1-800-288-4677)

ISBN: 978-1-4502-2921-0 (sc)
ISBN: 978-1-4502-2922-7 (ebk)

Printed in the United States of America

iUniverse rev. date: 04/28/2010

A man had an accident.

He lost his sense of time and emotional capacity.

This is his sixteenth attempt to communicate since the accident.

The scribes celebrate the birth of the lights in the season of death and the death of the lights in the season of birth.

2/21/2010 7:04:23 AM – The worst of times is the best time most of the time. Wisdom questions what tyranny demands. Maturity has to do with forgetting age not calculating it. No one is responsible for their age and age does not make one responsible. When one stops questioning they stop learning and then they start settling. Wisdom is relative to how much you seek to know. Understanding a detail is not as important as understanding the concept the details suggest. The concept the details suggest is the most important detail. Reason without ambiguity is dangerous. A friend to all has many enemies. A friend is hard to control and friendship is hard to let go of. All cities have wealth yet few cities have worth. Without wisdom, knowledge is just data. Most get paid for what they do because they don't get paid for what they think. All paying jobs corrupt the mind. True living is not work so no one works for a living. Honesty is a policy only the fearless can afford. Grief will either enrich you or enrage you. Bravery is achieved when fear is overlooked. Everyone has the nerve to become something but few have the nerve to be nothing. What you do is relative to what you think and what you think is relative to what you perceive. What you seek is more important than how much you seek. The ocean is not deep when you are on the bottom. Awakening is rude for all. Speaking your mind is more important than being accepted because acceptance at the price of censorship is slavery.

2/22/2010 9:22:47 AM - "All national institutions of churches, whether Jewish, Christian or Turkish, appear to me no other than human inventions, set up to terrify and enslave mankind, and monopolize power and profit."
- Thomas Paine

None of the large religious establishments are anything but profit machines used to scare people, the ones that sense time who are prone to fear, out of their money. If a religious institution does not speak of the tree of knowledge, written education, and in turn the remedy to the neurosis caused by it, the fear not remedy or variations of that, they are false and are to be avoided.

"Be kind, for everyone you meet is fighting a hard battle." – Plato

After one applies the remedy their purpose is not to be kind to the ones that sense time, the ones fighting the hard battle, their purpose is to push them down to the ninth circle of hell, treason because only in the circle of treason can one deny their self and thus escape hell, the neurosis state of mind caused by written education. The only way you get better after you apply the remedy is to experiment because you will be in the machine state. So as you experiment with your testimony you ponder the results and get better at your testimony. Be mindful you did not put the ones that sense time in hell, the neurosis; society put them in hell, your only purpose to assist them to escape and that and the door is in the 9th circle of hell, treason which denotes treason against their self which is what "deny yourself" means. The remedy relative to Socrates understanding was no true philosopher fears death so if one that has applied the remedy is running around being kind to people they will never be able to convince the people to face their fear of perceived death and thus "wake up" or escape the neurosis; the place of suffering, hell; the extreme left brain state caused by getting the written education as a child.

The rule of thumb is "Do unto others as you would have them do unto you." What this means is after you apply the fear not remedy and escape the neurosis caused by written education being pushed on you as a child you are obligated to saying anything you are compelled to say no matter how much it may hurt the feelings of the ones in the neurosis because if you were still in the neurosis you would want them to do the same. The ones that sense time are still in neurosis so their emotions are at very abnormally high levels anyway so if one goes around attempting to not hurt anyone's feelings by avoiding telling them they are in neurosis they will only deny their understandings. The beings in neurosis firstly do not know they are in neurosis and because of that they wish to stay in neurosis because they perceive it is normal so considering their feelings is not relevant to this situation. You did not put them in neurosis, society that pushed the education on them before their mind was developed did, your only obligation is to say what you are compelled to say to convince them to apply the remedy so they can escape neurosis and their feelings about what you say are not important because they are neurotic.

Neurotic: relating to, involving, affected by, or characteristic of a mild psychiatric disorder characterized by depression, anxiety, or hypochondria. Simply put they are mentally and thus emotionally anxious and thus mentally depressed. They are suffering because their right brain traits are in the subconscious state so one cannot allow that reality to interfere with one example to them what the education has done to them. They will resist and mock you and spit on you and call you everything in the universe but that is logical because they cannot think well in that neurotic state. You assume the machine state with the understanding they are not going quietly.

The fact you tell them their neurosis is evident because they do sense time and that aspect proves their right brain paradox is veiled, so that proves they are mentally unsound, is going to hurt their feelings because they are in neurosis and they cannot face reality well, so if you attempt to speak with the understanding you do not ever want to hurt their feelings, all you are going to do is be manipulated by them and you are going to censor your words so their abnormally high emotions are not infringed upon so being kind in your words is going to accomplish nothing. The rule of thumb is when you upset them and make them angry with your words you are on the right track because their anger or depression may push them down to the 9th circle of hell, treason and that is where you want to push them so they have a chance to apply the "deny yourself" or "fear not" remedy. You apply the remedy and assume the machine state and let them be destroyed by their emotions because of what you suggest relative to the remedy and the reason for the remedy. They are mentally unsound and you are not mentally unsound after you apply the remedy so treat them accordingly. You would want them to attempt to wake you up if the roles were reversed.

[1 Peter 5:14 Greet ye one another with a kiss of charity. Peace be with you all that are in Christ Jesus. Amen.]

This comment is relative only to ones who have applied the remedy, the kindred, the ones with no sense of time. This does not apply to the ones that do sense time for they are of the adversary. The deep reality of this situation is if you enforce or support or praise the ones in neurosis; the ones that sense time; they will never apply the remedy and if you do not do that they may go to the 9th circle of hell, treason and instead of applying the remedy their depression may get the better of them and they may literally "check out". The bottom line is you did not put them in that neurosis state the written education taught to them as children did, and that means if they remain in the neurotic state they are going to in one way or another harm everything they "touch" because they are mentally unsound and thus mentally non viable in that state of mind. This is no task for the weak minded so if you determine you are weak minded then you have not applied the remedy the full measure.

[James 3:18 And the fruit of righteousness is sown in peace of them that make peace.]

The ones that are at peace are the ones with no sense of time, they are of sound mind and are at peace because they can reason properly. They push ones that sense time into the 9th circle of hell, treason, and if that being survives that they escape hell and return to sound mind, unveil right brain, and in turn return to peace (harmony) mindfully. The "righteous" ones with right brain unveiled fully must convince their own fellow human beings in neurosis to defeat their fear of death on an absolute scale with the understanding the vast majority may defeat their fear of death literally once they are in a mindset of "submission" which is required to apply the remedy to the full measure; a mental state of meekness.

[Luke 12:51 Suppose ye that I am come to give peace on earth? I tell you, Nay; but rather division:]

[Nay; but rather division:] This comment is saying, if you go around after you apply the remedy and pretend everything is just fine it only proves you are afraid and need to apply the remedy until you have absolutely no fear. There are only two kinds of human beings on this planet. Ones that sense time which are the ones mentally hindered by the education and ones that do not sense time, ones of sound mind who have applied the remedy after getting the education the full measure, there are tribes that have no contact with civilization that have no written education or math so they have no sense of time or never got the neurosis but their numbers are marginal. The ones that sense time know not what they do and so they perceive mentally hindering the children the same way they were hindered is righteous and proper because they know not what they do and the ones with no sense of time attempt to stop them. That is the division the tree of knowledge as caused in our species.

"Be kind, for everyone you meet is fighting a hard battle." – Plato

Socrates main concept was no true philosopher fears death which is the remedy. Plato was his student, one of the youth Socrates was alleged to have corrupted, so to speak. This comment is good example of why words do not work. Plato is saying everyone got the education and they are in neurosis so they are trying to break free of the neurosis so be kind to them because they are fighting a hard mental battle. This means do not physically harm them but when everything is said and done one will never convince ones that sense time to seek the shadow of death and then fear not if they just tell them how wonderful they are.

This comment is Plato speaking about the trial of Socrates, his teacher, in Socrates Defense document.

"But far more dangerous are these, who began when you were children, and took possession of your minds with their falsehoods, telling of one Socrates, a wise man, who speculated about the heaven above, and searched into the earth beneath, and made the worse appear the better cause."

[who began when you were children, and took possession of your minds with their falsehoods,] This comment is of course relative to written education and it is not very kind yet still true. Plato is insulting the ones who brought charges against Socrates, the scribes.

[and took possession of your minds with their falsehoods]

Who took possession of your mind? The ones that sense time, the scribes. What is their falsehood? If you get all the reading, writing and math education as a child you will be wise, that is a lie, a falsehood. Because your frontal lobe does not develop until you are twenty all that left brain favoring education only makes you wise if you definition of wise is mentally hindered beyond my ability to explain in infinite books and perhaps beyond the vast majorities ability to fully negate on an individual level.

[Luke 12:51 Suppose ye that I am come to give peace on earth? I tell you, Nay; but rather division:]

This comment mentions the division the written education has created in our species.
Before written language and math there was no invention or method that would alter the mind or favor one hemisphere over the other to the degree written education does and this is largely in part due to this reality.

"In humans, the frontal lobe reaches full maturity around only after the 20s, marking the cognitive maturity associated with adulthood" - Giedd, Jay N. (October 1999). "Brain Development during childhood and adolescence: a longitudinal MRI study". Nature neuroscience 2 (10): 861-863.

The education was taught to children yet a child's mind does not develop until they are at least 20 and so this is what created this division of perceptions in the species.

X = the mental perception of a human being before written education and math, no sense of time perception dimension

Y = the mental perception of a human being after written education and math was invented, sense of time perception dimension.

So X was the norm before written education and math simply because there was no other condition or situation where the mind of a child could be altered to where they favored left hemisphere so greatly and at a young age that the mind and thus perception could be altered. The point being that the written education and math if taught only to a person over the age of twenty would perhaps not alter their mind and thus perception as greatly because the mind is developed at the age of 20ish.

So it is a combination of the fact the written education favors left brain and the fact it is taught to a child when they are very young in their mental development and also many rewards, peer pressure aspects are attached to it and also contact with others who have said neurosis and this combination is what alters the perception of the child. Because of this it is not so much the education as it is the circumstances in which it is taught and in this case when taught to a child starting at the age of seven when that child's mind does not develop until they are twenty there is a major effect on their mental development and thus perception and cognitive abilities. On top of this because the child is taught the education at such a young age their mind is altered but they are not even aware of it. Simply put the child's mind is in X state and the education is taught to them starting at the age of seven but the mind does not develop until the age of twenty so by the time that child is twenty they should still be in X state of mind but they are not because the education has altered their minds development and thus perception but that child cannot tell because the mind altering is very subtle and drawn out over a long period of time.

Without written education or before written education the entire species was in X state of mind. After written education there was a small group of humans who were known as scribes and they were in the Y state of mind. The complexity here is the very first people that learned written education were perhaps taught it after they were twenty so there did not appear to be any major unwanted mental side effects. So the very first group of human beings that learned math and written education were perhaps not affected by it mentally very much at all so they were still in X state of mind to a degree but then as time went on children were taught these inventions and that is when the mind altering started to happen because the mind is not developed until one is twenty and that is when the perception division started happening. So it is a situation where the adults learned these inventions and did not notice any bad side effects and so they taught it to their children and that is where the mental side effects started happening.

"A good decision is based on knowledge and not on numbers. "
Plato

On one level numbers are relative to money in this comment and on another level numbers is relative to math. Mathematics is left brain based so it encourages left brain so the better one is at math the more their right brain is veiled. The easy way to look at math is, math is based on parts and judgments and right brain is based on holistic aspects and is a poor judge or is not prejudice. So for example when you hear a person say "We do not have enough money in the budget to do that." They are making decisions based on numbers. The ones that sense time base perhaps everything on numbers and numbers are relative to money directly or indirectly so the ones that sense time make few decisions based on knowledge and so the ones that sense time make few good decisions. Look at it like this, if by chance one day I come up with some sort of convincing argument relative to the fact this written education does hinder the mind of a child the governments will not make a decision based on that knowledge and adjust education methods because the numbers, the money they will need to compensate all the people who were mentally hindered will sink them, so to speak. How will a person that has been in depression for years and years be compensated if I am able to show that depression itself is simply a symptom the right brain random access aspects have been veiled by the written education that person got as a child, so they would not be able to be depressed if that education had been taught properly. How will a mother be compensated for her son or daughter that killed their self as a result of depression? How will a person be compensated when they apply the fear not remedy and unveil right brain and realized their entire cerebral life was robbed from them? The governments are going to factor all those "numbers' and realize it is best not to tell anyone about the damage caused by traditional education because they can't afford the piper, so to speak. The deeper reality is the common people voted to push the education on all the children because it was pushed on them so they did this to their self. The blind leading the young into blindness is one way to look at it.

This man won a Nobel prize for his work in neurobiology. He said as plain as day.

X = "What it comes down to is that modern society discriminates against the right hemisphere." - Roger Sperry (1973) Neurobiologist and Nobel Lauriat

Y = "In humans, the frontal lobe reaches full maturity around only after the 20s, marking the cognitive maturity associated with adulthood" - Giedd, Jay N. (october 1999). "Brain Development during childhood and adolescence: a longitudinal MRI study". Nature neuroscience 2 (10): 861-863.

Z = " If you reflect back upon our own educational training, we have been traditionally taught to master the 3 R's: reading, writing and arithmetic -- the domain and strength of the left brain" -
The Pitek Group, LLC.
Michael P. Pitek, III

A = extreme left brain mental state neurosis caused by Y and Z
B = The remedy to negate A

Because of Y, education which is Z hinders the mind of the children and that is why X was suggested.
One obvious symptom of this mental hindering is the being has a very strong sense of time because the paradox aspect in right hemisphere no longer factors into the beings perception of time, hunger, fatigue, pain and taste to name a few.
When right brain is at 50% or in mental harmony with left hemisphere after the remedy to the education, tree of knowledge, is applied when the being thinks "how much time has passed?" the paradox aspect of right brain in the conscious state of mind says "Time has pass and no time has passed" and that is the minds final answer so one has no sense of time and this is what is known in ancient myths as the fountain of youth. The body reacts to the fact the mind does not sense time so stress and many other aspects that are relative to time are greatly reduced because a mind that is sound does not sense time. So one can understand how vast the mental damage of written education is on the species if one just asks people if they sense time, and if they say yes it is factual proof the paradox aspect of their right hemisphere and thus their right hemisphere traits are veiled so

greatly by the traditional education the right brain traits have been reduced to a subconscious state all together.

The devastating point is what one has to do to fully undo that damage caused by Z. This situation relative to Z + Y + X = A is like finding out you have stage four cancer and finding out what caused it but that is little consolation because the remedy that undoes A is very harsh and because it is very harsh many beings that have A simply are no longer mentally able to apply the remedy, B. It is very similar to a Doctor telling a patient "You have stage four cancer so we are going to give you chemotherapy and that alone may kill you but it may also save you." So the remedy (B) relative to the cure for (A) brings one mentally to the edge of death, the shadow of death, and then when they get there they allow it. If that does not sound very dangerous to you in your big sense of time state of mind it certainly should. It should concern you that you have to seek the shadow of death and then when it arrives you submit and fear not and lose your life mindfully just so you can negate the damage all those years of traditional education did to your mind.

No matter who you are, you are not above this reality:

Y = "In humans, the frontal lobe reaches full maturity around only after the 20s, marking the cognitive maturity associated with adulthood".

You started this education :

Z = " If you reflect back upon our own educational training, we have been traditionally taught to master the 3 R's: reading, writing and arithmetic -- the domain and strength of the left brain", at the age of six or seven and perhaps even started earlier.

Because you started that left brain favoring education when you were very young and because of this reality [the frontal lobe reaches full maturity around only after the 20s] there is no possible way you could be anything but mentally unsound and thus you have to apply the remedy or you will forever be mentally unsound and thus a threat to yourself and all of those around you, including children, including your own children.

An easier way to look at it is when you are born you are just like a brand new fetus and when you are 20 you are ready to be born, a mature fetus, mentally. So because the education was pushed on you at the age of seven, it is the same thing as if a pregnant mother has lots of mind altering drugs given to her when the fetus is in the first trimester. Simply put it will ruin the fetus' development.

So you were in the womb for nine months and then you were born but you were not mentally developed because [the frontal lobe reaches full maturity around only after the 20s] so instead of allowing you to develop society pushed this on you [: reading, writing and arithmetic -- the domain and strength of the left brain] and that factually affected your mental development. Because of this, it is impossible you could be of sound mind relative to left and right hemisphere giving equal signals; in fact your right hemisphere aspect is reduced to a subconscious aspect so the easiest way to look at it is your mind is like a crescent moon.
The left hemisphere signals are the dark signals on the moon and they cover the whole moon except for a small little area of light and that is your right hemisphere traits. So the bottom line of civilization is, once in a while a human being that gets the traditional education, starting at the age of seven or so negates the neurosis and wakes up and then they have an obligation to attempt to explain it to the rest of the species methods to try an undo the mental damage caused by the tree of knowledge which is traditional education, which is [reading, writing and arithmetic -- the domain and strength of the left brain].
My main purpose is not to wake you up because for the vast, vast majority the mental damage is irreversible because the being is totally convinced their perception after the education is normal so they only know this abnormal perception after the years of education so they are unable to apply the remedy because they do not even perceive they need to, so they are what is known as their own worst enemy. Your laws and rules and morals say it is proper to mentally hinder children although in your state of mind you do not realize that is what they say, it is called compulsory education law. I am mindful the ones that spoke about the dangers of the tree of knowledge in the ancient texts attempted war and attempted peace to sort this problem out and they all failed at the end of the day; they did not

convince civilization written education and math has devastating mental consequences on the minds of the children. My main purpose is to tell people the remedy as a form of testimony; I testify I accidentally negated the mental neurosis; and some perhaps apply the remedy and "wake up" and then you have another person whose purpose is to testify and the main purpose is to stop the ones that sense time, the scribes, from mentally hindering the children, the life spring of the species. I create warriors by telling them the remedy and then they understand the remedy and can explain it to others and they create warriors whose sole purpose is to stop the ones that sense time, the scribes, from mentally hindering the children. Our species is a house divided because we invented this written education which hindered the mind and we ignored the beings in the ancient texts requests to apply the fear not remedy, keep the covenant, after the education so the right hemisphere does not remain veiled. Whether the ones that sense time want to look at it like supernatural or whether they want to look at it from a natural point of view at the end of the day, the ones that sense time, the scribes are mentally harming innocent children and it is proper to attempt to stop them no matter what laws say contrary to that. The complexity is I accidentally negated the education induced neurosis and unveiled my right hemisphere traits and because of the extreme processing power and pattern detection I was able to look back on the accident and figure out exactly what happened so I can explain how the remedy can be applied and I also can explain why the remedy should be applied and these are facts and truth but in telling this truth civilization will perhaps go to war because they will not be able to argue with what I explain and so civilization perhaps will divide itself on two sides. There will be the ones who apply the remedy and take up the purpose to defend the children, and then there will be the ones who mock the remedy and continue to mentally hinder the children. The deeper reality is I can explain the remedy and how to apply it but I cannot determine how a person is going to react after they apply the remedy and unveil their right hemisphere. Some become militants and some become far more dedicated and they write books and explain it to a vast audience or become orators. Relative to my perception I am explaining how I accidentally reversed the damage caused by all that left brain education pushed on me as a child and relative to your perception I am assisting mankind in understanding the definition of the Red Sea.

Relative to my perception I am doing a service to people by explaining how they can regain their full mind after the education has hindered it and relative to you I am perhaps the most dangerous human being on the planet.

I am pleased if this is a lie: (X)[modern society discriminates against the right hemisphere.].

I am pleased if this is a lie: (Y)[the frontal lobe reaches full maturity around only after the 20s].

I am pleased if this is a lie: (Z)[reading, writing and arithmetic -- the domain and strength of the left brain], because then I am just writing infinite books that have no meaning and will not affect the species at all but if those comments are fact, then we are perhaps going to war against each other.

If Z is true and Y is true then X is true.

If Y is true and X is true then Z is true.

I decided early after the accident to go with the flow and what that means is I am completely upfront in everything I am thinking and no matter what happens as a result of that I am willing to accept it. I am not afraid of anything you are afraid of, is another way to look at it.

I want you to understand no matter what happens I should be this:

[S. V. (19) committed suicide by taking a deadly cocktail of antidepressants].

Since I should be that, I have determined it is best I go with the flow, so to speak.

What that means is I reached the 9th circle of hell treason, suicidal, and after being there for so long I finally got the nerve to not only take lots of pills but when I started to show signs of dying I let go. I was fully awake and showing signs of overdose and my mind said "You will die if you do not call for help" and I said to my mind "I do not care." So because of this there is nothing in this universe than can scare me or make me afraid because I was not afraid of death itself because my amygdala remembers I gave that answer and will no longer allow my hypothalamus to give me false fight or flight signals. No being is in front of with a threatening intent so I have no fear. What I write about may lead some to be afraid or some may be afraid to write these words and publish them on a world stage but that is not a literal actual threatening aspect. One may to look at it is I have no fear until I need to be afraid, when actual threats are encountered not perceived threats, like shadows.

Society is based on fear tactics. "You do this or this bad thing will happen to you.", "You do as we say or we will kill you or lock you in jail.", "You fall in line and follow the rules or we will punish you and you will regret not following our rules." My mind continues to remind me "You are not afraid of death ignore those fear tactics." So when I hear these fear tactics they do not work on me anymore. Neurologically speaking, I took these pills and they were not important they were just a catalyst that encouraged my hypothalamus to give me the fight or flight signal and in this case I perceived I was going to die so the hypothalamus was giving me the death signal, the maximum signal it can give, and when I ignored the signal the amygdala remembered that and it will never forget that so I am totally immune to fear tactics or pseudo fear. Because I am not yet warmed up, I am not use to this fearless state of mind, called consciousness, so I attempt to write things that I perceive I am afraid to write and publish them on a world stage just to see if after I publish them I will sense fear and I never do in part because I do not remember the details of what I write only the concepts. I do not remember exactly what I write but I am certain I am attempting to explain I woke up from the neurosis caused by the tree of knowledge, written education and math and attempting to explain the remedy to that neurosis. Everything else is just a detail and right brain or a being in sound mind is more concepts or parable focused and less detail focused. I am not anal retentive anymore, so to speak and thus I do not get flustered. This mental harmony state of mind is really a state of mind where the mind is fully aware one has to die one day and so no decision is made based on fear of death. If "society" around me was gone I could still go out into nature and live off the land because right brain, the god image in man, is able to assist me to determine how to survive on my own in nearly any situation with its vast pattern detection, intuition and lightning fast random access processing. Because fear is relative to panic and mental clarity is relative to concentration, when the fear is gone from the mind, concentration is optimum. I would stop reading now if I were you.
Without failure one is unable to detect patterns of victory.

2/25/2010 1:44:51 PM -

Relative to mammals females are the keepers of the offspring and men are aspects that assist them in that purpose. So we have written education and math, the tree of knowledge. These common proven facts explain a lot.

X ="In humans, the frontal lobe reaches full maturity around only after the 20s, marking the cognitive maturity associated with adulthood"

Y = [we have been traditionally taught to master the 3 R's: reading, writing and arithmetic -- the domain and strength of the left brain.]

Z = "What it comes down to is that modern society discriminates against the right hemisphere." - Roger Sperry (1973) - neuropsychologist, Nobel laureate

Because of X , Y mentally hinders the right brain which is what Z is suggesting.

So the tree of knowledge harms the offspring because it is taught to them in the first trimester of their mental development age six or seven, they don't develop fully until they are twenty, mentally, so education is like a mental abortion, it ruins the offspring. The women in the ancient texts did not take kindly to that because they are protectors of the offspring and that is why women traditionally were the last of the species to get written education, not because they are dumb but because if they get the "curse" the offspring will get it also. So the women sent the men who applied the fear not remedy to the tree of knowledge out to do battle with the scribes, the ones who pushed the education on the offspring. The women wanted to protect all the offspring because that is their purpose and that is what this comment is talking about.

[1 Samuel 18:7 And the women answered one another as they played, and said, Saul hath slain his thousands, and David his ten thousands.]

The women are the protectors of the offspring and they sent out Saul and David to protect all the offspring from the tree of knowledge. I do not expect many males will be able to relate to that reality but perhaps some females will be able to relate to that reality.

The story of medusa. Medusa's head is death, so one looks at death and then turns to stone or unveils right brain and goes into machine mode which means their emotions go back down to normal levels and they return to sound mind, or in the now. Same principle as "seek the shadow of death and then fear not". Both are remedies to the tree of knowledge, written education. Many are controlled by their fear and thus their ill functioning hypothalamus.

2/26/2010 7:59:51 AM –

When written education was invented there were not very many people who were taught it so what happened was there was a type of cult called scribes. These beings were paid well because at that time not many people knew how to scribe. Relative to the west script was invented 5400 years ago.

Samarian script is the earliest script but avoid focusing on details. It is understood women did not get the script and this line in the ancient texts reveals that.

[Genesis 6:2 That the sons of God(ones who applied the remedy, ones with no sense of time) saw the daughters of men(men = scribes, ones with a sense of time, ones who ate off the tree and did not apply the fear not remedy) that they were fair; and they took them wives of all which they chose.]

[saw the daughters of men.were fair] means they did not get the curse, did not have their right brain veiled..... [and they took them wives]

So the curse caused by the tree of knowledge, right brain traits being veiled, is relative to this comment:

[Genesis 3:14 And the LORD God said unto the serpent, Because thou hast done this, thou art cursed above all cattle,] [serpent,] a scribe, one who gets the education and does not apply the remedy so they have right brain veiled and thus are mentally unsound and no longer act like mammals or humans.

[Because thou hast done this] = ate off the tree of knowledge..

[thou art cursed above all cattle,} = why is one cursed?

Because:

1. [we have been traditionally taught to master the 3 R's: reading, writing and arithmetic -- the domain and strength of the left brain.]

So this is clearly left brain favoring.

2. ="In humans, the frontal lobe reaches full maturity around only after the 20s, marking the cognitive maturity associated with adulthood"

All this means is a left brain favoring invention is pushed on a child before their mind is even close to developing and then rewards and punishments (grades) are attached to it, and then money and promises of an easy life are attached to it.

So, think about these two comments.

[Genesis 2:17 But of the tree of the knowledge of good and evil, thou shalt not eat of it: for in the day that thou eatest thereof thou shalt surely die.]

[Genesis 3:4 And the serpent said unto the woman, Ye shall not surely die:]

[tree of the knowledge of good and evil,] Good and evil is seeing things as parts, a left brain trait. God see's everything as good or as one thing [Genesis 1:10 And God called the dry land Earth; and the gathering together of the waters called he Seas: and God saw that it was good.]

[called he Seas] is out of sequence should be [he called seas] so it is a sign post of authenticity, that aspect of the sentence is in random access, a right brain trait.

God see's everything as good or as one thing is a holistic perception and a trait of right brain or of a sound mind because right brain traits rule when the mind is at 50/50 and holistic outlook is a right brain trait.

So [Gen 2:17] is a comment by a being that has applied the remedy saying there are some problems with written education, the tree of knowledge, it alters your perception , it alters your mind and thus your spirit.

Then Gen 3:4 is a scribe, one that is cursed, saying, no there is no problem with the tree of knowledge.= [Genesis 3:4 And the serpent said unto the woman, Ye shall not surely die:]

Because of this reality:

: "In humans, the frontal lobe reaches full maturity around only after the 20s, marking the cognitive maturity associated with adulthood"

There is no way ever into infinity you can tell this education has had a bad side effect on your mind until after you apply the remedy because it started when you were seven and your mind was not even developed until you were 20. The only possible way you could have of knowing this happened to you is if someone woke up or negated this "curse" and was then able to give you symptoms of it, because they have contrast , they once were blind but now they see, they once were lost but now are found. Simply put, faith is having trust all this left brain favoring education pushed on you before your mind was developed veiled your right hemisphere aspects to a degree. If it even veiled right brain traits one degree your mind is unsound. A house, mind, divided cannot stand. The reality is, the right hemisphere aspects were veiled so much, ones perception is altered.

Simply put, because you perhaps doubt what I suggest relative to this written education, it proves your right brain intuition is veiled, because there are no people on this planet who have applied this remedy to a degree that I have spoken to since the accident that argue with what I suggest, other words, they know it because of intuition, and that is "soul", they are mindful of what happened to them. I am the new kid on the block and there are many far more along than I am perhaps. So you are relying on left brain simple linear aspects and that means you have to be told what to do, and that means your entire logic thread is perhaps this:

"My leaders have not told me written education hindered my right hemisphere traits so it has not", because you have silenced right brain intuition and so you cannot think for yourself.

Secondly your sense of time proves your right brain paradox is veiled so much it no longer even factors into your perception, and thus you have a strong sense of time. It is medically understood people with right brain leaning thoughts do not perceive time well. Ones who go the full measure with the remedy do not perceive time at all mindfully.

Your logic perhaps is left brain sequential and thus simple minded linear and so you cannot imagine that written education hindered your mind because your whole world perception would be shattered, so you resist it. All I can suggest is, I am an accident and accidentally applied the deny yourself, fear not remedy and it has only been 15 months, and I am fully mindfully aware the spirit of what I suggest is fact but I am also aware, I had no idea the tree of knowledge was written education 15 months ago.

Remember Jesus spoke to 5000 and only 12 followed him. It is not popular to tell people the education they got as a child mentally destroyed them. Isn't that interesting, Jesus spoke to 5000 and he did not end up with 5000 disciples. Relative to what you have been taught, all Jesus was saying is , I am God or Believe in god. If that is all he was saying he would have had more than 12 disciples. Who was he being mocked by?

[Matthew 27:41 Likewise also the chief priests mocking him, with the scribes and elders, said,]
[mocking him, with the scribes]

[Mark 1:22 And they were astonished at his doctrine: for he taught them as one that had authority, and not as the scribes.]
[for he taught them as one that had authority, and not as the scribes.]

Who is a scribe?

Anyone on this planet that got taught written education as a child and did not apply the fear not remedy so they are very adept at script, reading, writing and that includes math. You have to do math using a pen, and you have to write using a pen.

[Jeremiah 8:8 How do ye say, We are wise, and the law of the LORD is with us? Lo, certainly in vain made he it; the pen of the scribes is in vain.]
[the pen of the scribes is in vain.]

A scribe knows how to use written language and math but it cost them their right brain traits so they did not become wise they became mentally hindered.

[How do ye say, We are wise,] = You cannot possibly be wise if your right brain traits are hindered unless your definition of wise is factually mentally hindered and that is the definition of retarded.

Hindered: to delay or prevent the development or progress of somebody or something.

Delay: to impede the process or progress of; retard; hinder

What did that education and math delay? Your mental development.

Why? [In humans, the frontal lobe reaches full maturity around only after the 20s] + [the 3 R's: reading, writing and arithmetic -- the domain and strength of the left brain.] = Mentally hindered, delayed.

Simply put you are a scribe and you have to apply the deny one's self, fear not remedy and all your arguments into infinity will never change that fact. You need to stop trying to reason to the contrary because you are only capable of simple minded sequential left brain processing. You need to drop your nets and apply the remedy firstly. You need to seek the kingdom, right brain, the god image in man, first and then when right brain unveils all of this will make sense to you or will be added unto you.

[Luke 9:23 And he said to them all, If any man will come after me, let him deny himself, and take up his cross daily, and follow me.]

[If any man will come after me, let him deny himself,] Does this mean deny yourself a tiny bit, or deny yourself the full measure? If you do not understand the proper answer is deny yourself the full measure you should allow me to do your thinking for you and you just do exactly what I say because you are a scribe and that means you are your own worst enemy on every scale imaginable because you got the snake and that means your cognitive ability is "delayed" because cognitive ability is relative to the frontal lobe.

[Genesis 3:14 And the LORD God said unto the serpent, Because thou hast done this, thou art cursed]

Because you got written education your right brain is veiled and so you are the serpent because the god image in man, right brain, is dead in you, so you are wise to allow me to tell you what to do to get that serpent off your back. All the money in the universe is not going to get that serpent off your back so you now understand money means nothing, but if you wish you can try rubbing money on your head to see if you lose your sense of time and can remove that sense of time "mark" from your head.

This comment is important to focus on:

[Luke 17:33 and whosoever shall lose his life shall preserve it.]

If you go to a spooky place alone at night and your mind says "run like the wind or you will certainly die" and you say "No I won't run, I fear not" you deny yourself the full measure and thus you lose your life mindfully and thus preserve or restore your right hemisphere traits to a conscious state, and thus you find the kingdom. It takes about 30 days for it to fully restore and from then on out I cannot assist you and you are on your own because then you enter the battle. I recruit you into the battle by suggesting the remedy but after you join the battle you become a general, so to speak.

I will make this very clear. This remedy is not a game and once you apply it you will understand there are is no such thing as games in this narrow.

Game: an activity that people participate in, together or on their own, for fun.

Simply put you do not apply this remedy for fun. That's a nice way of saying from where I sit the armies of Goliath, the scribes, are vast.

[Mark 1:13 And he was there in the wilderness forty days, tempted of Satan; and was with the wild beasts; and the angels ministered unto him.]

After 30 days or so right brain will come online and it will minister to you: [forty days, tempted of Satan; and was with the wild beasts; and the angels ministered unto him.]

That means right brain will give you your instructions on how to convince everyone around you that you found the kingdom and you will find as I have found you essentially are mocked and doubted by the ones that sense time, the scribes, all the while, you will be fully aware what happened to you is happening to innocent children, and society is bragging how they make sure all the children get their "brand" of education with no suggestion of potential unwanted mental side effects. You will swiftly forget about the life you know now, and it will be like some bad dream, and it will seem like a past life because you will totally transform mentally or spiritually, and you will understand first hand what this comment means:

[Psalms 6:7 Mine eye is consumed because of grief; it waxeth old because of all mine enemies.]

Your grief is going to be equal to your wisdom and awareness, and your wisdom and awareness is going to be infinite and the more grief you experience the better you get at concentrating and if you are not able to concentrate you will collapse as a being or try to physically fight the scribes and perish.

What you know as your life is all false so let go of it, is what deny yourself means. Everything in your life right now, your goals and purpose will be erased and be meaningless after you apply the remedy because you will understand and be aware of where you are at, and what you were after you apply this remedy.

Your mental development was "delayed" so after you apply the remedy you start to develop your mind again and that development was stopped at about the age of six or seven, so you have a lot to learn and a lot of catching up to do as a being. Other words, education did not add anything to you it simply sopped your from mentally developing completely, and then you apply this remedy, and you are like a child of seven and have to learn how to be a human being. It is not important how old you are right now, your mental development was stopped factually starting at the age of six or seven and for some even earlier, the moment you started memorizing math tables and the alphabet.

[reading, writing and arithmetic -- the domain and strength of the left brain.]

The concept of resurrection or being born again or the transformation simply means, after you apply the remedy to the tree of knowledge, you resume your normal mental development or another way to look at it is you go from being mentally hindered and return to what is known as sound mind and that is a huge jump and take perhaps over a year relative to a calendar just to adjust to. It's like taking the antidote to a hallucinogenic drug that totally altered your perception that you have been under the influence of since you were ten so it is logical it is going to take a period to adjust.

After you apply this remedy you will pray with all your might for ignorance and your prayers will never be answered and so this is all you will know [Mine eye(awareness) is consumed because of grief;] Because you will be aware you are powerless to stop the ones that sense time from doing to the children what they did to you and when you feel right brain at full power your grief will multiply by the second and your days will last a thousand years and you will be in infinity, no sense of time.

23

So by applying this remedy you are going up against Goliath and his armies are vast and you are an army of one, because I cannot assist you after you apply the remedy, right brain will assist you. If you are showing any happiness after reading this section you clearly did not understand it.

10:55:47 AM –

There is the Old Testament and the New Testament. Testament suggests testimony. Testimony about what?

Testimonies of human beings who negated the mental side effects caused by written education, known as the tree of knowledge. Most testimonies were made by males because perhaps women did not get the education and math at the time period these texts were written as oft as males.

For example Jonah had a testimony and did not mention any other beings in these texts at all in his testimony.

His testimony can be summed up like this.

He applied the remedy partially but he was still showing symptoms of fear because he would not go to the ruler of the city to explain his testimony so he was still showing symptoms of the spirit of fear relative to : [2 Timothy 1:7 For God hath not given us the spirit of fear; but....,..of a sound mind.]

That is what the spirit of this text is saying:

[Jonah 1:1 Now the word of the LORD came unto Jonah the son of Amittai, saying,

Jonah 1:2 Arise, go to Nineveh, that great city, and cry against it; for their wickedness is come up before me.

Jonah 1:3 But Jonah rose up to flee(was afraid still)..]

.

So then Jonah understood he had to apply the fear not remedy the full measure.

On the boat there is this comment:

[Jonah 1:10 Then were the men (ones that sense time; scribes) exceedingly afraid(spirit of fear; a symptom of being a scribe)]

24

Then Jonah "did not try to save his life to preserve it"

[Jonah 1:12 And he said unto them, Take me up, and cast me forth into the sea]

This is a sacrifice, if you tell someone to throw you into a rough sea you are denying yourself. You are seeking the shadow of death. So Jonah is applying the remedy to the full measure.
So after he applied the remedy the full measure right brain "ministered to him" and for a second time said "Go and tell the ones that sense time, the scribes, your testimony, tell them you woke up from the neurosis caused by written education, the tree of knowledge."

[Jonah 3:1 And the word of the LORD came unto Jonah the second time, saying,
Jonah 3:2 Arise, go unto Nineveh, that great city, and preach unto it the preaching that I bid thee.]

[preach unto it the preaching that I bid thee.] This is just saying, say what you are compelled to say after you apply the remedy because you will be in the now, or the machine state so even you are not aware of what effect your words will have on others fully. That's a nice way of saying, you will be beyond your own understanding. One is unable to second guess their self when they are in the machine state. Things you say will catch up to you and make sense to you after you say them and some things long after you say them. Say as you are compelled to say and don't ask questions = [the preaching that I (right brain, the god image in man) bid thee.].

This time Jonah was not afraid because he lost the spirit of fear, he applied the remedy the full measure so he was of sound mind, he restored right brain.

[2 Timothy 1:7 For God hath not given us the spirit of fear; but.....(so no of spirit of fear means)...a sound mind.]

So Jonah woke up so well he convinced the King of a city that education veils right brain, the god image in man.

[Jonah 3:5 So the people of Nineveh believed God, and proclaimed a fast, and put on sackcloth, from the greatest of them even to the least of them. Jonah 3:6 For word came unto the king of Nineveh, and he arose from his throne, and he laid his robe from him, and covered him with sackcloth, and sat in ashes.]

Fasting is a form of denying one's self, and sack cloth is also a form of denying one's self, it's denying one's self, ones ego, its humiliation, tearing down the temple, the ego.
Notice how the scribes wear nice pretty clothes:
[Luke 20:46 Beware of the scribes, which desire to walk in long robes,]

So Jonah convinced this city to apply the remedy and then this happened.

[Jonah 4:1 But it displeased Jonah exceedingly, and he was very angry.]

Angry = grief

This is because Jonah understood written education was too "pleasing "of a golden calf and he could not stop it Relative to:

[Genesis 3:6 ... the tree was good for food, and that it was pleasant to the eyes, and a tree to be desired to make one wise,..]
.
[it was pleasant to the eyes, and a tree to be desired to make one wise] = perfect Trojan horse. It appears to have no flaws at all, yet it has major mental/spiritual flaws, it veils the god image in man, right brain traits and no being can accomplish much with the powerhouse silenced.
Thus this comment:
[Genesis 3:1 Now the serpent was more subtil than any beast of the field..] Subtil is a charm.
What was its charm? [it was pleasant to the eyes, and a tree to be desired to make one wise]

Desired to make one wise does not mean it does make one wise and that is the charm, the charm is an illusion. It appears to do something it factually does not do, in fact it does the complete opposite.

Wise: able to make sensible decisions and judgments on the basis of personal knowledge and experience.
The antonym of wise is foolish:

Foolish: showing, or resulting from, a lack of good sense or judgment.

So this comment [and a tree to be desired to make one wise] is really saying, the tree of knowledge written education, reading and math are desired to make one wise but instead they make one foolish because they veil the god image in man, the right brain traits and thus mentally "delay" a person's cognitive ability. None of this information will apply the remedy for you.

So then the book of Jonah ends with a question:

[Jonah 4:11 And should not I spare Nineveh, that great city, wherein are more than sixscore thousand persons that cannot discern between their right hand and their left hand; and also much cattle?]

[that cannot discern between their right hand and their left hand;] These people could not tell their right brain aspect was veiled because they were foolish because they got the education. One simply cannot tell in that sense of time perception dimension, and that is where faith comes in. So Jonah was asking, we have to destroy the entire species and start all over and hope we never mess with written education and math. He was pondering what Abraham and Lot concluded:

[Genesis 19:13 For we will destroy this place, because the cry of them is waxen great before the face of the LORD; and the LORD hath sent us to destroy it.]

Other words the curse is unstoppable on a species level, just stoppable on an individual level if one applies the fear not remedy.

So Jonah was so awake he convinced a king to apply the remedy as he was compelled to, and even after doing that he was still defeated and could not stop the curse and so he considered the literal war against the ones that sense time. We never know what he did and never will know what he did but it is certain he was experiencing much grief.

2/27/2010 12:08:49 AM - The Greek word for hieroglyphics is demotic. This is relative to when Moses was in Egypt. One very important aspect to understand about right brain is this:

[Rights think and learn in visual, kinesthetic and audio images; need to visualize a picture so they can recall the facts.] This is relative to why the Bible has so many parables.
The Bible has parables in the Torah aspect as well as the New Testament.

For example:
[John 2:19 Jesus answered and said unto them, Destroy this temple, and in three days I will raise it up.
John 2:20 Then said the Jews(the scribes; ones that sensed time and said they were Jews, not true Jews), Forty and six years was this temple in building, and wilt thou rear it up in three days?]

Jesus is saying it took you 46 years to build that temple and if you tear it down and I will rebuild it in 3 days. That is a concept comment. Right brain deals with concepts not details. Jesus is saying although you are old in age if you follow me and deny yourself and "lose your life mindfully" you will preserve your mind the kingdom and unveil right hemisphere after you ate off the tree of knowledge. So Jesus was speaking in concepts but the scribes, the ones with right brain veiled assumed he was not, but the proof he was is that one of his disciples clarifies what Jesus was saying.
I will repeat that, one of Jesus' disciples clarifies what Jesus was saying so one of his disciples was saying "No, No Jesus did not mean literally tear down the literal temple as in the building"

[John 2:21 But he spake of the temple of his body(mind).]

Then Jesus said quite clearly, to a being that applied the remedy, go sin no more.

[John 5:14 Afterward Jesus findeth him in the temple(sound mind, this being applied the remedy and rebuilt his temple, he unveiled right brain after education veiled it), and said unto him, Behold, thou art made whole: sin no more, lest a worse thing come unto thee.]

[temple of his body(mind).] = [findeth him in the temple (sound mind)]

So if anyone attempts to understand these texts without right brain unveiled they will simply take everything literally, but not everything is literal, many stories are concepts and that is how beings that have right brain unveiled speak oft.

[Their thoughts are frequently in code] One might suggest Revelations has lots of code in it but also the entire texts have codes in them. That's a right brain trait because right brain is not good with details so it speaks in concepts and thus codes or parables.

I do not think anyone is possessed by the devil, I tend to lean towards what Timothy said:

[2 Timothy 1:7 For God hath not given us the spirit of fear; but of power, and of love, and of a sound mind.]

The spirit of fear ones on the left have is not their conscience.
They will say "that music is evil, that word is evil, that picture is evil", and then assume they have a conscience but that is not their conscience that is the spirit of fear.
Conscience or soul is right brain intuition. I mean one can sense something without seeing anything. Faith is seeing the unseen and that is what intuition is.
So Just before Jesus died he said "they know not what they do", the ones with a sense of time know not what they do. Only being with an unsound mind knows not what they do. Only lunatics harm children with written

education and do not even sense they are doing so, so they know not what they do. If you are aware you are mentally harming children with written education call and let me know and I will take care of the rest because I am looking like a shark for a reason to stop writing these vanity books.

I tend to lean to the logical reality that Mankind invented written education and math and they were great tools but then we started teaching them to small children and then their negate side effects came into being and it snow balled from then on out and here we are 5400 years later wondering why everything is so "interesting".

[J. P. (12) committed suicide by hanging]
Twelve year old children hanging their self? That is indeed interesting. Let's all pray that is not because as a child he got lots of left brain favoring education pushed on him as a result of the compulsory education law because then we have lots of people that need to be tried for involuntary manslaughter and brought to justice and if not then law doesn't matter at all, so anarchy will rule. Granted I feel off the train of thought.

[2 Timothy 1:7 For God hath not given us the spirit of fear; but of power, and of love, and of a sound mind.] So what gave people this spirit of fear? The tree of knowledge, written education, in bending the mind to the left it made the hypothalamus go a bit wacky and so it started to make people very afraid and Abraham figured that out in the 15th chapter of Genesis.

[Genesis 15:1 After these things the word of the LORD came unto Abram in a vision, saying, Fear not, Abram: I am thy shield, and thy exceeding great reward.]

What happens to one if they fear not, which is apply the fear not remedy, the lose one's life mindfully to preserve it remedy?
They get an [exceeding great reward.]. What is that reward? They restore their right brain aspects and return to sound mind, and lose the spirit of fear.
Since [For God hath not given us the spirit of fear] then the spirit of fear is not of God or is abnormal.

If you are afraid to say certain words and listen to certain music you have the spirit of fear and that is as simple as it is. Relative to your perception you may perceive you do not listen to certain music or say certain words because you have morals or a conscience, but morals and conscience is right brain intuition and if you sense time, that trait no longer factors into your perception, so in turn you are just afraid of those words you are do not say. It is not logical you are going to hell if you say a certain word because if you sense time your right brain is veiled so you are in hell, the place of sorrow, you are mentally unsound to the degree you are nonviable mentally and that is why the remedy is kind of important to apply. It is logical you may doubt that.

2/27/2010 7:45:27 AM –
[Revelation 5:1 And I saw in the right hand of him that sat on the throne a book written within and on the backside, sealed with seven seals.]
[And I saw in the right hand of him that sat on the throne] – Right hand denotes one that has applied the remedy to the full measure, so they sit at the throne (sound mind) relative to the master of the house(mind) and they have the spirit of God, the God image in man unveiled, right hemisphere.

[a book written within] This is relative to the book of life. This means not everyone who gets the tree of knowledge can apply the remedy to restore right brain traits, in fact the number is quite slim, but this only means all that left brain favoring education is devastating and many perhaps cannot undo its damage, they are trapped by their own altered perception, extreme fear. Simply put the only reason you will not go to a spooky dark abandoned house in the woods alone at night with no lights is because your hypothalamus has turned you into a being that gets fight or flight signals from the hypothalamus just from thinking about going to those "spooky" places, mentally sound minded human beings fear nothing, not the devil, not words, not music, not pictures, not ghosts and certainly not the shadow of death. If you want the slothful watered down version of the remedy simply go meditate in a room all alone for the rest of your life. Only human beings can apply the full measure remedy, don't take it personally. Now you can stop reading my private diaries.

X ="In humans, the frontal lobe reaches full maturity around only after the 20s, marking the cognitive maturity associated with adulthood"

Y = [we have been traditionally taught to master the 3 R's: reading, writing and arithmetic -- the domain and strength of the left brain.]

Because of X , Y creates this left brain leaning state of mind, the place of suffering, one that is mentally unsound from all that Y education is in the place of suffering because they have the right brain aspects veiled. Simply put if a human being mentally has either hemisphere veiled or silenced even one degree they are suffering because nature intended both aspects to be at 50% or in exact mental harmony.

[Revelation 5:2 And I saw a strong angel proclaiming with a loud voice, Who is worthy to open the book, and to loose the seals thereof?]

This is a question and it is asking, what human being is able to understand the ancient texts? The answer is, only a person that has applied the remedy and restored right brain traits because pattern detection, complexity, intuition is required to understand the ancient texts, those are all right brain traits.

[Who is worthy] any person that applies the "fear not" or "deny one's self" remedy the full measure is worthy.

[Revelation 5:3 And no man in heaven, nor in earth, neither under the earth, was able to open the book, neither to look thereon.]

This is John saying he was not pleased because the "men(scribes)" were unworthy to understand the texts. A "man" is a person that got the education and did not apply the remedy, a person that does apply the remedy is a Master of the house, the mind, because they return to sound mind, left and right brain traits at 50% in harmony. They are also known as Lords or under the influence of the Lord, the right brain, the god image in man. They are just sound minded human beings but in contrast to the scribes who have their right brain powerhouse veiled they appear to be "wise men".

[Revelation 5:4 And I wept much, because no man was found worthy to open and to read the book, neither to look thereon.]

This is just repeating the above comment. A person who did not apply the remedy is unable to understand the education has hindered them mentally because they have this thing called pride and ego and those aspects will not allow them to "look at their self" and judge their self or the invention written education and math. Another way to look at it is, if you cannot ponder that perhaps all that left brain favoring education hindered your mind during your childhood you are in dire straits because your pride and ego are way to strong as a result of that extreme left brain state and that is hindering your ability to think logically. Your emotions are turned up so high you cannot think clearly, is another way to look at it.
As emotions decrease cognitive ability and thus concentration increases.

[I wept much] Is relative to this comment:
[Ecclesiastes 1:18 For in much wisdom is much grief: and he that increaseth knowledge increaseth sorrow.]

[For in much wisdom is much grief] John had lots of grief because he was unable to reach the ones who had fallen from grace, the ones who got the tree of knowledge and were in the place of sorrow relative to [he that increaseth knowledge increaseth sorrow.], the ones that sense time. I am fully mindful I cannot win relative to convincing the species written education factually ruins the mind of the children and thus has ruined the mind of the adults also, so I just suggest the full measure remedy because it does not matter much if I suggest things "properly" or not.

[Revelation 5:5 And one of the elders saith unto me, Weep not: behold, the Lion of the tribe of Juda, the Root of David, hath prevailed to open the book, and to loose the seven seals thereof.]

This is saying someone will eventually apply the remedy and then they will understand the ancient texts and be able to explain them, but this does not mean everything will be solved or fixed, it just means eventually someone breaks free of the neurosis caused by written education because

33

the mind seeks harmony. Even though written education veils right brain traits, the mind is still trying to undo that, or right brain is still trying to get back to 50/50 so eventually someone breaks free of that and can understand the ancient texts.

[behold, the Lion of the tribe of Juda] My last name is pronounced Roar like a lion, but many human beings have applied this remedy after John wrote this so this is perhaps just an accident, that my last name Rohrer is pronounced roar like a lion. Relative to my perception. I get spit on more than anything else so I am not exactly jumping up and down with elation. No good deed goes unpunished kind of thing. I tell people I accidentally applied the fear not remedy and it is the true remedy in concept to the neurosis caused by the tree of knowledge and I get spit on. Funny how that works out. Of course I am dealing with neurotics so it is logical they should spit on me, after all I am attempting to convince them to mindfully kill their self. That certainly blew it.

[Revelation 5:7 And he came and took the book out of the right hand of him that sat upon the throne.]

This is saying a leader scribe has his right brain veiled so a leader in society cannot understand the ancient texts because they are still of the world. This is relative to; a rich man cannot find the kingdom.
Revelations is not about what is going to happen it is John speaking in code, a right brain trait explaining the situation he was in at the time and because we was in prison he could not just come out and say exactly what he wanted to say so he spoke in code.
Bottom line is, once you get the tree of knowledge you have to apply the remedy and if someone does not agree with that it is because they are blind to reality, so they should apply the remedy. One has to face the log in their eye (apply the remedy), so they can see (restore their senses, intuition and pattern detection), firstly.

[1 John 2:18 Little children, it is the last time: and as ye have heard that antichrist shall come, even now are there many antichrists; whereby we know that it is the last time.]

Right brain influenced and left brain influenced equally =Sound minded child, a child before they get the tree of knowledge which favors left brain and thus veils right brain.

So a child of God is a young child that still has right brain traits in the conscious state.

So they are a right brain influenced container= RBIC

Left brain influenced container is a person that got the education and in turn have right brain traits veiled=LBIC

So a child is a RBIC and an adult which is a LBIC will see that child and seek to make that child like they are, so they will give that child the education to make that child a LBIC and the adult a LBIC will perceive that is logical and proper and thus after thousands of years of that cycle repeating we are a lunatic species. A species divided against itself, against nature, against our own families and our own neighbors because we see way too many parts and are essentially as a species as mentally unsound as one can be ever. Beings that sense time have to take strong mind altering drugs just to experience a moment of sanity or mental clarity, and that is how mentally unsound we are as a result of the education. So doing very powerful drugs are the only chance for many beings that sense time to experience creativity, a right brain trait. I am not depressed about this situation. I am attempting to do something about it relative to explaining it, but I am in the now or the machine state so all I can do is continue to write to teach myself, to detect more patterns, to be able to explain it better.

So [1 John 2:18] is saying.

[Little children (RBIC) be mindful even now there are many anti-christs (LBIC, scribes)]

So an Antichrist is simply a LBIC because they do not have right brain traits in their conscious state, so they see RBIC as bad or ill or evil but that is logical because right brain traits are totally opposite of left brain traits. Really what John is saying is repeating this comment:

35

[Jeremiah 8:8 How do ye say, We are wise, and the law of the LORD is with us? Lo, certainly in vain made he it; the pen of the scribes is in vain.]

John is saying beware little children, the scribes and their pen(their education) is in vain because in the process of learning the education it favors left hemisphere, and in turn veils right hemisphere traits, the god image in man so it does not make you wise [How do ye say, We are wise] since learning script makes one mentally hindered.

[How do ye say, We are wise, and the law of the LORD is with us] This saying how can you say you are wise and the Lord, the god image in man is with you after you veil it, right brain, with all that left brain favoring education? How can a mentally unsound being be wise? How can a being with the God imagine in man veiled, right brain, be of the Lord? And the answer is, it is impossible they can be, so they must apply the remedy to the tree of knowledge. Of course no LBIC would agree with that because they would have to eat lots of crow and swallow their infinite pride to admit that, so it's kind of this being who wrote this is pondering to himself more than talking to anyone else.

10:52:49 AM –
http://wilybadger.files.wordpress.com/2008/11/hortus_deliciarum_-_hell.jpg

A medieval called Hortus Deliciarum has a painting depicting hell.

If you look on the right side margin of the painting you will notice 9 bodies. These bodies represent the 9 circles of hell. The actual painting is only showing 4 circles.

The comment "it is easier for a camel to go through the eye of a needle than foe a rich man to find the kingdom." That is what the first level of hell is, the first circle. That is limbo. That is the top level depicted in this painting. Notice the beings in that level on the left have a snake surrounding them or wrapped around them. So the people in this first circle ate off the tree of knowledge, and had the god image, right brain veiled, and on top of that they are "of the world". They love their life so to speak so they are completely absent or blind from what the tree did to them, so they really have no way to deny their self, because they are pleased with how they are.

Simply put a very wealthy person with lots of material things is least likely to do this:
[Mark 8:34 ...Whosoever will come after me, let him deny himself,...]

This is relative to the comment "The meek shall inherit the earth and also blessed are the poor in spirit". Simply put a person with a sense of time that has luxury and money is not likely to be meek or poor in spirit(depressed) so they are not likely to deny their self, which is what the remedy is.
The next level down in the painting things start to get rough. You will notice some of the beings are being pierced with some sort of pike, so they are suffering a bit more than the ones in the first circle/level. The point is, as one goes further down into hell they suffer more.

The third circle in the painting/level shows people being boiled so they are suffering even more than the ones in the previous 2 levels, circles.

Now the 4th level represents the 9th circle of hell, this circle is treason. If one denies their self :
[Mark 8:34 ...Whosoever will come after me, let him deny himself,...]
They commit treason. So one has to go through hell to get to heaven and the door out of hell is in the 9th circle, treason. Jesus said knock and the door will be opened. What that means is one has to be in the mindset of treason, then they knock, which is one applies the remedy, the deny ones self, fear not remedy, and the door or exit from hell will be opened (their right brain will unveil or open) and they can escape hell, the place of suffering (unsound state of mind). All one is doing in escaping hell is restoring their right brain aspects and they return to sound mind so they can think clearly and life becomes very easy so they are no longer suffering, so they simply return to sound mind or consciousness. They become cerebral "giants" and less materialistic as a result.
In the painting in the "9th circle" the 4th level in the painting, one can see a saint, prophet or what is known as the good shepherd on the left hand side

and in the 9th circle. They are in that circle because only the "meek" have a chance to apply the remedy.

Meek = depressed or suicidal, which means these beings do not even believe they have a right to continue living, but that is a symptom right hemisphere is starting to unveil. These depressed or suicidal are the only ones that have a chance to "wake up" so they are the most valuable of all and that is why that prophet is in the 9th circle of hell in this painting, he is shepherding them to wake up.
So this hell concept is what any human is in after they get the education, they are of unsound mind and thus suffering and only the ones that get to the 9th circle mindfully have a chance to apply the deny one's self remedy. This battle to escape hell one an individual level is what is known as the holy war or the Jihad. This child did not do so well in her Jihad and perhaps got a bit too much "education" a bit too fast.

[A. D. (16) took her own life and her last myspace post said 'I want to die.]

"I want to die" is exactly what one wants to say when they find the shadow of death, that is what "meek" is, but this is not fantasy land and many beings literally end up becoming fatalities as the result of attempting to restore right brain traits. Simply put society is killing young children by pushing all that left brain education on them long before their frontal lobe even develops.

Thus the comment "The meek shall inherit the earth (earth being, have a chance to "wake up" and escape hell.) One has to go through hell to get to heaven and the exit of hell is in the 9th circle, treason, and once there one has to deny their self which is what the remedy is.
Simply put:

If you go to a spooky dark place alone at night and you mind says "run or terrible things will happen to you" and you do not run, you commit treason against yourself, and that is what deny yourself means, essentially you are telling your hypothalamus 'I want to die', and that is what the remedy is to the tree of knowledge. It is a onetime thing and takes one second in the right situation.

[Mark 8:34 he said unto them, Whosoever will come after me, let him deny himself.]
Be mindful the kingdom is within which means this battle it in your mind and in your spirit, and your spirit after getting the education, the tree of knowledge, does not want to "deny itself" so you as a being must be aware of that, and do what you do not want to do. It all comes down to self control. It is most important not to give up and experiment with this deny yourself remedy because that left brain aspect wants you to give up and wants you to never deny yourself because if you do right brain comes back to power and left brain hates that prospect.

Be mindful John Paul II whipped himself and slept naked on the floor and that is a form of denying one's self, it's prostration and submission, but this mindful deny one's self is the full measure "treason" against one's self. Even listening to music you do not want to listen to is a form of denying one's self. even saying the word "perhaps" a lot is denying one's self because ambiguity is a right brain trait, so saying "perhaps" often favors right brain , and you will find ones that sense time do not like that word being said to much. Left brain dislikes ambiguity; right brain has doubts, moments of doubt, so to speak, so saying "perhaps" in fact favors right brain.
Freud said "neurosis is the inability to tolerate ambiguity" The words "perhaps" and "maybe" suggest ambiguity, so even saying those words as much as you can no matter what, favors right brain and is a form of denying one's self. I do not recommend you literally harm yourself, or whip yourself, because the kingdom is within so this reaching the kingdom, unveiling right brain, is completely a mind exercise not a physical exercise.

[1 Corinthians 3:18 Let no man deceive himself. If any man among you seemeth to be wise in this world, let him become a fool, that he may be wise.]

If what you read relative to this remedy appears to be unwise, you better attempt as hard as you can to become a fool.

[seemeth to be wise in this world, let him become a fool]

If you think this remedy I suggest is foolish and you don't want to do it because you perceive you are wise, you better become a fool. You learn to do foolish things if you think this remedy is foolishness. You make it your goal in life to do foolish things, because in your state of mind, sense of time state of mind, you think being a fool is stupid. You think denying yourself is stupid. You think being wise is smart, so you have to learn to become a fool. This is only until you apply the remedy it is not permanent. Once you apply the remedy you are truly wise or of sound mind.

[seemeth to be wise in this world, let him become a fool]

As awareness and comprehension of a situation decreases hope increases. Fame is fleeting but wisdom is terminal. The more situations one can adapt to the easier life becomes. This is why right brain pattern detection, fast random access processing and intuition are so valuable because they allow one to detect a situation and adapt to it swiftly and this is contrary to the ability to change slowly. Left brain is pleased with rules and directions but those rules and directions inhibit adaptation and thus ability to change. For example a being with a sense of time loses their job and because they do not have all these right brain aspects they cannot change swiftly or adapt swiftly so they perceive losing their job is the end of the road. If one can adapt swiftly to any situation they do not really have any problems. A problem is a situation one cannot find an easy way to solve. Solving a problem is relative to pattern detection, swift processing of information and intuition to decide which information is valuable to solve that problem and swift is relative.

[J. S. (49) committed suicide by ligature strangulation after losing his job.]

A being with right brain unveiled has a lot of ambiguity, a right brain trait so losing their job so to speak would never be a situation of distress because they would always look at it as a challenge. It is elementary a sound minded human being can adapt to any situation so the worse thing that would ever happen is they would have to return to the wild and live in the wild and that is no problem at all for a sound minded human being because with right brain unveiled they can easily adapt to any situation and their hunger is greatly reduced because their mind is stream lined and does not create lots of drag so they need less food to survive. The prospect of living in the wild to an unsound minded being is a nightmare because they could not adapt to that situation. If a human being looks at living in the wild as bad or dangerous then they are mentally unsound because that is where human beings came from. Human beings did not have cities at first. They lived in the wild. So human beings should be totally at home in the wild unless something has happened to their mind where they are no longer comfortable living in the wild or unable to adapt to the wild. It all comes back to one factor alone. Once a child gets enough left brain favoring education their right hemisphere aspects start to veil or silence and they are doomed because human beings need all of their mental aspects from both hemispheres at all times and at full power and if any of those aspects from either hemisphere are veiled even slightly that human being is in danger because without all of those mental traits from both hemispheres at their disposal simple tasks relative to living become difficult tasks.

Mammal: a class of warm-blooded vertebrate animals that have, in the female, milk-secreting organs for feeding the young. The class includes human beings, apes, many four-legged animals, whales, dolphins, and bats. Are apes and bats and whales evil or bad because they live in the wild? If not then it is impossible to assume human beings are evil or bad if they live in the wild. If you cannot understand we are mammals then something has altered your perception to the point you are out of touch with reality itself. Human beings are nothing but mammals but the written education has altered their perception to the point they assume they are greater or less than mammals. How can a human being be more than a mammal when they are just a mammal? Perhaps you are embarrassed to be a mammal. Perhaps someone told you that mammals are evil. Perhaps someone told you that animals are evil. Perhaps you just hate animals and so you hate yourself. No human being is above a whale or an ape or a bat because they are all mammals. A whale can hold its breath under water for hours and that trumps your ability to add numbers and spell words, so you are not smarter than a whale. A whale does not go around harpooning human beings to make some money so who is the smarter of the two mammals? Does that bother you that all you will ever be in your entire life is a run of the mill mammal? I am certain you grit your teeth when someone says to you "We are just mammals and thus animals. " If you hate the fact you are nothing but an animal that is horrible news relative to you because that is all you will ever be is an animal. If any being on this planet suggests we are more or less than mammals they are just completely out of touch with reality. Do you think all of your attempts at rules mean's you are not a mammal? Do you think all of your education means you are not a mammal? You are just a mammal and you are not even a special mammal. The closest star system to earth is 4 light years away and that means you could not be more alone and isolated than you are right now. Perhaps you wish to leave earth because it keeps reminding you that you are nothing but a mammal. You want to be everything in the universe but a mammal and you will never be anything in the universe but a mammal. You do not like the word mammal and you hate the word animal because you hate yourself. You spend all of your effort trying to prove to others that you are not an animal and that is why you are an unhappy animal. Never take the advice of mammals that suggest they are not mammals or more than mammals. A chimpanzee putting a stick in an ant hole to get ants does not prove that is no longer a chimpanzee. A human being spelling a word or adding numbers does not prove that human being is no longer a mammal. There are no mammals in the universe that are not animals. If you are more than an animal then you should turn yourself into science because a mammal has discovered a new form of life.

Look at it like this.
Mankind had a sound mind, left and right brain traits in harmony or equal and in that situation right brain ruled, it has more powerful aspects, example: lightning random access processing, intuition and vast pattern detection, left brain has none of that. Then written education came along and favored left brain and in turn veiled the power house right brain.

[we have been traditionally taught to master the 3 R's: reading, writing and arithmetic -- the domain and strength of the left brain.]

So left brain hijacked right brain and ruled the mind and finally it ruled over right brain and it is very stubborn and does not want to go back to 50/50 because at 50/50 right brain rules and left brain hates that prospect because left brain is "jealous" of right brain, the powerhouse, the god image in man.

Left Brain
Sequential - sequential files are very slow in processing
Rational - this is relative to knowing by seeing proof or being told what to think
Analytical
Objective
Looks at parts

Right Brain
Random - Random access files are very quick in contrast to sequential files
Intuitive - this is instinct or conscience or the soul, it's like knowing without seeing, thinking for one's self, not needing to know what to think or do
Holistic -
Synthesizing
Subjective
Looks at wholes

Just in these elementary comparisons one can see why left brain, Cain, would be jealous of right brain, the God image in man.
So the tree of knowledge [we have been traditionally taught to master the 3 R's: reading, writing and arithmetic -- the domain and strength of the left brain.]
Is what caused the hijacking, and that happened 5400 years ago and our minds as a species have fallen from grace, or are unsound and have been ever since, but sometimes people escape that and attempt to explain how others can wake up, and they do not fair very well because left brain hates

the prospect of going back to second fiddle behind the god image in man, right brain.

Forget the people involved, this is strictly a battle of our minds for power and the people are just containers.

It is like I accidentally found this great drug that is free and lasts forever and is fantastic and enables one to have a very powerful mind and when I tell people how they can achieve this state of mind they say shut up dick.

The number one resides at the end of infinity starting from zero.

2/28/2010 11:40:44 AM -

[Luke 17:33 Whosoever shall seek to save his life shall lose it; and whosoever shall lose his life shall preserve it.]

Left brain is simple minded and contrary right brain is complex.

A person with a sense of time will read this:

[and whosoever shall lose his life shall preserve it.] and come to one conclusion. Those who die will live. This gives off the impression of supernatural. This is because left brain has no ambiguity or doubt so one can only see one translation and cannot ponder or consider many angles. Jesus was not saying if you die you will live literally because that makes no sense at all. If you die you are dead .So one has to consider the alternative meaning.

[and whosoever shall lose his life shall preserve it.]

One eats off the tree of knowledge so they have the curse so their life is death, they have an unsound mind so they are in the place of suffering, so the only possible remedy to that would be they have to die unto their self mindfully, which is what deny one's self means.

$X =$ the spiritual state of a person after the tree of knowledge, cursed, under the influence of Cain, left brain, the evil one, in the place of suffering, hell.

$Y =$ state of mind after one applies the deny one's self remedy. Sound minded, right and left brain traits at 50/50, one finds the kingdom, escapes the place of suffering

Z = deny ones self, the remedy, seek the shadow of death and fear no evil, or fear not, shadow being the operative word, submit, prostrate, bow.

So now if we put those variables into this line by Jesus:

[and whosoever shall lose(Z) his life(X) shall preserve it(Y).]

So then this line is saying, whoever denies their self in X state of mind using Z remedy will return to Y state of mind as they were as a child and thus be a child of God.

So Jesus explained it flawlessly, but the catch is, if one has right brain veiled, they will hear but not understand. What that means is these ancient texts were hidden because they are battle plans against the ones that sense time, the scribes. The ones that sense time, the scribes are the adversary. For example, these texts are the history of the ones with no sense of time and their battles against the ones that sense time, but the ones that sense time found them and determined they are not battle plans against them, because well, they are a bit on the slothful side, a bit blind one might suggest, and wouldn't know battle plans against them even if they published them on a world wide scale for thousands of years.

There are two versions of history, the scribes version is mankind invented math and written language and everything got way better. The ancient texts version is mankind invented written language and math and fell from grace. Both versions are totally opposite versions and only one version is truth and the other version of history is a lie. Perhaps one should ponder that carefully.

You have been told God himself destroyed Sodom and Gomorrah and that is true as long as your definition of god is a being who applied the fear not remedy and was under the influence of the god image in man, right brain. Abraham and Lot say as plain as day they destroyed the cities of men who push the education on the children and in turn veiled the right hemisphere in the children and put the children in the place of suffering.

45

[Genesis 19:13 For we(Abraham and Lot) will destroy this place(the cities of the "men", the ones that sense time), because the cry of them is waxen(they are growing in numbers) great before the face of the LORD; and the LORD(right brain calculated there was no way to stop the curse but to kill the ones cursed) hath sent us to destroy it.]

3/1/2010 1:09:22 PM - The meek may regain sight and the arrogant flee from the light.

These are some sequential logical conclusions relative to what I suggest on a religious forum.

[ralphinal] So, it all comes back to saying that if you are smart, have an education, can read and do math, you are damned. God wants us all to be uneducated, bare-foot and pregnant forever.]

My response:

Written education and math is a tool, a man made tool. With all tools one can either use them properly and get benefits from the tools or not.
As long as one applies the fear not remedy after they get the education then they restore right brain traits and everything is fine. The catch is, once one does this they can no longer use written education and math well, and that is the proof written education and math can only be used well by people who have not applied the remedy, and thus have not kept the covenant, and thus sense time, and thus are of unsound mind.
Is a world full of unsound minded people better than a world where everyone is living in caves but have sound minds?
That is the what selling your soul to the sinister is all about.
Society has this world and it has its education but it also has this:

Gina G. (16) and Vanessa D. (15) committed suicide by jumping in front of a train and it is thought they made a suicide pact with other teens
Brittany P. (14) committed suicide for unknown reasons

Michael P. (14) committed suicide by hanging from the clothes rod in his closet

Laren W. (14) allegedly took her own life

What you are looking at is the results of what happens when the education is pushed on a small child that do not even have their mind developed until the age of twenty. What you are looking at is what happens when the right hemisphere is veiled and thus complexity, ambiguity, intuition and pattern detection is veiled. A small meaningless problem arises and because the mind cannot cope the being determines its best to just kill their self. It is still far deeper than that. When right brain random access is veiled, one can maintain a mindset of depression for long periods and when right brain is not veiled one cannot. If one can maintain a mindset of depression one can then maintain a mindset of suicidal thoughts because the lightening fast random access processing of right brain is gone from their thoughts. It is still deeper than that, a side effect of having right brain veiled is ones hypothalamus starts sending lots of false signs of fear. Fear is what all these emotions you perceive are relative to.

For example: a girl breaks up with a guy and that guy fears the loss so he harms himself or harms that girl.

A person fears saying a cuss word because they fear they will go to hell if they do.

A person fears eating certain foods because they fear going to hell if they do.

The bottom line is FEAR.

The mind is bent to the left by education and a side effect is extreme fear.

A person loses their job and they have no mental capacity any longer due to the education to adapt so they see that is the end of the road for them.

[Conley W. (38) shot himself and his wife in a murder suicide after he lost his job.]

Right brain never perceives loss or winning, it is endless, it never gives up, but left brain gives up easily. This being above lost his job and exhibits a left brain trait, giving up. In reality since he was mindful of death, suicide, he could have sought out the shadow of death in his mindset and then feared not and he would have applied the remedy, but this is not fantasy land, when one perceives depression and suicidal thoughts they are not aware those are symptoms right brain is trying to unveil itself. They perceive they should really kill their self but in fact they should just seek the shadow of death and then fear not when it arrives. Remember the 9th circle of hell is treason, Suicide is treason, the meek are the suicidal, so this being lost his job and went right to the 9th circle of hell, treason, and like most, he did not survive that trip. Education kills people when not taught properly.

[Genesis 2:17 But of the tree of the knowledge of good and evil, thou shalt not eat of it: for in the day that thou eatest thereof thou shalt surely die.]

The above being found out what this comment means and he let us all know he understood what [for in the day that thou eatest thereof thou shalt surely die]
A human being is no longer mentally viable when right brain is veiled, it is impossible they could be. A house, mind, divided cannot stand because it is built on sand, it is unsound.
.Ones that sense time are never ever capable of anything but left brain sequential simple minded conclusions because the fact they sense time proves the right brain paradox aspect no longer factors into their perception and so that means complexity, pattern detection, intuition no longer factors into their decision making processes at full capacity so their decisions are unsound.

[God wants us all to be uneducated, bare-foot and pregnant forever}

Perhaps God wants us to be sound minded human beings and infinitely wise like we are when we are born, but this education tool we invented veils the complex aspect of our minds and if we do not apply the fear not, deny one's self remedy we as a species are nothing but mental abominations who cannot think ourselves out of a wet paper bag.
We cannot go back now. We as a species sold our souls, all one can ever do on an individual level is focus on the log in their eye and that means

attempt to apply the remedy so at least they can return to sound mind and that is as good as it gets in this narrow.

We can never go back to how we were as a species before we fell from grace by eating off the tree of knowledge. As a species our tree if rotten to the core, but on an individual level ones can make their rotten tree a fruitful tree again by applying the remedy and restoring right brain to its proper place in the spirit or mind.

It is better to have a sound mind and live in the dirt than to have riches and live blindly.

This is not an opinion:

X ="In humans, the frontal lobe reaches full maturity around only after the 20s, marking the cognitive maturity associated with adulthood"

This is not an opinion:

Y = [we have been traditionally taught to master the 3 R's: reading, writing and arithmetic -- the domain and strength of the left brain.]

This is not an opinion:

Z = "What it comes down to is that modern society discriminates against the right hemisphere." - Roger Sperry (1973) neuropsychologist, Nobel laureate

Modern society is civilization.

Because of X , Y mentally hinders the right brain which is what Z is suggesting.

Look at this comment:

[we have been traditionally taught to master the 3 R's: reading, writing and arithmetic -- the domain and strength of the left brain.]

If this comment said : [[we have been traditionally taught to master the 3 R's: reading, writing and arithmetic -- the domain and strength of the right brain.]

We would still be in the same situation. If written education favored right brain we would still be mentally unsound. The only way we would be safe is if this comment said, "favors left and right brain equally"

But the factual reality is :[reading, writing and arithmetic -- the domain and strength of the left brain.]

We are knowingly or unknowingly mentally hindering children and I was one of them and you were one of them and the only difference is I accidentally applied the ancient fear not remedy to the tree of knowledge and accidents count in this narrow.

I am pleased if the ones that sense time never suggest they understand the spirit of what I suggest because that tells me my argument is getting good. What is a government going to tell the mother of those children above when I convince people education in veiling right brain is why those children became depressed and thus suicidal and thus killed their self? I am pleased if you do not understand anything I say. You may say "explain it better" but what you are really saying is " please incite a world revolution against the powers that be on earth" because you may not care much about the offspring but I am mindful the females care and if the women become enraged the men are going to battle to protect the offspring on the females behalf.
The better I get at explaining it the closer the species gets to the "red sea" and I am mindful you perhaps do not believe that but I fear not, because my only purpose is to do as I am compelled to do. I have faith in the flow and that is where I go.
I am compelled to speak this truth I have discovered above everything else, above even me.

Sammasambuddhas attain buddhahood, then decide to teach others the truth they have discovered.

The disciples applied the remedy Jesus suggested and they told the truth they had discovered even when they understood it would cost them their lives.

John the Baptist did also. Jesus did also. They were all fully aware of what would happen. Jesus had the last supper because he was aware his argument was very good and the ones that sense time were drawing close, the ruler scribes.

[Mark 1:22 And they were astonished at his doctrine: for he taught them as one that had authority, and not as the scribes.]

The disciples and Jesus knew if they kept talking they would die, and they did get slaughtered. Simply put the rulers scribes in society would never be trusted again if it came to light written education when pushed on young children makes them dumb, fearful and easy to control. They would have to stop anyone who suggests that because it is truth and if truth gets around the ruler scribes control is in jeopardy. Control freaks only fear losing control. Control is a left brain trait and freedom or few rules is a right brain trait.

Society is just a control structure with lots of caged animals and once in a while a caged animal escapes his cage and explains how the other caged animals can escape their cages. Moses said quite clearly "Let the people you have mentally turned into slaves with the tree of knowledge go" and the Pharaoh didn't like that suggestion very much.

[Exodus 7:14 And the LORD said unto Moses, Pharaoh's heart is hardened, he refuseth to let the people go.]

Simply put control freaks do not want to let go of control.
[Pharaoh's heart is hardened] = left brain influenced, got the education and did not apply the remedy, left brain covets and is controlling = [he refuseth to let the people go.] Let the people be free because they are born free, why control others, we are all equal and free. Only a control freak would hate the sound of that.
END

[God wants us all to be uneducated, bare-foot and pregnant forever.]

The above comment is relative to the comment: Mankind is afraid of flat ground not mountains. The deeper reality is in the extreme left brain state a person has to do something to perceive accomplishment and this is what Dante suggested was going up and down stairs in his Inferno writing.

[God wants us all to be uneducated] This being is really saying [God wants us to be mentally sound] but he does not know that is exactly what he is saying. He perceives uneducated is evil or bad, because the entire premise of education is a human being is stupid when they are born and thus they have to be educated or they die or are evil or stupid but that is illogical because we did just fine for tens of thousands of years with no written education or math at all. So this being has determined written education and math in fact does make one wise when in reality it is all left brain favoring education and it does mentally hinder the mind of children to an absolute degree and if he was aware of that he would have said. [God wants us to be mentally sound] instead of [God wants us all to be uneducated]. So the spirit of what he is suggesting is accurate as long as one flips it and considers the absolute reverse and that is an indication he is in an alternate perception dimension. It has never been about the written education and math it is about teaching it to seven year old children and after that is done the remedy is one has to seek to mindfully kill their self to negate the damage it causes or they are stuck with 10% of a mind when they should have 100% mind, so that is the fundamental flaw of education. You will find it is a bit more difficult to mindfully kill yourself to the full measure and if you get lucky and accomplish that in your lifetime you will understand why education is fundamentally flawed. The remedy is a lot of work just to get back to zero. There is a certain "rush" to hurry up and educate all the children. It is a symptom civilization has determined the faster they push that left brain favoring education on the child the better and that is the reverse of reality, the longer that child's mind is left alone so it can develop the better.

3:18:12 PM – Think about how many laws are relative to this one law. Disturbing the peace. This law is totally relative. For example if you go outside of your house in a ballerina outfit and start dancing eventually someone will call the police and complain about something and the police will show up and say "We got a complaint and we are here checking up on it." The reality is, after one gets all that education they are in extreme left brain state and so they are nothing but control freaks. They will complain and that is a form of control. Go complain to the police and tell them something is disturbing your peace and they will do your control freak bidding for you. The deeper reality is in the extreme left brain state caused by education one see's parts very strongly and that means they are very prejudice. That means they have aversion to things and when they get the aversion if that thing does not go away it mentally harms them. So they may say "I hate that color, that music, that sound, that picture, that view." That is because in the extreme left brain state they are seeing parts as in some things are pleasing and that means some things are not, so they are prejudice. Racism is a direct result of the education bending people's minds to the left and what's interesting about that is the tribes who never got education and were taken advantage of by the "scribes" did not hate the scribes they just were wise enough to stay away from lunatics. If there is any music or color you do not like, it is proof you are mentally unsound because you should be indifferent or pleased with all color and all music and all sounds. You should be neutral to all colors and music and sounds and since you are not you are suffering needlessly as a direct result of the unwanted mental side effects of the education being taught to you as a child before your delicate mind was even developed.

4:41:02 PM - Luke 6:19-31

The point of this parable is that Lazarus was meek. He was like Job, he was not having very good luck at life so to speak. That is the frame of mind one has to achieve in order to apply the "deny oneself" remedy to the full measure. So simply put the suicidal and depressed are the meek and have a chance to follow what Jesus said "Deny yourself;" and every other single person in the world is in various stages of arrogance. So Lazarus was raised from the death. "Dead" is the state of mind one is in after they eat off the tree of knowledge, written education, they have right brain veiled, so they are mindfully suffering and thus are in the place of suffering or what this passage says..[this place of torment]

The whole concept that after one applies the remedy is they will be at peace is not truth. With the tree of knowledge comes sorrow and with wisdom, applying the remedy, comes grief.

[Ecclesiastes 1:18 For in much wisdom is much grief: and he that increaseth knowledge increaseth sorrow.]

Do you perceive Jesus was happy to go around and tell people to deny their self? Do you think Jesus was pleased to go around and tell people they had to "lose their life(mindfully) to preserve it"?

If one is happy about anything they should be happy the fact they are happy only proves their ignorance is perhaps incurable.

Lazarus was not raised from the dead as in literal death. Lazarus was raised from mental death the tree of knowledge caused and Jesus assisted him to apply the "deny one's self" remedy and Lazarus did deny himself because he was in the proper state of mind, he was depressed and willing to "let go" and so he followed Jesus' advice and then he was raised back to life, which is sound mind, and that means sound spirit.

Avoid assuming because you can say the word Jesus you have applied the remedy because Jesus did not say "Say the word Jesus" Jesus factually said:

[Mark 8:34 And when he had called the people unto him with his disciples also, he said unto them, Whosoever will come after me, let him deny himself,..]

Jesus said to everyone, deny yourself and that means to the full measure which means you have to totally let go of this life you have relative to after you ate off the tree of knowledge, education, and that is mindfully totally let go.

That means you have to seek the shadow of death in a spooky place all alone at night and when your mind says "You will die if you do not run" you deny yourself and fear not and fear not evil. Until you apply the remedy you are vanity. So whatever you are praying to after you got the education and before you applied the "deny yourself" remedy is certainly not God. Perhaps you should ask your cult leader is that is truth.

"Where the willingness is great, the difficulties cannot be great."- Niccoló Machiavelli

A ninety degree angle is a death sentence to fools and an inspiration to the wise. The incline of the hill is not as important as the inclination of the climber. Having motivation when facing impossibility is what will is. Becoming great is easy, being great is not. Risking everything for nothing requires willingness. The most difficult part of being great is to let go of your desire to be great. One cannot solve life's problems one can only seek to not see life as a problem. Willingness to fail is more important than desire to win. Self respect is relative to the narrow one finds their self in. If you stop questioning you stop having quests.

"And those dancing were thought to be insane by those who could not hear the music." – Nietzsche

What you don't hear is what you should listen for. The blind cannot see how many are blind and the ones with sight cannot see how to fix that. The blind cannot see how many are blind and the ones with sight cannot bear to see that. Completely insane people never question their sanity. Questioning your sanity may lead you to the truth. One risks irrelevance if they stop taking risks. If you are insulted by what others think you are insulted by what you think. Shame has more to do with fear than conscience.

Another question by one on a religious forum:

[Prodigal Son1]What 'cult' are you speaking about in your 'ramblings'?]

My response:

1. The tree of knowledge is written education and math. It veils the God image in man, right hemisphere.
Proof:
[we have been traditionally taught to master the 3 R's: reading, writing and arithmetic -- the domain and strength of the left brain.]

So society itself or civilization pushes this education on children starting at the age of seven. Because the mind is not developed until one is over twenty, the damage relative to veiling right brain is devastating.

Proof:
"In humans, the frontal lobe reaches full maturity around only after the 20s, marking the cognitive maturity associated with adulthood"

So because any being that got this education has right brain veiled they are simply left brain influenced containers. They see a child that is of sound mind and see that as "bad" so they determine to "fix" that child under the guise of "Let's make sure all the children get educated" and "no child left behind"

So Civilization is simply a cult, and relative to the ancient texts, the cult of the serpent. So a person is born, they get the education and they become a cult member and the right hemisphere is veiled and they want to make sure the right hemisphere is veiled in their own children and also everyone's child because misery loves company.

Proof:
"What it comes down to is that modern society discriminates against the right hemisphere." - Roger Sperry (1973)

What is modern society? Civilization.

What is right hemisphere? The god image in man.

How does civilization sin against the God image in man and thus God?
Via the tree of knowledge which is : [we have been traditionally taught to master the 3 R's: reading, writing and arithmetic -- the domain and strength of the left brain.]

So all of civilization is the cult of the serpent and they veil the god image in man in children but because they had their right brain veiled as children they have no intuition, a right brain trait, to detect that, because intuition is the soul.
Civilization sold its soul and the soul of its children and so it does not even detect it is harming children at all with education it believes it is helping them, so it is anti-truth.

This is why Just before the cult killed Jesus for telling this same truth he said [Luke 23:34 Then said Jesus, Father, forgive them; for they know not what they do.]

This means Jesus certainly did not forgive the cult for doing what it does to children, he was saying God you forgive these beasts but I certainly do not.
Only mentally unsound or insane people know not what they do, and that is civilization, they had their right brain veiled so they are insane and they are harming innocent children on an industrial scale and they have no right brain intuition to even understand that is what they do, so they are not really humans in that state of mind, they are possessed or beasts as the ancient texts suggest.

[Genesis 3:14 And the LORD God said unto the serpent(one who got the education the tree of knowledge, and did not apply the deny one's self remedy after words), Because thou hast done this, ((((thou art cursed)))) above all cattle, and above every beast of the field; upon thy belly shalt thou go, and dust shalt thou eat all the days of thy life:]

Thou art cursed, and your sense of time proves your right brain paradox no longer figures into your perception of time which is why your sense of time is so strong.
So Jesus said Deny yourself, because yourself is the serpent after you eat of that tree of knowledge, education. I find great humor in that.
You may want to ask your cult leader if that is truth.
END

9:05:04 PM - There are two people who got the education, the tree of knowledge and they are asleep.
One who has applied the remedy to the tree of knowledge will explain to both of them the deny one's self remedy. One will hear the remedy and only see darkness so they will remain asleep.
One will hear the remedy and they will see it as sunshine and they will apply it wake up and leave the slumber.

I am mindful explaining the remedy is like planting a seed.

Often the seed falls on the trail and never takes hold.

Often the seed fails in the rocks and is burned up in the sunlight.

Often the seed falls in the soil but the birds come and take it away.

Often the seed starts to take hold but then the vines grow over it and it withers.

Seldom the seed , the remedy, is heard and one applies the remedy and then they become a sower of the seed and continues the infinite loop of planting the seed, suggesting the remedy..

There are two beings with buckets.

One being has a hole in his bucket and one being has no holes in his bucket.

Both beings hear the fear not remedy and the being with the bucket that has holes cannot catch the concept of the fear not remedy so he ignores it and assumes it is foolishness.

The being with the bucket that has no holes starts to become curious about the remedy and asks more questions about the remedy until his bucket is full. Each question he asks about the remedy fills up his bucket until his bucket is full then he applies the remedy. The being with holes in his bucket has an easy load and the being with a full bucket has a heavy load because there are many with buckets that have holes. The bucket fills up drop by drop until the being is forced to let go, forced to apply the remedy.

3/2/2010 7:58:55 AM –

[Acts 8:9 But there was a certain man, called Simon, which beforetime in the same city used sorcery, and bewitched the people of Samaria, giving out that himself was some great one:

Acts 8:10 To whom they all gave heed, from the least to the greatest, saying, This man is the great power of God.

Acts 8:11 And to him they had regard, because that of long time he had bewitched them with sorceries.]

Sorcery : the supposed use of magic

bewitched : to affect somebody or something using a supposed magic spell

Neither of these comments are sorcery or about supernatural.

X ="In humans, the frontal lobe reaches full maturity around only after the 20s, marking the cognitive maturity associated with adulthood"

Y = [we have been traditionally taught to master the 3 R's: reading, writing and arithmetic -- the domain and strength of the left brain.]

These texts are about two things. The tree of knowledge which is Y, and the need for the fear not remedy or deny one's self remedy or the seek the shadow of death and fear not remedy or the lose one's life mindfully to preserve it remedy, because of X.

Any human being on this planet that suggests they have supernatural knowledge is what is known as sorcerer and a sorcerer that suggests they will heal you or pray to supernatural to benefit you is one that bewitches you. You take the money out of the equation and you will find out very swiftly who the sorcerers are and who the ones that speak truth are.

How much money should I charge you since you were just a small child when Y was pushed on you and because of X your mind has been hindered and in all reality you may not even be able to undo that damage unless you apply the fear not remedy the full measure because it is quite a self control exercise just to get your mind back to how it was when you were a child before the education?

Without your right brain intuition, pattern detection, complexity and swift random access processing at full power, and your sense of time proves it is not at full power because the paradox aspect of right brain no longer factors into your perception , you are nothing but a gullible sucker and a prime target for a sorcerer.

[To whom they all gave heed, from the least to the greatest, saying, This man is the great power of God.]

This comment is saying this sorcerer is making people give him money and he says some words and the people who have right brain veiled eat it up. I do not detect supernatural, ghosts, lizard men or aliens.

[Acts 8:12 But when they believed Philip preaching the things concerning the kingdom of God, and the name of Jesus Christ, they were baptized, both men and women.]

[kingdom of God] = right brain = kingdom is within, not ghosts and supernatural which are without. So the kingdom is within and relative to the mind and the (Y) effects the mind, and the remedy to correct that is to deny one's self, and baptism is one way, you dunk your head under water to get that hypothalamus to give one the death signal and then one can ignore it and that restores the kingdom, right brain traits after Y veils it. I see nothing supernatural about that in fact I am dealing with beings that are so mentally damaged by the tree of knowledge they perhaps cannot even grasp elementary cause and effect relationships anymore.

If you cannot grasp that this:

X ="In humans, the frontal lobe reaches full maturity around only after the 20s, marking the cognitive maturity associated with adulthood"

Factored in with this:

Y = [we have been traditionally taught to master the 3 R's: reading, writing and arithmetic -- the domain and strength of the left brain.]

means you might have gotten a bit too much left brain favoring aspects when your mind was still developing so perhaps you are perhaps mentally unsound, then you are perhaps completely out of touch with reality on all levels.

Before you speak about supernatural you need to grasp simple elementary cause and effect relationships first. I want you to attempt to use your mind and convince yourself that

X + Y = mentally sound as in right and left brain traits are in perfect 50/50 harmony.

If you are capable of convincing yourself that X + Y = mentally sound then that proves you are mentally unsound and no longer able to reason and so it would make sense you would believe in sorcerers that suggest ghosts, aliens, lizard men and demons and thus sorcerers that ask you to give them money to save you from the "spooky stuff".

Perhaps you should just ponder the spirit of these comments because if you attempt to come to a conclusion you perhaps will only come to left brain simpleminded sequential conclusion. One might suggest your right brain complexity and thus complex conclusions went bye- bye many years ago.

Which of these do you think is the truth?

X ="In humans, the frontal lobe reaches full maturity around only after the 20s, marking the cognitive maturity associated with adulthood"

Y = [we have been traditionally taught to master the 3 R's: reading, writing and arithmetic -- the domain and strength of the left brain.]

X + Y = left brain favored
X + Y = mental harmony; both aspects in harmony
X + Y = right brain favored

Your answer will tell you if you are capable of reasoning at all anymore.

3/2/2010 10:10:09 AM – I am mindful the ones that sense time that mock what I suggest relative to the written education are in fact not actually mocking me. They are simply in such deep denial they are saying to their self when they spit on the spirit of what I suggest "Please do not let this doctrine this being is suggesting be true." They are attempting to make me shut up because every time I type something they become a little less ignorant. I am starting to understand what the ones that sense time pattern is. The ones that sense time cannot argue with the spirit of what I suggest so

61

they simply are reduced to mocking what is say by focusing on details but they never attack the actual concept of what I suggest. They suggest I am stupid because I cannot use commas but they cannot argue that traditional education is left brain favoring. They cannot argue that concept so they focus on details that are totally unrelated to that concept in hopes that will make it so they do not have to face that concept.

A parent will say to their child "I will never knowingly harm you." I am suggesting if you are a parent you unknowingly harmed your child by pushing this education on them when they were seven and you unknowingly did it because your parents pushed it on you and unknowingly harmed you. I am not concerned about that but you perhaps may be. I am concerned about the ones you haven't unknowingly harmed yet. Simply put you are considered damaged goods with a slim chance of recovery so you do not even factor in the equation anymore at all. You are a terminally ill patient and I see no reason to exert much energy on a terminally ill patient. My purpose is more along the lines of an ounce of prevention. Whatever I have to do to ensure you do not unknowingly harm more children like you were harmed is on the table. That is a nice way to say all bets are off.

Please be mindful you are pleased to see all the children get the education at the earliest possible age.

[Genesis 6:7 And the LORD said, I will destroy man whom I have created from the face of the earth; both man, and beast, and the creeping thing, and the fowls of the air; for it repenteth me that I have made them.]

[And the LORD said, I will destroy man] .. man = the ones that sense time = the ones that get the education and do not apply the remedy; the ones with right brain veiled; the scribes.

[And the LORD said, I will destroy man.. for it repenteth me that I have made them.] Please be mindful the "Lords", the masters of the house(mind), the ones that applied the remedy regretted the ones that sense time. Please be mindful Nature herself regrets the ones that sense time. Please be mindful the universe itself regrets the ones that sense time. Please be mindful you sense time. Please be mindful this book is not in the fiction section. Please be mindful everyone you know senses time. Please be mindful your parents sense time. Please be mindful the police sense time. Please be mindful your elected leaders sense time. Please be mindful your religious leaders sense time. Please be mindful God himself regrets the ones that sense time. [for it repenteth me that I have made them.] Please be mindful God himself made a huge mistake in allowing the ones that sense time. Please be mindful you sense time. Please be mindful God made an error by allowing the ones that sense time and he regrets his grievous error. [for it repenteth me that I have made them.] Please be mindful God is upset with himself for allowing the ones that sense time. Please be mindful you sense time. Please be mindful God regrets himself for allowing the ones that sense time.

[And the LORD said, I will destroy man(the ones that sense time).. for it repenteth me that I have made them.] My only purpose is to convince the ones that sense time to mindfully kill their self. How does that make you feel? Do you wish to put pills in me so I will not convince you to mindfully kill yourself? Does it please you my purpose is to convince you to mindfully kill yourself?

Repent: to feel regret about a sin or past actions and change your ways or habits.

[And the LORD said, I will destroy man(the ones that sense time, the scribes).. for it repenteth me that I have made them.]
God himself sinned when he allowed the ones that sense time. The ones that sense time made God sin against himself. God sent beings who attempted to convince the ones that sense time to deny their self and thus mindfully kill their self so that God could atone for his sin against himself which was allowing the ones that sense time to exist. Please be mindful you sense time.

Please be mindful you cause God to sin against himself. [the LORD said ...for it repenteth me that I have made them.] = Repent: to feel regret about a sin. Please be mindful God repents for allowing the ones that sense time to exist. Repent: to feel regret about a sin.
[for it repenteth me] Do you believe the ancient texts are lies or truth? Do you believe the bible is a lie or the truth? Do you believe the wise beings in the Bible are liars or tell the truth? Are you able to determine the truth

when you hear it? Is this truth or a lie? [Luke 17:33 ; and whosoever shall lose his life(mindfully) shall preserve it.]

Is it truth or is it a lie? Do the beings in these ancient text lie or do they tell the truth? Do you perceive these texts want you to save your life mindfully or lose your life mindfully? Since God himself repents that he allowed the ones that sense time it is logical the beings in these texts want the ones that sense time to mindfully kill their self. Please be mindful you sense time. You are better off mindfully killing yourself than breathing one more breath because every time you take a breath you make God repent that he allowed you to breathe. Do you perceive I stutter? Do you perceive I am going on a speaking tour to convince people to mindfully kill their self? These words are my speaking tour. How much money can I make by convincing people to mindfully kill their self? My only purpose is to convince you to mindfully kill yourself so that God will stop feeling so bad that he sinned against himself by allowing you to exist. Please be mindful you sense time and thus God repents that you sense time and breathes his oxygen. God repents against himself because you breathe his oxygen. How much wisdom do you have now? How much does the ability to add numbers together matter now? How much does your ability to use commas matter now? How much does your grade point average matter now? How much does your money matter now? How much do you matter now? [the LORD said ...for it repenteth me that I have made them(the scribes, the ones that sense time).] Please be mindful you sense time. [Luke 20:46 Beware of the scribes,..]

Your people intelligence is no match for my inability to use commas properly.

3/2/2010 7:17:51 PM –

"Children are innocent
A teenager's fucked up in the head
Adults are even more fucked up
And elderlies are like children"
Porno or Pyros - Song: Pets

[Children are innocent] – Before the written education – sound minded
[A teenager's fucked up in the head] – After several years of education – mentally unsound
[Adults are even more fucked up] – After college, in full blown neurosis – fully mentally unsound
[And elderlies are like children] – The effects of the education start wearing off in old age – going back to mentally sound just before one dies unless the remedy is applied sooner.

Children and the elderly are united against a common enemy.

3/3/2010 4:54:57 PM – Sometimes a female mammal of one species will come across baby mammals of another species and take care of them. Sometimes that female mammal will even nurse the babies of another mammal. Consider the concept relative to child that finds a baby bird that falls out of its nest or finds a stray dog on the street. That child may suggest "Let me take it home and take care of it." And an adult may respond "No leave that animal where it is." or "We don't want that dirty animal in our home.". What is happening in this situation is what is called pride or ego. In Latin the word "I" is spelled EGO is capitals. The reason that female mammal will nurse the babies of another species of mammals is because that female mammal does not see any separation or see parts, or does not see a difference between a baby of its own species and a baby of another species. A human child does not see the difference between a baby bird, a baby dog or baby human because they do not have an ego yet. Simply put the education, tree of knowledge, is what creates ego and thus pride and thus separation and thus this "god complex". Is the species of dog worse, better, or equal to the species of cats considering both are mammals? Since both are mammal they cannot be different unless one starts to notice the details and parts. Self consciousness is what ego and pride really is so human beings are not suppose to be self conscious in a sound state of mind but if something alters their perception as a child, written education, they can become very self conscious and thus full of pride. This reality is what has created a dominate frame of mind relative to human beings compared to all other species. We are dominate as a species because we are able to kill every other species that gets in our way but in reality we are monsters because we kill every other species that gets in our way because we have so much pride and thus self consciousness so we perceive we are above other mammals and we factually are not. It is as simple as, if every other animal died off we would die off so we are equal to every other animal. If any one species of animal dies off we would not die off but if all species of animals died off we would die off. If we were truly dominate or better than other species we would survive even if every other animal species died off. There are single cell organisms in our stomachs and if they became extinct we would die off because we rely on them and have relied on them to live our stomach so we are not even above them we are reliant on them and at best equal to them. This pride is all a result of having the mind bent to the left by the tree of knowledge and this pride is what gives us as a species this "god complex" relative to our value. A sound minded mammal lives in harmony with their environment which means they do not perceive they are greater than their environment and an unsound minded mammal lives in disharmony and that can play both ways. For example, a mentally unsound mammal may see their environment is greater than they are and thus not drink water because they see water is greater than they are so they are in disharmony. They may not eat certain things and so those things may become over populated and that may result in harm. On the other hand a mentally unsound mammal may destroy everything their path and see their self as better than everything else. So both of these disharmony aspects means one is out of sync mindfully with their environment and neither position can last. If one respects all other animals over their self they will never kill any and thus they may die and if they have no respect for any animals they may kill them all and thus they may die. So this written education has altered our perception as mammals and has thus made this aspect pride and thus self consciousness so powerful we perceive we are the kings over all other animals and at the same we are aware if the other animals die off we factually will die off also. Once the mind is pushed out of harmony everything relative to that is pushed out of harmony. We over populate because every single parent perceives they have to have lots of kids because their pride is so strong they believe having kids is a sign of power and prestige. Another way to look at it is people have children because they perceive we may go extinct if we do not. If we stop having children for twenty years many believe we may go extinct so they have lots of children but that is only because their mind is completely out of harmony. Many have children so they can show their parents they are wise or show their friends they are wise or show people around them they are wise or hip or of value but it has nothing to do with sensibility it is all relative to pride and self consciousness caused by being conditioned into a mentally unsound state by the education. One sinister aspect is the parents have children and want them to get a better education than they got but the "brand" of written education the way it is taught to young children factually mentally hinders the children so in that respect the scribe parents have children so they have something to abuse but the parents are in neurosis and have no idea that is the only reason they have children. The abused tend to become abusers and children are the easiest to abuse. This of course is relative to the reverse thing, Civilization judges a person's worth relative to how much education they got and in reality world the amount of written education a person gets is relative to how mentally hindered they are. Scribe parents will brag about how young their child was when they taught them the ABC's and how to count and they are factually bragging how fast they mentally abuse their child so having children at this stage is nothing but having children so one can abuse them because one was abused as a child via the same education. It is understood in civilization written education is [Genesis 3:6 ...a tree to be desired to make one wise,] and I accidentally found out it is a tree that mentally veils right brain traits and makes ones fear go through the roof and factually mentally hinders one and thus makes one mentally retarded. If you doubt that apply the remedy and when right brain unveils and you will feel like going to war with civilization for its crime against you but be mindful they are factually in deep mental neurosis and have no idea what they are doing and to top it off they have all the weapons and laws on their side.

The ones that sense time are so mentally ruined they factually hinder their own offspring to a devastating degree and have no idea that is what they are doing at all. Some will ask me to prove it and I realize they want me to prove to them they mentally hinder children and in turn mentally kill the children. I am mindful all my proving it to them will perhaps do to them is make them want to either mindfully kill their self or literally kill their self. If one is not fully aware of that they do not understand what I am saying. Some suggest honesty is the best policy. In this situation relative to written education being honest means one has to tell people they support knowingly or unknowingly mentally killing children and literally killing children knowingly or unknowingly as a result of the education being taught to children at such a young age and due to the fact in the extreme left brain state of mind ones emotions are turned up far too high from the education one may suddenly realize what they have done and go right to the 9th circle of hell and end their life literally. This is logical and expected in the vast majority of cases. One might suggest it is a rude awakening for some and they will either face the reality and take the mental anguish, deny it and stay in denial or mindfully implode and perish, but there are no other possibilities. I am mindful I am telling human beings that are not in the emotional state to be able to handle harsh reality such as the reality relative to written education so I am mindful I may actually be killing people mindfully or literally just by arranging words in a certain fashion to excite emotions. I have explained this situation to some people related to the psychology field and after I was finished with my explanation they said "We got it all wrong and I am very depressed now." That does not mean they will apply the remedy that only means they are on their way to the 9th circle of hell, treason, depression, suicidal thoughts. What this means is I a mindful I may actually be knowingly killing people as a result of telling them the truth and being honest, so clearly honesty is not always the best policy unless ones policy is to potentially indirectly kill people as a result of being honest. Apparently that reality is irrelevant to me at this point. I decided to go with the flow and let the chips fall where they may and so that is the only relevant aspect to me at this point. Perhaps I should not be concerned over spilt milk from leaking containers. Some prefer lies and denial to death even though both eventually lead to death.

3/3/2010 9:49:59 PM –
[Psalms 25:9 The meek will he guide in judgment: and the meek will he teach his way.]
[Psalms 37:11 But the meek shall inherit the earth; and shall delight themselves in the abundance of peace.]
[Matthew 5:5 Blessed are the meek: for they shall inherit the earth.]

[Zephaniah 2:3 Seek ye the LORD, all ye meek of the earth, which have wrought his judgment; seek righteousness, seek meekness: it may be ye shall be hid in the day of the LORD'S anger.]

Meek = the depressed and suicidal; they are ones with a sense of time that do not believe they even have a right to be alive. Depression and suicidal thoughts are end symptoms right brain is attempting to unveil after the written education has veiled it. With right brain unveiled and at 50% power in the mind alongside left hemisphere it is impossible to be depressed because right brain random access lightning fast processing will not allow the mind to ever rest on any thought for more than a moment relative to a clock. This means a mindset of being depressed or suicidal is not possible at all ever, when right brain is unveiled fully. So this comment: [Blessed are the meek] means the depressed and suicidal are blessed because they are in the proper frame of mind to unveil right brain after written education, the tree of knowledge, has veiled it. This is relative to the eastern concept of the remedy because detachment is the frame of mind that is required to apply the remedy. This detachment is not about throwing everything you have away, in fact it is more relative to not allowing these "material" aspect's in one's life interfere with ones thoughts when they seek the shadow of death. For example if ones thoughts are concerned about losing their money and wealth then when their hypothalamus says "death is coming" in that spooky dark place one goes to, they will run. Another way to look at it is a suicidal person has to be mindful of death and then get to a mind set of letting go of everything they know in their life to reach a mindset to let go of life. One is simply not going to go to a spooky place alone at night if they have any attachments they perceive they may lose in their thoughts. The ones that sense time cannot let go of attachments because a left brain trait is coveting and so they "fear" they may lose control of these things they covet if they go to that spooky place and something "kills" them. This is relative to the concept "you are your own worst enemy". This remedy takes no money and no great mental power to apply in reality. One gets the death signal from the hypothalamus and they perceive panic and they perceive they should fear and run but instead of exerting effort one relaxes and does nothing and that is the remedy in full and it takes one second but relative to the fact a being that senses time has

69

great fear and is thus scared easily, it is nearly impossible for them to apply. This does not mean the ones that sense time are scared as a being as much as it means the ones that sense time have a hypothalamus that is very, very sensitive because their mind has been bent to the left because of all that left brain favoring education they got as children before their mind was even developed. The ones that sense time listen to their hypothalamus when it gives them these "death" signals and the point of the remedy is to not listen to their hypothalamus and that is essentially what the concept of fear not is all about. If you hear a song and something in that song makes you feel like that song is bad or evil I am suggesting that is your hypothalamus lying to you. If you hear a word and that word makes you feel like that word is evil or bad I am suggesting that is your hypothalamus lying to you or, sending you false "fear" signals. So the point of self control would be to face those fears. If your mind says that song is evil or that word is evil then say that word or listen to that song until your mind stops saying that song is evil or that word is evil. You may perceive those songs or words are evil because you perceive you have morals but I am mindful you do not have morals you have a hypothalamus that is afraid of bad hair cuts. If you have any morals at all you would dedicate your entire life to stopping the ones that mentally hinder innocent child's minds with written education so you factually do not do that so you factually do not have morals in fact you have such an absence of conscience you do not even believe years of left brain favoring education push on the delicate mind of a seven year old children does not damage that child's mind and mental development so I am mindful you are absent of a conscience on all levels. You have a conscience as long as the definition of conscience is void of all conscience and that is an indication of how mentally devastating the years of written education has had on the development of your mind. You perceive once you apply the remedy and you regain your conscience you will be so fantastic but in reality after you apply the remedy and regain your conscience you have to deny your conscience because all of your friends are asleep and are asleep to the fact they mentally hinder children's minds with the education and with their influence on the children and there is nothing you can do about it so you have to actually avoid subscribing to your conscience once you get your conscience back because in this narrow it will destroy you. You will not go insane but you will seek to escape the reality of consciousness when surrounded by lunatics. What you will find when you apply the remedy is our species messed around with this great invention written education and veiled its right hemisphere and after thousands of years everyone has their right hemisphere veiled essentially and they are mentally no longer in a state of mind that could be describes as anything but insane. Our species takes the children and makes them insane so the children will be like the adults are and so the entire species is essentially insane because of this invention written education and math. That can drive a person who is fully aware of it mad relative to they just want it to go away, they cannot handle that kind of heat, they cannot face that kind of misery. Because of this it is important to be mindful of what focus on the log in your eye is all about. Simply put you are a human being and no human being can take that kind of misery especially when they are conscious and fully mindful of it so one has to develop mental strategies to convince their self the species is just an illusion and this helps one deal with the reality our species ruined itself unknowingly with this left brain favoring invention. The magic of right brain though, is it processes thoughts very fast and in random access so one is not going to struggle with this reality as long as they do not go halfway or lukewarm with the remedy. Seek the shadow of death and fear not, that is a full measure remedy. Those that lose their life mindfully preserve it, that is a full measure remedy. The dunking under water version of the remedy is a full measure remedy. This full measure version of the remedy ensures one wakes up swiftly relative to a year, as in one warms up swiftly. One goes through many mental stages of waking up in that year but they go through them swiftly. Once the heightened awareness, right brain intuition, kicks in after right brain unveils, going swiftly through the stages is paramount. These full measure remedies ensures one goes to heaven in a chariot and if one messes around and does not go the full measure they may get stuck up the mountain so to speak and one does not want to get stuck somewhere up the mountain. You may understand some things I say but in your sense of time state of mind if you felt the heightened awareness with your emotions turned up to the level they are you would go right to the 9th circle of hell and you perhaps could not take that kind of suffering and you perhaps would literally kill yourself or harm others, this is because your emotions are through the roof after all that education. So although the machine state appears sad to you if you get stuck with heightened awareness and still have strong emotions you will implode. There are many examples of beings and even some Saints that applied the remedy one way or another and could not take the heat in the kitchen because they perhaps did not go the full measure. For example: [Jonah 4:3 Therefore now, O LORD, take, I beseech thee, my life from me; for it is better for me to die than to live.] Socrates said something along the lines of, For me to die and them to live, which is better God only knows.

In a true vacuum if you applied the remedy and had the heightened awareness you would be at peace but because you are aware of the 'ways" of society after you apply the remedy right brain is going to be in your conscious state and it is going to detect patterns and use its intuition and before even six months relative to a calendar you are going to be fully aware what is happening and then you will be fully aware there is not a whole lot you can do to stop what is happening relative to what this written education does to the mind of children. Whatever you perceive is going on relative to the species relative to your sense of time state of mind, you are factually totally ignorant. The little hope aspect is that if you apply the remedy the full measure you will warm up swiftly and reach the machine state swiftly then you achieve this indifference state of mind.

This being clearly understood what was going on relative to the education.

"The tree of knowledge is not the tree of life! And yet can we cast out of our spirits all the good or evil poured into them by so many learned generations? Ignorance cannot be learned."

Gerard De Nerval

[Ignorance cannot be learned.] All this means is, a human being cannot be taught to be ignorant but after they get all that left brain favoring tree of knowledge, their right brain is veiled and then they are ignorant, mentally hindered, mentally hindered means mentally retarded and that is what ignorance is. He was quite a comedian. He ended up in poverty and he hung himself but it was not because he was depressed it perhaps was because he could not stand the heat in the kitchen, the heightened awareness. This is why this comment is so important [Revelation 3:16 So then because thou art lukewarm, and neither cold nor hot, I will spue thee out of my mouth.]

No lukewarm. You either stay asleep or use the full measure remedy because you want to be in the machine state in this narrow and what the machine state really is, is, the right brain is unveiled fully to 50% in harmony with left brain and so your thoughts are going so fast and they are random access you cannot maintain a set state of mind or very long relative to minutes relative to a clock so you will be able to stand the heat in the kitchen, so to speak.

[The tree of knowledge is not the tree of life!] What this comment means is, you can spell well and do math well but that only proves you have no mental life or activity to speak of relative to a sound minded human being that has both hemispheres working in harmony. That is one pattern I notice about all these beings that have applied the remedy to one degree or another. They are all comedians and the only ones that get the jokes are the ones that have applied the remedy to a degree. I attempt to avoid being a comedian because I did not find it funny to do to myself all the things I did to myself in the ten years in the 9th circle of hell, depression, and perhaps you will understand how funny I did not find it infinitely sooner than you think. After all my only purpose is life is to convince you to mindfully kill yourself so never assume that my purpose in life is anything other than that. No matter what I say ever, it is simply a ploy to convince you to mindfully kill yourself with the understanding you may have a bad accident and literally kill yourself. How you feel about that is totally irrelevant at this point in infinity. Granted I fell the tracks off.

[Psalms 25:9 The meek will he guide in judgment: and the meek will he teach his way.]

This comment is a sign post.
[The meek will he guide in judgment] It is out of sequence so it is proof right brain random access factored into this comment. The comment should be relative to proper sequence [The meek he will guide in judgment] Other words if a child wrote a sentence in English class [The meek will he guide] without a question mark at the end, the English teacher would rush the child to the psychologist and see how many pills the psychologist could cram down the child's throat to "fix" the child.

Clearly this type of grammar is a symptom of mental illness relative to ones that are mentally ill, called society. [The meek will he guide in judgment] It is rather sinister but only if you are not a machine.

[Maggie C. (14) took her own life after being constantly bullied]
Perhaps I shall destroy them all because of what they have done to you with their wisdom education princess. The suffering you are powerless to stop is your enemy. Rules are to be bent, broken or avoided but never lived by because rules are absolutes and hinder ones options and thus one's ability to adapt.

3/4/2010 8:23:07 PM - [1 John 2:18 Little children, it is the last time: and as ye have heard that antichrist shall come, even now are there many antichrists; whereby we know that it is the last time.]

There are at least 1800 references to children in the Torah and New testament.

That is because of this reality relative to the tree of knowledge, written education and math.

This is not an opinion:
X ="In humans, the frontal lobe reaches full maturity around only after the 20s, marking the cognitive maturity associated with adulthood"

This is not an opinion:
Y = [we have been traditionally taught to master the 3 R's: reading, writing and arithmetic -- the domain and strength of the left brain.]

This is not an opinion:
Z = "What it comes down to is that modern society discriminates against the right hemisphere." - Roger Sperry (1973) - neuropsychologist, Nobel laureate

Modern society is civilization.

Because of X , Y mentally hinders the right brain which is what Z is suggesting.

The reason children are mentioned so often is because if a person gets the education after their frontal lobe has developed it perhaps would not veil their right brain. A child gets education at a young age and in the times of the ancient texts it was mostly males and because of this [In humans, the frontal lobe reaches full maturity around only after the 20s..] it means the left brain was favored and so the right brain was not favored and slowly became silent.

[and as ye have heard that antichrist shall come, even now are there many antichrists;]

John is saying to children, what David said.[Luke 20:46 Beware of the scribes]

John is saying children there are many scribes and they will push the written education on you, and John is calling them anti-christ's because they have right brain, the god image in man veiled because they got the written education and did not apply the fear not remedy.

[now are there many antichrists; whereby we know that it is the last time.]

This aspect of the comment is saying, "we know it will be the end of no sense of time once you get the education" Simply put a beings ability to sense time is factual proof their right brain paradox no longer factors into their perception because it has been veiled by the written education.

Simply put, the quick and the dead are real people, and the quick are the ones who applied the fear not remedy and they have a sound mind so they are mentally quick in contrast to the ones that have right brain veiled and they are the mentally dead, hindered.

[Revelation 11:18 And the nations were angry, and thy wrath is come, and the time of the dead,]

The time of the dead. The ones with right brain veiled sense time, and they are the dead, mentally unsound, thus THE TIME OF THE DEAD; the mentally dead (hindered) sense time.

One version of history is mankind invented written language and math and became mentally wise and one version is mankind became mentally hilarious and I accidentally discovered which version was the truth.

3/5/2010 9:03:31 PM – One huge red flag about Socrates relative to written language is he did not write any books and also at the time written education was new and he considered it a revolution and a bad thing, something along the lines that oral communication was more personable but this complicates things because one of his main points was "No true philosopher fears death." And that is the fear not remedy and he would not know that unless he applied the remedy and he would not need to apply the remedy unless he was taught written education or taught to write first. For example the tribes in the Amazon do not have written language so they certainly would not know the fear not remedy because if one never gets the written language training one could never "wake up" from it and discover the fear not remedy is how they "woke up". So the Sumerians invented written language roughly around 3400 BC and that would be in line with about 5400 years ago but in Greece language was copied from the Phoenicians and this was long after the Sumerians invented written language so relative to Socrates time around 2500 BC written language was very new to that area of the world and this is why Socrates suggested written language was a revolution and he spoke out against it and this would explain why the ruler scribes of that time would want him to be silenced. So Socrates was very similar to what the beings in the Torah were relative to suggesting the dangers of written language, the tree of knowledge only the beings in the Torah were suggesting its dangers perhaps much earlier because written language came to the middle east much earlier than it came to Greece. So the pattern here is regardless of when written language was invented in a certain area of the world there was a time when there were skeptics or beings that spoke out against it and slowly these critics of written language we silenced. So this means since Samarian language was invented somewhere around 5400 years ago about 3400 BC the Torah may in fact date back that far. What this means is Abraham and Lot may have been around much earlier than is suggested which is 800 BC , they may have been around more like 3000 BC just after written language started to catch on. This is logical because any child that was taught written education would show signs of right brain attempting to unveil itself and that is depression and suicidal thoughts and so eventually someone would be waking up or having a good accident. Other words it is not logical people who were being taught written education were not waking up for thousands of years after written language was starting to catch on. So although it may appear Moses was around just after Abraham and Lot the reality is he may not have been around for perhaps a thousand years or more after Abraham and Lot. This is the very first suggestion of the fear not remedy perhaps in the history of mankind relative to being a remedy to the mental side effects of written education.

[Genesis 15:1 After these things the word of the LORD came unto Abram in a vision, saying, Fear not, Abram: I am thy shield, and thy exceeding great reward.]

So Socrates was in another part of the world where written language was not even invented until long after it was invented in the middle east and that means Abraham was the first human being to suggest the remedy to the tree of knowledge and also gave a parable or story explaining how it was to be applied and this may go back as far as the invention of written language 5400 years ago. So before there was even any understanding about the brain or the hypothalamus Abraham detected the primary psychological symptom of getting the written education, fear, and then the remedy, fear not and he even demonstrated this remedy on his own son Isaac in the Abraham and Isaac story and this may be as far back as 5000 years ago and that is testament to how powerful right brain pattern detection, intuition, lightning random access processing speed is. So Abraham got the written language and then broke free of the neurosis and figured out what had happened and then made this comment.

[Genesis 15:1 After these things the word of the LORD came unto Abram in a vision, saying, Fear not, Abram: I am thy shield, and thy exceeding great reward.]

Then Abraham tested his understandings by applying this fear not principle on is son Isaac and so he was the first psychologist, neurologist that had a complete grasp of the mental damage caused by learning written education. Essentially he understood the mental side effects and so he understood because the damage caused by written education was on a mental level he understood it could only be remedied on a mental level, which means no literal medicine could fix it, it had to be a situation where mentally a person perceives fear to the extreme, perceived fear of death and then they have to allow that or not fight that or submit to that, or fear not. I am mindful Abraham was so sane or so conscious the beings that got the written education could not figure out what he was even suggesting at all. He was so far beyond the beings mentally that got the written education and were in the neurosis they perhaps had no idea what he was talking about because he did not have any terms to explain it other than cerebral terms. For example how would one explain the mind or the brain, perhaps 5000 years ago.

Here are some comments related to the mind and are both comments by Abraham.

[Genesis 23:8 And he communed with them, saying, If it be your mind that I should bury my dead out of my sight; hear me, and intreat for me to Ephron the son of Zohar,]

[Genesis 26:35 Which were a grief of mind unto Isaac and to Rebekah.]

I am mindful this is all relative to the invention of written language and so the whole concept of supernatural is not logical relative to these texts considering written language is not supernatural. Since mankind fell from grace 5400 years ago and that is saying written language hinders the mind and when we started embracing that relative to this area of the world and started acting strange relative to the fact learning written language at a young age hindered the mind, supernatural is absent from that entire line of thought. If one puts their hand on a stove and burns their hand, that is not supernatural. If asbestosis causes lung cancer that is not supernatural. If in learning written language your perception and thus your mind is altered and you start exhibiting symptoms of that relative to your deeds and fruits that is not supernatural. This is why the main key to these texts is in the first three chapters and those first three chapters discuss the tree of knowledge and because the three main religions in the west all mentions the first book or the Torah in one way or another that means they are all relative that key in the first three chapters, the tree of knowledge, written education. What is really happening relative to the beings that wrote these texts is they were conscious and they were talking to beings that got the written education and thus were unconscious and so they were far beyond the understanding of the beings they were attempting to communicate with. So from Abraham to Moses to Jesus to the disciples and to Mohammed and others which all applied the remedy in one way or another, they were simply beyond the understanding of the ones that got the written education and did not apply the remedy because all of said beings were conscious and of sound mind and so a mentally hindered unconscious being cannot understand a sound minded conscious being fully. Simply put a conscious sound minded being is beyond the understanding of an unconscious mentally hindered being and written education favors left brain so one becomes mentally hindered. There are not written languages in recorded history that are in right brain random access so the mental neurosis is identical no matter what "brand" of written language one is talking about and thus the remedy is identical. Because the remedy is identical no matter what kind of written language or math one gets, that makes it much easier. So the fear not remedy in concept is universal on a world wide scale and is applicable to all written education and math induced neurosis anywhere. This is why Jesus told the disciples to go and tell the whole world the message because the remedy was applicable to every country because at that time perhaps all countries had written education. So Abraham solved all of today's problems relative to the species relative to this written education induced neurosis when he wrote this comment [Genesis 15:1 After these things the word of the LORD came unto Abram in a vision, saying, Fear not, Abram: I am thy shield, and thy exceeding great reward.] and as a species we just now realized it and that would be the proper definition of foresight. Now that I am very infinitely complacent I will very infinitely digress. One thing is certain, the majority of beings that sense time and are thus in the neurosis are firstly not even aware they are the neurosis and secondly the neurosis itself hinders their ability to apply the remedy even if they want to. So these wise beings appeared supernatural in their wisdom in contrast to the ones that were in the neurosis and these wise beings were saying "No it's not me, there is nothing special about me I just applied the fear not remedy and have god on my side (meaning right brain unveiled fully)." And the ones in neurosis were saying "Oh and he is humble and meek and wise." when in reality the wise beings were telling the truth, they were just conscious and thus appeared extremely wise in contrast to the ones that had right brain veiled by the education. - 11:24:13 PM

3/6/2010 7:12:55 AM – Ponder this intellect aspect of left brain because intellect is not really accurate to describe it because it is really a focus on details. An intellectual is essentially a person that can understand and think and reason but that is assumed to be in part a person that is good with details but that really has very little to do with intellect. For example a historian is really just a person that is very good with details and left brain is all about details and so contrary to that right brain is very good with concepts and details are not really that important on many levels especially relative to this written language situation. For example these dates and events and names relative to this written language neurosis are not very important because they are so far removed. If I suggested written language was invented 300 years ago and a guy named Joe discovered the fear not remedy to the written language neurosis those details would all be inaccurate but the concept of fear not as a remedy to said neurosis is the concept that is accurate and the only aspect that is relevant. Other words it is not important when written language was invented, it is not important who discovered the fear not remedy and it is not important where the remedy was discovered because the concept of the remedy is all that is important relative to right now. What is on a person's plate is the remedy itself and all the details or reasons one should apply the remedy is not going to assist one to apply the remedy. In school they will suggest a person that can spell well and use grammar well is quite an intellect but in reality it is just that person is very good with details a left brain trait. This whole concept about who is wiser and which country is wiser and which area of the world is wiser is really a symptom of left brain detail focus and that means our species is full of many detail focused anal retentive beings when it should be full of more concept and holistic focused beings. The very fact we even have countries at all is a symptom of this left brain detail focus and this fixation on detail is what creates the separations, not morals or intelligence. Economics itself is a result of this left brain details fixation. For example there are not really people living in different countries that is just a superficial detail separation and the internet proves that. When I speak to people in chat rooms I do not even ask them what country they are from but often the ones with a sense of time are interested in those details. One way to look at it is the written language has made us very left brain heavy and thus very detail focused and all of the details we are focused on as a species creates very many separations and all the separations encourage many rules and laws and divisions and that only encourages left brain aspects even more. In any given country they have favorite or certain foods relative to that country for example but if one removes that detail then it is reduced down to, in any given country they eat food and even further, in any given country there are people. So this left brain education is what actually creates all this separation because left brain is focused on details. Neurosis is the ability to sense time mindfully and the inability to understand that is abnormal.

3/7/2010 1:47:16 PM– [Genesis 3:1 Now the serpent was more subtil than any beast of the field which the LORD God had made. And he said unto the woman, Yea, hath God said, Ye shall not eat of every tree of the garden?]

One should be mindful the reason this comment is speaking to women [And he said unto the woman] is because women are keepers of the offspring and once the women eat off the tree of knowledge all the children are the serpents, so to speak. Simply put, if the men eat off the tree that is not as important because men are not keepers of the offspring, men are protectors of the women but the women are keepers of the offspring, the women have more of a connection with the children than the men do. So in this reality the easiest way to the children is through the women. For example:

[Genesis 24:16 And the damsel was very fair to look upon, a virgin, neither had any man known her: and she went down to the well, and filled her pitcher, and came up.]

[And the damsel was very fair to look upon, a virgin, neither had any man known her] This means this woman was fair because she had not eaten off the tree of knowledge and no man had known her which means she had not had any contact with the men, the ones that sense time, the ones that had eaten off the tree of knowledge, the scribes. This contact aspect works like this. Think about a tribe that does not have any written education but then the ones that sense time come in contact with them and before you know it that tribe is doing things for money and acting like the ones that sense time. Another example is when you hear about wars fought by children. The children do not have the education but some being that has had the education comes in contact with them and begins to manipulate them and the next thing you know he has the children fighting a war for him for material gains. A child that has not gotten the written education is very impressionable because they are very trusting. Right hemisphere is very trusting because it has very little prejudice so a being of sound mind with right brain in the conscious state is very trusting.

[and she went down to the well, and filled her pitcher, and came up.] This comment is suggesting this women who was fair, did not get the education, and had never been with a man, one that senses time, was very wise. She filled her pitcher with water which means she was wise hearted.

[2 Samuel 20:16 Then [cried a wise woman] out of the city, Hear, hear; say, I pray you, unto Joab, Come near hither, that I may speak with thee.] [Judges 5:29 Her [wise ladies] answered her, yea, she returned answer to herself,..]

So in this comment wise woman is a woman who either did not eat off the tree of knowledge, did eat off the tree of knowledge and then applied the fear not remedy, or a women that was around men, the ones that sense time and then applied the fear not remedy. The complexity here is that once a person is over the age of twenty and then applies the remedy they are wise to the ways of the ones that sense time so it is very unlikely they become under the curse again but that of course is not an absolute. This concept of contact is very important to be mindful of. One example would be at one time Native Americans did not have guns then they meet the ones that sense time and eventually the Native Americans did have guns. Some may see this as the Native Americans adopted the cultural ways of the "white man" but in reality it is the transference of the curse into the impressionable, the sound minded.

Think about it like this equation.

X = food
Y = money
Z= deeds required to get X or Y
A = Education

So the ones that sense time are all about control because that is a left brain trait, coveting, so they control the natural resources, food and water, and then they require that a person needs money to get access to those natural resources. So then a person is required to do things Z to get Y to get X and A is a supposed sure way to get Y and thus X.

So, A + Z = X,Y
This is a basic carrot and stick tactic. "If you want money and food and luxury you are going to need an education." So this concept is based on the premise that education is ones salvation or ones ticket to money and thus food and water. Traditional education veils the right hemisphere so in reality this concept is a method to ensure everyone becomes a left brain influenced container and nothing more.

[Now the serpent was more subtil than any beast of the field which the LORD God had made. And he said unto the woman,]

This comment is simply saying eventually the men, the ones that sense time, put women in a situation where if the woman wanted food and water and luxury the women had to get the education. This is why in the history of recorded mankind women have always been mistreated because they resisted getting the education. The premise of civilization is if a person does not have their brand of education they must not be intelligent because civilization has determined education is a true measure of intelligence when in fact it is only a true measure about how mentally unsound one is.

The better one is at math and writing and using all the rules and directions associated with them the further left brain is favored and so the more mentally unsound one is.

Giedd, Jay N. (october 1999). "Brain Development during childhood and adolescence: a longitudinal MRI study". Nature neuroscience 2 (10): 861-863.
"In humans, the frontal lobe reaches full maturity around only after the 20s, marking the cognitive maturity associated with adulthood"

Let's look at this word in the above comment cognitive.
Definition of cognitive : relating to the process of acquiring knowledge by the use of reasoning, intuition, or perception.

" If you reflect back upon our own educational training, we have been traditionally taught to master the 3 R's: reading, writing and arithmetic -- the domain and strength of the left brain" -
The Pitek Group, LLC.
Michael P. Pitek, III

This traditional education favors left brain and in turn veils right brain traits so it alters ones perception.
[acquiring knowledge by the use of .... perception.]

This traditional education favors left brain and in turn veils right brain traits and one right brain trait is intuition.
[acquiring knowledge by the use of ..., intuition]

The antonym of reason is insane because other words for reason are sanity and good sense. So in order for a human being to make a good sense or reasonable decision they need all the traits of left and right hemisphere in equal parts. For example: To make one decision the mind needs these left brain traits linear logic, ability to see parts, simple minded perception, objective perception, analytical perception, rational perception and then right brain traits pattern detection, intuition, random access perception, holistic perception, ambiguity, paradox, complexity. So in order to make any decision no matter what it is all of these aspects from both hemispheres have to be equal. If one of these traits from either hemisphere is stronger than any other traits the decision or the reasoning ability is altered so one loses their ability to reason and thus loses their good sense.

So for example, before the accident I had no idea written education and math had bad mental side effects but then after the accident all of these right brain traits were added back or restored to my reasoning ability; intuition, pattern detection, complexity, ambiguity and paradox and now it is very obvious and very easy to understand all of that left brain favoring education on top of the fact the frontal lobes does not develop fully until one is twenty is a huge red flag. It is very obvious and very logical that this equation is logical and reasonable and sound.

X = "What it comes down to is that modern society discriminates against the right hemisphere." - Roger Sperry (1973)

Y = "In humans, the frontal lobe reaches full maturity around only after the 20s, marking the cognitive maturity associated with adulthood" - Giedd, Jay N. (october 1999). "Brain Development during childhood and adolescence: a longitudinal MRI study". Nature neuroscience 2 (10): 861-863.

Z = " If you reflect back upon our own educational training, we have been traditionally taught to master the 3 R's: reading, writing and arithmetic -- the domain and strength of the left brain" -
The Pitek Group, LLC.
Michael P. Pitek, III

Because of Y, education which is Z hinders the mind of the children because of X.

It is very logical the reality of Y coupled with the reality of Z is going to affect cognitive and reasoning ability because cognitive ability is relative to perception and intuition and since Z effects both of those aspects reasoning itself is going to be affected in an unwanted way.

Now a person's ability to senses time is an indication their perception has been altered as a result of Z(Y). Since a person's perception has been altered that means their cognitive ability has been altered because cognitive ability is relative to perception.

[Definition of cognitive : relating to the process of acquiring knowledge by the use of .Perception.]

Another way to look at it is, if Z never happened to a human being at a young age their perception would not be the same as it is after they get Z at a young age and so their reasoning and thus cognitive abilities would not be the same because perception is relative to reasoning. What this means is the only reason you do not detect without anyone telling you Traditional Education(Z) mentally hinders people is because you got traditional education (Z) and your cognitive ability and thus your reasoning ability and thus your good sense has been altered in an unfavorable way. Another way to look at it is because as a child your frontal lobe was not at full power and because you had all that left brain favoring education pushed on your at far too young of an age you were turned from a being that had good sense and the ability to reason to a being that lost its ability and cognitive reasoning skills so you were made insane because you are not capable of reasoning with an entire hemisphere of your mental aspects veiled. Simply put one cannot make a reasonable decision when their right brain intuition, complexity, ambiguity, paradox are not at full power. Because society itself all got this education all of their cognitive abilities are on the level of insanity. The entire civilization will be asked a simply question: "Should we educate the children with traditional education (Z)" and all of civilization will answer "Yes that is wise" so all of civilization is making an insane decision or an unreasonable decision because their cognitive abilities are all altered so they are not able to make a good sense or reasonable decisions. What this means is because civilization cannot make a reasonable decision they decide all the children get the education and so that is an unreasonable or insane decision and that ensures another generation that does not have the cognitive ability to make good sense reasonable decisions will be created. Civilization will see a tribe living in nature that has no contact with traditional education and civilization will make the decision to assist that tribe to get the traditional education

(Z) and that is an unreasonable or an insane decision but civilization will perceive that is a reasonable decision because they are far too insane to determine what a reasonable or unreasonable decision is.

Is pushing this : [Z = " the 3 R's: reading, writing and arithmetic -- the domain and strength of the left brain" -On the mind of a child considering this reality : [Y = "In humans, the frontal lobe reaches full maturity around only after the 20s, marking the cognitive maturity associated with adulthood] a reasonable decision or an unreasonable decision?

Is pushing this : [Z = " the 3 R's: reading, writing and arithmetic -- the domain and strength of the left brain" - On the mind of a child considering this reality : [Y = "In humans, the frontal lobe reaches full maturity around only after the 20s, marking the cognitive maturity associated with adulthood"] a good sense decision or a bad sense decision?

Civilization has decided Z + Y is a reasonable and sound minded decision when in factual reality that decision is total insanity and the farthest thing from reasonable decision that is possible and civilization does not even perceive that so civilization is completely insane because their perception and intuition has been altered as a result of said traditional education and intuition and perception are relative to cognitive ability and that means their ability to reason has been severely hindered. Simply put modern society is a lunatic asylum. Because of that it is important you do not attempt to make a decision relative to applying this fear not remedy relative to trying to make a logical conclusion or question if it is the proper thing to do because you are not capable of reasoning and perhaps not capable of making a good sense decision. The solution is to do exactly what you do not want to do because what you want to do is unreasonable relative to applying the remedy. This means you have to think in total reverse of how you think. You perceive it is unwise to go to a dark spooky place at night alone and you think it is unwise to do that because you are unreasonable and thus insane in your cognitive ability because of the education you got as a child. Simply put if you got this before you were twenty [reading, writing and arithmetic -- the domain and strength of the left brain"] you are unable to reason because your perception and intuition has been altered so you cannot make decisions based on good sense or based on reality until you apply the remedy and restore the right brain traits back to your decision making processes. Even as you read this you are attempting to deduce if what is suggest is true and so you are attempting to reason and you are not able to reason. The only chance you have is to throw down everything you are thinking and go out and apply the remedy and think of nothing else but applying the remedy because if you attempt to think about anything else you will "reason" your way out of applying the remedy because in your altered state of perception caused by the education you are insane and thus can only make unreasonable decisions. Because the education has made you insane the only solution is to do insane things because insane things are sane things. Going to a dark spooky place alone at night and then when your mind says "Run, spooky things are coming to kill you" and when that happens you do not run, appears to be insane to you but in reality it is absolute sanity.

11:41:49 PM – An email to someone about something.

X = "What it comes down to is that modern society discriminates against the right hemisphere." - Roger Sperry (1973)

Y = "In humans, the frontal lobe reaches full maturity around only after the 20s, marking the cognitive maturity associated with adulthood" - Giedd, Jay N. (october 1999). "Brain Development during childhood and adolescence: a longitudinal MRI study". Nature neuroscience 2 (10): 861-863.

Z = " If you reflect back upon our own educational training, we have been traditionally taught to master the 3 R's: reading, writing and arithmetic -- the domain and strength of the left brain" -
The Pitek Group, LLC.
Michael P. Pitek, III

Because of Y, education which is Z hinders the mind of the children because of X.

A fetus develops in 9 months
A child that is born takes about 20 years for the frontal lobe to develop

So this means education(Z) starting at age 7 is the same thing as injecting a pregnant mother with drugs during the fetus' first trimester

Fetus 1-3 months first trimester
Child 1 -7 years first trimester relative to the fact the frontal lobe takes 20 years to develop and it is relative to cognitive reasoning , so the education kills the kids mentally

So with the education society is mentally aborting the children and the reason they are not aware of it is because they got the education and so their right brain intuition is nearly silenced.

So a person is born fully conscious with left and right hemisphere working in harmony or at 50/50,
then at the age of seven a child is taught traditional education and that favors left brain and so the being is pushed out of mental harmony because the mind does not even develop fully until the age of 20 , so they are made unconscious or pushed into neurosis.

So my accident was , I broke that neurosis and figured out how I did it in hindsight and returned to consciousness left and right brain working at 50/50.

The problem with that is "modern society" is civilization and because they essentially all get the education they are in neurosis and because their right brain intuition is veiled they are not even aware what the education does to the mind of the children just as their parents were not aware of what the education did to their mind so "modern society knows not what it does.

END

3/8/2010 7:36:29 AM – I have been pondering the reason I even at this stage still write in diary format. I am mindful I am telling you things and concepts no human being you will ever know could tell you but even saying that I still do not want one single human being on this planet to assume I am talking to them. I ponder some of the beings that have applied the remedy to a degree and they are out in the world and they are speakers or communicating with others to various degrees and they are all caught up and on some mission or crusade relative to suggesting this remedy to the species. I detect the patterns and for example Moses in some ways detached from the people in the very end when he went off to die alone on the mountain. Jesus and the disciples were certainly among the people, Socrates was among the people but also to a degree detached because he never wrote any words and everything we know about him is from witnesses. Now Buddha had a small group of beings he spoke to but he apparently never made large speaking engagements with large crowds so to speak. It is even recorded that Buddha went home to his wife and children after he applied the remedy and then left them perhaps because he realized he could not reach them. This detachment aspect gives the impression that detachment unto itself is the purpose. Detachment gives the impression one is walking down the road of life and then they have to detach as if detachment itself is just some random aspect that one just does out of the blue but in reality the mental damage is so great as a result of that education being pushed on one at such a young age this detachment aspect is the only cure. The cure to regain the right hemisphere aspects could have been anything but it just so happens to be this extreme mental detachment aspect applied to the maximum degree in the right situation that is the cure, that undoes the damage that frees or unlocks the mind. There are many comments about the world and avoiding the ways of the world in the ancient texts and this is relative to detachment and is not relative to the world as in nature but relative to the world as in the ways of the ones that sense time which is society or civilization. I was watching a show about an aircraft carrier and one of the pilots was right brain leaning so to speak and he came into a room full of other pilots and the person talking said "This pilot is one of those right brain focused people and he is in his own mindset so we kind of leave him alone." That is an indication of this separation and division and thus the detachment aspect. It is as if before the accident I wanted to be a part of the world but it never panned out and now I cannot mindfully even relate to the ways of the world or society so the world is not even real anymore and that is the result of the complete detachment mentally from the world ones achieves with the remedy. For example this comment :

[1 John 2:15 Love not the world, neither the things that are in the world. If any man love the world, the love of the Father is not in him.]

The spirit of this comment is absolute detachment from society mindfully of course not literally, of course it could be considered literally. If one considers the mindset of a suicidal person or a depressed person and then substitutes the word "world" in this above comment for society and society meaning the ways of the ones that sense time, the scribes.

[Love not (society) , neither the things that are in (society).] One can clearly see this is the mindset of a suicidal person because the only thing that keeps them from killing their self is their attachment to "the world" and so a depressed person is attempting to detach from the world, society and that is the remedy to a neurosis, detachment, mindful detachment. So this indicates depression and suicide has nothing to do with depression or suicide, it just so happens to be an end stage to unveiling right brain traits after traditional education veils right brain traits. So the only kind of people that are considering or pondering doing this : [Love not (society) , neither the things that are in (society).] are the meek and thus the meek, the depressed and suicidal, shall inherit the earth and earth meaning they detach from the world which is society or the ways of the ones that sense time, the scribes. So what one has to do to restore their right brain traits is to mindfully detach from society and ones they do that and apply the remedy they cannot reattach to the ways of society. This is all in the mind and on a cerebral level of course. For example I do not see money as evil but because money is based on numbers and right brained does not see numbers because they are parts so I do not mindfully notice the difference between 1 dollar and a billion dollars because the numbers require judgment to sense the value. One thing interesting about this society concept is that society lives on this assumption it is wise. Society with all its technology and science and medicine and politics and money is wise for example but the absolute truth is society and all its wisdom still has yet to figure out written education and math pushed on the mind of small children interferes with those children's mental development and thus hinders their minds so society in that respect society in all of its glory is not even at the level of basic elementary understandings. You can take everything in society and place it on a scale and then on the other side of that scale factor in society's inability to even question if traditional education and math may hinder a child's mind and you will see societies perks are all cancelled out. Simply put, who cares what society has accomplished when at the end of the day it still mentally ruins all the children's minds with its wisdom education. What has society done that is going to make up for the fact it mentally ruins all the children with its wisdom education? Do not even answer that. You perceive I am supposed to listen to the directions of a society that is not even at the mental state to detect they ruin their own children mentally starting at the age of seven. As a species we take a knife and drive it into our heart and then we put on nice clothes so people will think fondly of us in our casket.

[Ezekiel 22:27 Her princes in the midst thereof are like wolves ravening the prey, to shed blood, and to destroy souls, to get dishonest gain.]

This comment sums it up nicely. Society is a complete lunatic that destroys everything in its path, ruins the minds of the children and causes needless suffering because of that as a result of the traditional education methods and at the end of the day all of its gains mean nothing. Society cannot mentally ruin the children and then assume it can recover from that. This is why as a species we are completely vain at this stage. That means we have to completely scrape about 99 percent of what we understand. Who gives a rat's ass about space, technology, medicine, nature when we still mentally kill our own children on an industrial scale. I do not mean ruin the children's minds like just slightly I mean destroying the children's minds relative to completely aborting the children's mind. If you just take the children at the age of seven and just kill them literally at least I will not have to write in my books you are a cold hearted cruel torturing bastard from hell. The fact you assume I am kidding or not accurate only proves to me how mentally ruined you factually are as a result of all that left brain education. My only purpose is to convince the entire species to mindfully kill itself so you keep that in mind at all times. I do not even need to leave my isolation chamber to convince six billion people to mindfully kill their self. I am one of the little children you "fixed" with your wisdom education and so my only advice to all of society itself is you would be wise to keep your distance because my mind does not even acknowledge you as a life form any longer. That means your mindful death does not even resister in my mind at all. I suggest I will convince you to mindfully kill yourself and you perhaps have a heart attack from hearing that and I do not even acknowledge that's an event at all and that's the disconnect. You piss yourself like a little frog does when someone picks it up and that is an indication all that education you got a child turned you into an emotional nightmare. You smack a child for saying a cuss word. You pay money to people to insult your own child if your child does not spell properly as the ones you pay money to suggest they better do. You are factually closer to a mental abuser of innocent children than a human being in your current state of mind. It is not important what your cult leader or political leader or your shrink says, the most positive thing you can do in your sense of time state of mind is to mindfully kill yourself completely. If anything is left of your current self after you mindfully kill yourself you have to try again because that means you didn't get all the rot out. You have to keep trying to mindfully kill yourself until you can no longer register time at all and then you have to attempt to convince everyone else around you to mindfully kill their self and then you remind them you would not want them to mindfully kill their self if you didn't love them so much. This is why the word hope is not even real relative to this situation we are in as a species. That is an indication of what this written education invention has done to our species. You sit there and worry about money and your health and your material things and I sit here and ponder various ways I can convince you to mindfully kill yourself on an absolute scale. You worry about money and I am only trying to convince you to stop killing all the children. I have not reached the level of intelligence that you are at because I am in this delusional world where I perceive children are more important than money. I am not as intelligent as you are because you understand money is more important than God himself and thus more important than the children of God. This is all you do to children with your wisdom education [Ezekiel 22:27 destroy souls]. You rob their minds and thus destroy their soul, intuition, and you are in such a deep neurosis you doubt that. There is no other human being on this planet that writes books speaking out against the devastating effects of written education on the mind of children and that is because every other human being on this planet is nothing but scared little dogs. They perceive their worthless life has worth so they allow the children to get mentally ruined. There are no other human beings on this planet that speak out against written education because they still perceive their life has worth, they still have hope. They are not quite at the stage of meek. They have not quite let go. They have not quite reached the mental clarity state to understand one is unable to live in a lunatic asylum that our species is, so one should seek risk and thus seek mindful death. The words I write are what the mind is capable of when one does censor their thoughts like a scared dog. I don't fear six billion lunatics with weapons instead I concentrate on that reality and convince them to mindfully kill their self using my words. We are either going to mindfully kill ourselves as a species or literally kill ourselves as a species and I do not detect any difference in the two options. You perceive radical is skipping a meal. You perceive radical is saying a cuss word. You perceive radical is disagreeing with someone. You perceive radical is coming up with a witty comment. You perceive radical is correcting someone's spelling. You perceive wisdom is understanding when to start a new paragraph. You are not pleased with the word "kill" because it subconsciously reminds you that you were mentally killed as a child as a result of all that left brain education and so you react emotionally when you read or hear the word kill. The word "kill" suggests death and you attempt to avoid that topic because it subconsciously reminds you of the abuse you experienced mentally as a child. You do not want to submit you were mentally abused as a child at the hands of the education because then you would have to face the reality you were tricked or were a sucker or were a fool and that would hurt your pride. You would not have pride if you didn't get the education you would be able to look at what happened as an honest observer but instead with your pride you look at the mental hindering as a personal thing. Once you apply the remedy you are going to have to condition yourself to be an honest observer because if you start taking things personally you will not be lasting long in this narrow. You have to get it into your head our species destroyed itself mentally with this written education and math invention and there is perhaps no way to correct that on a species level. Everyone you know in your life from your friends to your relatives all got the education and once you apply the remedy you will not be able to convince them to apply the remedy and if you take that reality personally it will destroy you. Your friends and relatives had the same damage done to them as you had and so your inclination is to avenge them and that is what pride is. Your only option is to detach yourself from that abuse of your family and relatives and become an honest observer. The courts do not give a dam if all of your relatives were mentally abused and hindered into hell. The police do not give a dam if your relatives or you were mentally hindered into hell. No one gives a dam that your got robbed of your mind or that your relatives got robbed of their mind because they are all lunatics and thus were robbed of their minds the same way you were. You are going to have to understand this entire control structure relative to justice and righteousness and honor is all just a lie and thus an illusion. The only justice there is in this narrow is that you can apply the remedy and restore your mind and that is as good as it will ever get. You can have your mind back and all you have to do is mindfully detach from the entire society to do it. This is relative to the one reality alone and that is, do you care more about your mind or your friends? Do you care more about your mind or you peers? Do you care more about your mind or your money? If you care about your friends, your peers, your money or your wealth you will factually not apply the remedy the full measure. You have to mindfully detach from all of that crap in order to apply the remedy the full measure. Considering your mind does not even develop fully until you were twenty and considering that left brain education started when you were seven or earlier you are mentally unable to grasp how mentally damaged you are. What you perceive as mental clarity is actually mental hindering to the point of retardation and your sense of time proves that. Your sense of time proves you are mentally retarded. Your mind was bent so far to the left your right brain traits do not even factor into your thought processes at all anymore. You have to do heavy drugs to feel right brain to come up with an idea or be creative and even then the idea is foolish. You are thinking people that sense time have come up with some interesting inventions but in reality they have not. They have not even entered the level of mental clarity to be aware the written education and math hinders the mind and that is the basic understanding any human being with even slight mental clarity should be aware of without even trying. All they have invented are trinkets of stupidity because while they peddle their trinkets of stupidity they are unaware they are allowing innocent children to be mindfully destroyed so they are not even at a level one could suggest they are anything but mindfully absent. They appear lifelike but I assure you they are dead in contrast to the mentally living. They are in a coma in contrast to ones that are conscious. Everything you have ever learned in your life no matter what it is has to be burned because it is all wrong and is thus foolishness. Everything you have learned in your life is a lie. Everyone you know is a lunatic and factually mentally unsound and thus mentally hindered and thus mentally retarded. Since they do not even understand what the tree of knowledge is and the remedy to negate its mental effects they cannot be anything other than a lunatic because that knowledge is elementary knowledge. One is either mentally dead or mentally alive and the entry level to being mentally alive is to understand what the tree of knowledge is and to understand the concepts relative to the remedy to the tree of knowledge and one can only achieve that mental level if they apply said remedy. So now you can determine who is mentally alive and mentally dead just by asking them what the tree of knowledge is. If they do not know exactly what that is they cannot possibly be anything but mentally dead. So now you know how to distinguish between the quick and the dead. Of course after you apply the remedy your right brain intuition will allow you to determine exactly who the quick and the dead are without even saying a word. You need to let go of all of your delusions because they are infinite and will take some time to let go of. If you continue to read my private diaries that gives me the go ahead to rip you mentally to shreds and I assure you I will rip you mentally to shreds. I will tell you a little secret. The vast majority of human beings in the neurosis cannot ever be recovered so never ever assume you can reach any more than a .0024% fraction of them and so it makes no difference what you say no matter what because the vast majority are simply fatalities. That takes off the pressure. Simply put you can have an argument no being in the universe could argue with but that means nothing because in the end the remedy is one has to mindfully kill their self and the ones in neurosis are afraid of bad hair cuts so they simply will not apply the remedy ever. Never assume I am special I am a human being and no matter what I am not intelligent enough to defeat this neurosis on our species. It is simply beyond my ability. That does not mean I give up it just means I am fully aware of what I am up against and it means I am not attempting to "act" or give off this impression of being some great perfect being because that means nothing in contrast to how powerful this neurosis is. I can dance in ballerina outfit or convince you I am supernatural but that does not mean beings in neurosis are going to go out and mindfully kill their self. This creates a situation that deeds and words are not really the resting factors. Freud did not blow it because he did cocaine, it was simply the neurosis is way too deep and that means very few are ever suppose to escape it at all. It is fatal to the vast majority no matter what anyone says ever. That aspect must be looked at as a positive thing because it means one can relax and not be so premeditated in their words and deeds. When all else fails, adapt. What is, is. Now back to the punishment.

[Pacbox: "Still at it Rohrer? It's nonsense. Give it up. You're argument holds no water and never will. It's made up out of thin air."]

When an airplane takes a nose dive the first class passengers are the first to hit the ground.

2:47:09 PM – Apparently this comment is one I tend to have some luck explaining to the ones that sense time so I keep rephrasing it a bit different in the off chance at least one thing I suggest to them sinks in.
[Ephesians 5:18 And be not drunk with wine, wherein is excess; but be filled with the Spirit;]

This is very elementary. This is the reality. A person gets years of left brain favoring education known as reading writing and mathematics starting at an early age nearly 15 years before their frontal lobe fully develops so this education bends their mind to the left because their mind is still developing. Try to look at the mind in a child like bread baking in the oven and the right half of the bread has a lid covering it and the left half of the bread, the mind, has no lid so the left half swells or is much larger than the right half as the bread cooks. So the bread comes out after baking, after education, and it is not uniform. The drinking itself or drug use is a logical way to relive the suffering one is in with the mind that is not uniform and at the same time it unveils the right brain traits juts a bit while the drug or drink lasts. So the euphoria itself one experiences when they drink or do drugs is not a high from the drugs it is a high from unveiling right brain a bit and this is evident because some artists are known to do drugs to enhance creativity and creativity is a right brain trait. So this comment [Ephesians 5:18 And be not drunk with wine, wherein is excess; but be filled with the Spirit;] is saying, if you simply apply the fear not, deny one's self remedy, you will find the kingdom, which is unveil right brain after the tree of knowledge, written education has veiled it, and then you will always feel that euphoria you feel when you drink or do drugs. So this comment is not a rule or command it is in fact elementary logic. It is saying, if you drink after you get the education you will feel good but it is in excess because all you have to do to feel that exact same sensation all the time is to apply the fear not remedy and then you won't need to drink to feel good or escape the place of suffering, hell, which is having a mind with the complex aspect of it, right brain, veiled as a result of education. Simply put, after one applies the deny one's self, fear not remedy, drinking or drugs will no longer cause euphoric effects hardly at all because the only reason they cause mental euphoric effects is because they unveil right brain a bit while they last. So this comment is not saying "Do not drink" it is saying "You can apply the remedy and unveil right brain and then you won't be mentally suffering so you won't need to drink" It is saying "It is proper to want to feel right brain because after all you were born with it and the education veiled it, but if you just apply the remedy, you will not kill yourself and become drug addicted attempting to keep feeling right brain traits." So in summary in case you do not know what the sinister is, Society takes a child and bends their mind to the left and veils right brain using education and they do it unknowingly, and then when that child gets older and does drugs to escape that mental place of suffering they lock that child in jail and call them a druggie and loser and failure.

So this comment is a riddle.
How is one [filled with the Spirit;]

The remedy [Luke 17:33 and whosoever shall lose his life (mindfully) shall preserve it(be filled by the spirit(unveil right brain after education, the tree of knowledge veils it)).

So the comment is saying Do not drink wine but instead : lose his life (mindfully) shall preserve it(be filled by the spirit(unveil right brain after education the tree of knowledge veils it)).

Which is simplified by saying do not drink wine but instead listen to what Jesus suggested and apply the deny one's self remedy. So it is perfect Logic not a rule.

Jesus was known as the Lord of Logos/ Lord meaning master of the house which is a being of sound mind.

Logos is a persuasive strategy by the use of logic and reasoning.

Example:
[Acts 13:12 Then the deputy, when he saw what was done, believed, being astonished at the doctrine of the Lord.]
[astonished at the doctrine of the Lord(Master of the house, mind).] Why?
He had a persuasive strategy by the use of logic and reasoning.
Why?
He applied the remedy and returned to sound mind and thus a sound mind has a persuasive strategy through the use of logic and reasoning.
When or how did he do that?
[Mark 1:10 And straightway coming up out of the water, he saw the heavens opened, and the Spirit like a dove descending upon him:]
Using John the Baptist's water version of the fear not remedy:
[coming up out of the water, he saw the heavens opened] Means his mind opened back up which means his right brain aspect unveiled using the water version of the remedy. Simply put if you put your head under water your hypothalamus will eventually give the death signal telling you to go

to the surface and if you ignore that signal you will apply the remedy but the psychological complexity is one has to believe they will drown so one has to have a person they do not trust hold them under water. That version of the remedy makes the spooky location version look rather inviting I would think.

[Mark 11:18 And the scribes and chief priests heard it, and sought how they might destroy him: for they feared him, because all the people was astonished at his doctrine.]

[was astonished at his doctrine.] = a persuasive strategy by the use of logic and reasoning.

[Mark 12:38 And he said unto them in his doctrine, Beware of the scribes, which love to go in long clothing, and love salutations in the marketplaces,]

[And he said unto them in his doctrine, Beware of the scribes] = written language has some serious mental issues and since it was a convincing argument just like Socrates had the "powers that be among the scribes" saw these beings as threats.

Socrates also had a similar ability to argue well as noted at his trial. This of course is just the result of right brain traits. For example a person of sound mind has the ability to use random access thoughts to find the eventual conclusion to any argument and then when speaking to one with a sense of time, left brain influenced, which can only think in sequential thought's , they can be out maneuvered. It is just simple logic a person that has one hemisphere veiled even slightly cannot compete with a being that has access to full power of both hemispheres.

[Pacbox: "Still at it Rohrer? It's nonsense. Give it up. You're argument holds no water and never will. It's made up out of thin air."]

3:56:59 PM – It is important to understand the tactics one must use in speaking with the ones that sense time. The rule of thumb is when speaking in a psychology chat room use the neurological and psychological explanations of the remedy and then throw in a some religious scripture and in the religion chat rooms stick with the religion scriptures but throw in a little psychology and neurology and that way you make the psychologists religious and the religious beings psychotic. This conversation I had in a psychology chat room was very telling because it is the desired results one should get if they dot all the "I's" so to speak. What this means is one becomes so proficient from experimenting relative to explaining this situation to the ones that sense time one actually is fully aware of every question ones that sense time could be thinking and then one answers those questions before the ones that sense time even ask them. This is relative to just telling them everything they could need to know and then if one does that right the ones that sense time will become depressed and that is a symptom their pride and ego is starting to go so they become humble and meek. That is the entire point of all of it because one will never apply the remedy unless they are depressed because the remedy is one denies their self. Simply put ones that sense time never will be meek unless they are humbled and the ones with no sense of time cannot be meek or humble they can just say things that give that impression to observers. The easy way to look at it is right brain when at full power at 50 percent has so much ambiguity and thus doubt that one cannot feel meek or humble. Feeling meek or humble means one feels depressed but depression is not possible with right brain unveiled because it is processing random access thoughts so swiftly as in seconds relative to a clock so being in a state of humility is factually not possible and this goes the same with anger and all the other emotions so one tends to appear like they are exhibiting many emotions but in reality they cannot maintain any one emotion for even a few moments like seconds relative to a clock. The ones that sense time will not let go of all their delusions unless they are meek and humble and thus depressed. People that are depressed are willing to considering throwing everything away or letting go of everything so that is the desired state of mind one has to be in to deny their self which is what the remedy is. So I am chatting in this chat room, psychology, and being in the machine state I am typing so swiftly they cannot even comment hardly so they are reduced to listeners and once in a while they throw in a comment like :

[[Jamon^] Do you realize you are crazy or are you blind to it and truly believe you're speaking ordered thoughts?]

This comment is a classic example of how ones that sense time are saying one thing but in reality meaning another thing, he is saying, do you [truly believe you're speaking ordered thoughts?]
I have right brain and left hemisphere traits in my conscious state so it is totally logical I should speak in random access comments because in a 50/50 contest right brain traits rule over sequential left brain traits. So this being is saying in reality [I see you are speaking in random access thoughts] but he is not aware that is what he is saying, he perceives I am "crazy" because he is use to people who speak in left brain sequential thoughts because he has never met anyone that has negated the written education induced neurosis fully. He assumes a person of sound mind is crazy because if they are not everyone he knows is crazy. If I am not mentally unsound then everyone he knows is mentally unsound including him. This is an indication of how far along this education induced neurosis is in all of civilization. This neurobiologist won a Nobel Prize and he said : "What it comes down to is that modern society discriminates against the right hemisphere." - Roger Sperry (1973)
This Jamon in this chat room is included in "modern society" subset and he suggests I am exhibiting crazy traits. If I was in a psychologists office and was talking like I do they would start explaining all the pills they should put me on to "fix " me because that is what they do to children when the children act a little hyper and show right brain traits. Simply put a being with both hemispheres operating in harmony exhibit traits that appear like illness to beings that have right brain veiled and any being that was taught traditional education and math as a child has right brain veiled to either a great degree or a vast degree and the only way to solve that is to apply this mental fear not remedy in one way or another and there is absolutely no exceptions and one knows they applied it fully when they completely lose their sense of time. The ones that sense time perceive emotions will solve a problem but they never have an they never will so the logic is the

less emotions the more problems one can solve or the more mental clarity one achieves and thus one is better able to solve problems. I have to go through a few insults from the ones that sense time until I get to a point in my explanation where they start shutting up and just listening. I perceive I put them in a trance. They are hearing things they have never heard in their entire life from anyone ever and it slowly starts to make sense to them and they go into a trance of just wanting to hear more. It is like charming a snake. That didn't come out right, but I doubt it. One of the keys to the focus on the log in your eye concept is, one cannot make up for the ones that sense time neurosis so they have to make up for that by concentrating and achieving a mental clarity that bridges that gap.

[Do you realize you are crazy or are you blind to it and truly believe you're speaking ordered thoughts?]

3/9/2010 9:52:41 AM –
All I can say is written education and math taught to children long before their minds develop is not worth it and when you get to the point of applying the remedy which is mindfully killing yourself just so you can get the mind you had as a child back you will understand what I am talking about.

[16:41] [The_Eccentri] wonder what happend to that one guy
[16:41] [ecstasy] what guy
[16:41] [The_Eccentri] he was talking like 4 hrs str8
[16:41] [The_Eccentri] TRohrer
[16:41] [ecstasy] oh yes
[16:41] [ecstasy] i am reading his posts
[16:41] [ecstasy] :)

These beings are talking about what I explained to them and it is essentially the same thing I explain in the books relative to the mental implications of the written education and math on the delicate mind of children and they were children so in that respect I am talking about them.

[16:41] [The_Eccentri] there intresting though
[16:42] [The_Eccentri] very enlightning
[16:49] [ecstasy] i am very dissapointed and pretty much depresed
[16:49] [ecstasy] never felt like this in my life
[16:50] [ecstasy] I thougt i was the strong type of guy
[16:50] [ecstasy] but in the end ... we are always wrong

This comment : [[16:42] [The_Eccentri] very enlightening]is relative to this comment in the ancient texts: [Ecclesiastes 1:18 For in much wisdom is much grief:] and the evidence is in this comment : [[16:49] [ecstasy] i am very disappointed and pretty much depressed]

What this means is because I am getting warmed up well enough I am able to shatter their world perception and they can never go back so all they can do is go to the 9th circle of hell, treason and apply the remedy or they will forever remain in the ninth circle of hell and perhaps end up killing their self eventually. Perhaps you understand why I write my books in diary format. The main reason I do not fear death is because death is not as bad as having to tell my fellow human beings they were mentally hindered as children and then having to tell them they have to mindfully kill their self to just get back to sound state of mind.

[[16:49] [ecstasy] never felt like this in my life
[16:50] [ecstasy] I thougt i was the strong type of guy]

What I have accomplish with words is I have altered this beings entire outlook on everything for the rest of his life. Every time he hears "We leave no child left behind we educated all the children " he is going to gnash his teeth. Every time he hears some beings say "When people get education they have a better life." He is going to gnash his teeth. Whenever he hears "We are going to build schools in third world countries so all the children get the education" he will gnash his teeth. He will either literally kill himself or mindfully kill himself which is apply the remedy and his chances of applying the remedy is .0024 percent so I ask you, how valuable is your written education and math now? You were charmed by that written education and math and you spread it all over the world and now you have to pay the piper and you perhaps will not be surviving that payment plan. It took me four hours relative to a clock to shatter this being's entire perception of the world and my purpose is to get my argument down to a paragraph and then a sentence and then one word. Fear not is already taken, deny yourself is already taken, submit is already taken so I have to concentrate and discover one word that will bring the ones that sense time down to the ninth circle of hell, treason. I am leaning towards "bow". Let's plug it into the remedy.

Walk through the valley of the shadow of death and (bow). I do not detect it is better than fear not, submit or deny yourself but it works.

Bow: to accept something and yield to it, often unwillingly.

Walk through the valley of the shadow of death and (yield).

Yield: to admit defeat and surrender.

Once a being's illusions are shattered they have no ground to stand on. The beings that spit on the spirit of what I suggest are not mentally prepared to have their illusions shattered.

[ecstasy] I thougt i was the strong type of guy]

He thought he was the strong type of being but he will not thought that anymore during this lifetime. All you can do is hope that when this being applies the remedy if he able to, when he wakes up he decides to write books or paint pictures or go on speaking tours instead of going on a head hunt. You hope as hard as you can when this being wakes up and fully understands what he was robbed of, his right brain traits, he does not decide to go on a head hunt. I am not intelligent enough to be able to determine how a person is going to react when they apply the remedy and fully realize they got raped into hell as child and robbed of their life, liberty and pursuit of happiness. If that scares you or concerns you that is simply too bad. You are not calling the shots anymore as if that has not occurred you by now. I am uncertain who your leader is but they are not calling the shots anymore and I am certain of that. The one with the most convincing argument is the only vote that counts. That's unfortunate. Now I will discuss something of value.

1:43:50 PM − Relative to the frontal lobe. Firstly the frontal lobe does not develop fully and thus the mind does not develop fully until one is around the age of twenty. The left brain education starts at around the age of seven and this frontal lobe is relative to dopamine-sensitive neurons and contains many of them and that is relative to the cerebral cortex which is relative to perception. Cognitive ability is relative to reason, perception and intuition. So the dopamine-sensitive neurons in the frontal lobe are relative to mental clarity and thus relative to cognitive ability. So the left brain favoring education pushed on a child at the age of seven alters the child's perception and cognitive ability because the dopamine-sensitive neurons in the frontal lobe cease to function properly and that means the child is made mentally unsound or mentally insane. Another way to look at it is, the frontal lobe and cerebral cortex aspects are working properly on a physiological level but on a mental level because the left brain favoring education was pushed on the child before the child's mind developed means the mental state of that child is very abnormal. Dopamine is relative to rewards, attention, concentration, long-term memory, planning, and drive, motivation, and outlook. Dante spoke in Inferno something along the lines of the ones whose heads are pointed backwards and they go up and down stairs. After one applies the remedy and the right brain traits are restored back to the center rewards are no longer registered at all and this means drive is unlimited and this is relative to the ancient texts comments about the quick and the dead, and drive is relative to sloth. Something is seriously wrong with your mind if you need a reward to do something. So this up and down stairs concept means ones with a sense of time jump through hoops to get a reward and when they fail at jumping through the hoop they become sad. The ones that sense time do very well until an unknown obstacle arises and then they have complete mental shut down. Right hemisphere is the master of adaptation and it needs no directions or instruction's ever because it uses its intuition to experiment and thus teaches itself and this is relative to a sound mind. In school a child gets an A and by that time their mind is bent to a degree to the left and they feel pleased and then when they get an F they are displeased and so they try harder with the left brain favoring education so they can get another dopamine injection when they jump through the hoop and get another A. In some countries the children that do poorly at school perceive they are not intelligent and then kill their self. This is relative to Japan and also relative to all countries. When the rewards stop the motivation stops and that is the reality of having right brain veiled. When the rewards are gone or not achieved depression sets in and that is what going up and down stairs is. Take everything from a person that senses time as in their money and house and family and friends and material things and they perhaps will determine its best to kill their self in short order because those rewards are what motivates them. This dopamine is in fact what the story of Job is all about. Job lost all his rewards but he did not panic and kill himself because right brain when unveiled does not register rewards or loss because everything is a concept when one has a sound mind. In a sound state of mind there is no reward's so there is also no loss of motivation when rewards are absent. One simply is motivation with no concepts of rewards or punishments so one just does and this is why the ones in the Torah were made slaves and why many beings that never got the education made great slaves. They are essentially machines in a sound state of mind and they do not register rewards or failure they just perform and accomplish and nothing stops them and nothing intimidates them and nothing but the task at hand is relevant. They are in the now, the machine state. A reward is relative to something of value and a value is relative to numbers and right brain does not know what a number is. This in my 16th book in 16 months but when I think about 16 my mind says "What is sixteen?" and the ambiguity of right brain says "Perhaps nothing perhaps" and so I do not detect I have written any books at all and so my mind reacts to what it perceives so I feel no stress because my mind perceives I have written zero books. The ones that sense time will do one job or one task and then need to rest and that rest is their reward and so they do a task and then need a reward and then do a task and then need a reward but in a sound mind state when right brain is unveiled ones only does and never perceives the need to rest or get a reward ever. If the mind does not perceive it did a task then your mind will not perceive it needs to rest. If the mind does not perceive it is hungry the body will not perceive it needs to eat. This is all relative to the dopamine and the dopamine is relative to the cerebral cortex and the cerebral cortex is relative to perception. I would make a perfect slave because my mind does not even register what a reward even is. If the Africans were lazy we never would have made them slaves. If

Pharaoh did not make lots of money off the tribes he never would have made them slaves. Because society pushes the education on everyone as a child they simply create beings that are slothful and need rewards to be motivated. The entire concept of climbing up the ladder of success is based on rewards for producing but a being with right brain unveiled produces without the need to ever be rewarded because right brain is pleased to experiment and come to further understandings into infinity and never ever asks for a reward or asks to be acknowledged because those are value based aspects. I am not writing books slower since I started I am writing faster and my mind has yet to acknowledge I have even started to write at all and so I show no physical symptoms of fatigue or stress because the mind is relative to what the body experiences. If your mind tells you that you are hungry your body will start exhibiting symptoms of hunger and if you mind tells you time has passed your body will exhibit symptoms of time passing such as fatigue and if your mind tells you that you have accomplished a task you will need a reward to be motivated to do another task. If you write a book and then start charging money for it because you perceive that book took you effort to write, that is your mind telling you it took effort. If you write a book and your mind tells you it took no effort at all you may attempt to give that book freely because you perceive it is not worth anything because it took no effort to write and on top of that right brain does not know what a number is. Life should be as easy as milk but the education alters the mind and thus perception and makes life a perceived difficult task that is in realty effortless. There is a problem with this dopamine situation relative to how it works in the mind once the mind is bent to the left by the education. This left mind bending education alters a person's perception.

Schizophrenia

A person starts to sense time, sense great hunger, sense fatigue when in reality they should not be sensing those things so strongly if at all so the education makes any human being that gets it schizophrenic. Schizophrenia is a mental disorder characterized by abnormalities in the perception or expression of reality. Your sense of time is through the roof to the point you are a nervous wreck and that is how schizophrenic you are. Your emotions are turned up so greatly you have a nervous breakdown when you lose your job or lose a loved one and that is how schizophrenic you are. Some examples of Schizophrenia relative to perception of time.

[B. P. (15) hung himself on the anniversary of his Mother's death], An anniversary is relative to perception of time.
[A. H. (20) committed suicide by gunshot on Christmas Day]

Right brain does not know what Christmas day is because it does not know what a day is because it does not know what an hour is because it does not know what a minute is. These beings got all that left brain education and they started to do this : [Galatians 4:10 Ye observe days, and months, and times, and years.] and then in one way or another they decided to kill their self based on their perception of this [Galatians 4:10 Ye observe days, and months, and times, and years.] They mindfully observe time and so they determined at this certain time they perceived it was wise to kill their self so they would have some attachment to that period of time that was nothing but an illusion in their unsound mind caused by the education.

[Schizophrenia is a mental disorder characterized by abnormalities in the perception of reality.] = [Galatians 4:10 Ye observe days, and months, and times, and years.].

So you are schizophrenic and you are allowed around children and you give the children the same education you got and then the children become schizophrenic so you factually cannot be trusted around children but the people who would make that determination are also schizophrenic because they got the education also so they allow the children to be harmed by you.

[K. S. (18) lit himself on fire in a cemetery on Halloween night].

It is a very easy concept to understand. The fact this being sensed time means his right brain paradox was veiled by education so he was mentally unsound and so he was exhibiting mentally unsound behavior. So he killed himself in a cemetery on Halloween night with the understanding somehow that point in time or that date in time would mean his death was of value but on a deeper level, all suicides are simply human beings that got the education and they are attempting to defeat their fear of death because that is the only way to unveil right brain but in many cases it does not work out for them because they take that defeat your fear of death and they really defeat their fear of death in a literal way. So the education altered this beings perception and then this being acted on that perception, sense of time, and killed their self based on that perception of time and so the education killed this being.

One of the more devastating ways the education kills people is it veils their right brain and then they seek drugs to relieve that suffering state of mind they are in because the drugs release the dopamine because when the mind is sound the dopamine is at full power all the time so one cannot even feel euphoria from drugs use so drugs use itself does not do anything except make one feel some physiological effects so the beings that do drugs are simply attempting to feel good because they feel bad because their right brain was veiled by education and they just want to feel what it's like to be in sound mind. Simply put, they do drugs and perceive they are getting high but in reality they are feeling what being sound minded is like for the duration of the drugs and only to a slight degree because the education damage is so great it takes over a year to fully adjust to consciousness after one applies the remedy.

So they perceive they are getting high but in reality they are feeling right brain traits for the duration of the drug so they are [Schizophrenia is a mental disorder characterized by abnormalities in the perception of reality.] They are trying as hard as they can as a being to feel right brain traits after education has veiled them and they tend to end up killing their self in the process and then society says they are worthless drug addicts.

[J. B. (14) died of a suspected methadone overdose]
[K. G. (27) died of an accidental heroin overdose]
[O. K. (33) allegedly died from a drug overdose]
[S. W. (29) allegedly committed suicide by overdose]

I am mindful I have a very strong case for all out war, but perhaps I don't fight schizophrenic lunatics that have no conscience perhaps.

3/9/2010 8:05:11 PM –
[Psalms 23:1 <<A Psalm of David.>> The LORD is my shepherd; I shall not want.]
First David was mentioned in the New Testaments

[Mark 12:37 David therefore himself calleth him Lord; and whence is he then his son? And the common people heard him gladly.]
[Mark 12:38 And he said unto them in his doctrine, Beware of the scribes, which love to go in long clothing, and love salutations in the marketplaces,]
[Mark 12:39 And the chief seats in the synagogues, and the uppermost rooms at feasts:]
[Mark 12:40 Which devour widows' houses, and for a pretence make long prayers: these shall receive greater damnation.]

[The LORD is my shepherd] Simply means David applied the remedy and so he unveiled right brain and so David was a Master or Lord or the house/mind. So David in this comment is saying right brain serves me well and then he says, [I shall not want.] "Want" is a craving or desire such as lust, greed, envy, jealousy, coveting and control which are all mental symptoms one has right brain veiled. The easy way to look at it is when right brain is unveiled fully one cannot maintain a set thought for more than a moment because right brain random access thought processing is so fast one cannot maintain a mindset of greed, lust, envy or simply put, wants. [I shall not want.] denotes sense of time because a want is relative to craving something in the future. "I want money", "I want attention", "I want a big house.", "I want control." Etc. I shall not crave, meaning no sense of time or being in the now

.
So Mark 12:37 is saying David called him Lord, which means David called right hemisphere, the god image in man, Lord and so ones that applies the remedy become influenced by right brain because it rules when the mind

111

is at 50/50 harmony so David was a Lord or spokesman for the Lord and thus a Master of the house/mind. So David said :[Mark 12:38 And he said unto them in his doctrine, Beware of the scribes] Any human being that gets the written education must apply the remedy because in order to learn the ability to scribe one has their right brain veiled, relative to being taught that invention before their frontal lobe develops at the age of twenty plus. The scribes are the ones that are material and control focused and this comment is saying they are the ones that rule over the people, and this is relative to the time because not all people at this time were scribes, in David's time, or were taught written education and they were known as the tribes.

[which love to go in long clothing(material focus), and love salutations in the marketplaces(self indulgence and thrive on praise of others which denotes ego and thus pride, pride is a psychological symptom of the education induced neurosis,]

[Mark 12:39 And the chief seats in the synagogues(religious scribes, ones that sense time thrive on power), and the uppermost rooms at feasts(this suggests rulers scribes):] The point of this comment is that the ones that sense time see parts, a left brain trait, so there is this artificial labeling that sets them at the top and in power and thus they use the artificial scale of power to suggest they are somehow better than someone else or in higher esteem. For example a person with a Doctorate degree is understood to be in higher esteem than someone that only has a high school education. A Pope is understood to be in higher esteem than a priest. A President is in higher esteem than a Senator. A supervisor is in higher esteem than a clerk. A Rabi is in higher esteem than a common Jew. This is all a symptom of being in the left brain state or influence because left brain only see parts. This is relative to what Moses was suggesting to Pharaoh: [Exodus 2:14 And he said, Who made thee a prince and a judge over us? intendest thou to kill me, as thou killedst the Egyptian? And Moses feared, and said, Surely this thing is known.]

[Who made thee a prince and a judge over us?] "Us" being the human race, human beings. Since we are all human beings it is not logical someone can be ruler over others. Of course one that gets the education is under the influence of left brain, Cain, and Cain is controlling and makes demands and covets and lusts and craves for power, and in the case of the Pharaoh , power over other people. Of course it also works the other way around , a person under the influence of left brain wants to be told what to do because a right brain trait is intuition, which means when right brain is unveiled one can think for their self so that being does not need to be ruled over, so to speak. So Moses was saying to this Ruler scribe Pharaoh, "Who made you the boss over everyone?" and like any tyrant or control aspect would respond when they fear their control may be in jeopardy [Exodus 2:15 Now when Pharaoh heard this thing, he sought to slay Moses. ....] So Moses was just like a child saying "You are not the boss of me or us" and this left brain influenced ruler, scribe, said "I will kill you because I am the controller." It is along the lines of absolute control corrupts absolutely but the deeper reality is once a person gets the education and in turn has right brain veiled, they are all about control, coveting, greed, envy, lust which are all forms of control. Society is not a control structure because that is how human beings are, we are a control structure society because the tree of knowledge , written education favors left brain and in turn silences the right brain intuition and that aspect allows us all to think for ourselves, of course this is not a conspiracy, this education is a Trojan horse or a gold calf that outwardly looks flawless but inwardly it hinders the mind to a vast degree. Human beings do not need anyone to tell them what to do unless their right brain aspects like intuition, pattern detection, lightening processing have been veiled or turned off. Moses was kind of saying "If I am not the leader then you certainly are not the leader" and that ruler scribe, the Pharaoh said "Kill that guy now because that attitude is a threat to my power and thus my control over my slaves."

[Mark 12:40 Which devour widows' houses, and for a pretence make long prayers: these shall receive greater damnation.]

[Which devour widows' houses] This means destroys families, the males tended to get the education and the women did not and so the men were "cursed" and so the family was cursed, which left the women, a widow, because her husband had the "curse". Think about a male who is sent off

113

to fight some war for a ruler so the ruler can gain more power and thus more control but the men who fight end up dying and thus leave a widow. Nearly all wars in history are about control and control is coveting and that is a left brain trait and right brain loves freedom, and despises rules and control. If one has right brain unveiled they are pleased with freedom and if one gets the education and thus has right brain veiled they are pleased with control and thus coveting and thus being told what to do. Moses would have said this to any government in the world [Exodus 2:14 And he said, Who made thee a prince and a judge over us?] and any government in the world would say the same thing Pharaoh said :[Exodus 2:15 Now when Pharaoh heard this thing, he sought to slay Moses. ....] because all leaders got the education so they are all left brain focused and thus based on controlling aspects. A left brain influenced being, one that senses time, craves to be controlled or craves to control and a being with no sense of time, right brain influenced, sound minded, does not want to be controlled and does not want to control and that is why the Africans were turned into slaves because they were free and met the ones that sense time and the ones that sense time took that as a sign of weakness and in turn controlled them. Pharaoh saw the tribes, the ones that did not get the education at that time, and saw them as easy to control and so he made them his slaves. The ones that do not sense time are hard workers and never expect a reward because they are pleased cerebrally. This is why a parent will tell a child "Do not trust strangers" because a child trusts everyone. The Africans trusted the ones that sense time just like the Incas trusted the Spanish and just like the tribes trusted the Pharaoh. One cannot trust the dust.

[and for a pretence make long prayers: these shall receive greater damnation.] This is simply relative to this comment among others [Revelation 2:9 .... I know the blasphemy of them which say they are Jews(religious), and are not,....]
Simply put, once a human being gets the written education they have to apply the remedy and if they do not they are separated from the god image in man, right brain and thus separated from God. There are no exceptions ever. The complexity is once you apply the remedy there is nothing to pray for because you have the sprit in you and one cannot get anything better than that, relative to [The LORD is my shepherd; [I shall not want] = (have

nothing to pray for).] and thus before you apply the remedy you are not praying to what you think you are.

[these shall receive greater damnation.] This comment is relative to the rich and the powerful relative to the ways of the world, the ones that sense time. They are the rich and so a camel can do the impossible long before these "rich rulers" will be able to apply the remedy because they are totally oblivious to the fact their right brain was veiled by the education. Only the meek, the depressed are aware something is not right but they often cannot put their finger on it.

[Psalms 23:2 He maketh me to lie down in green pastures: he leadeth me beside the still waters.] This is simply suggesting more traits of having right brain unveiled. One's mind is at peace relative to one has no sense of time, no sense of fatigue, no sense of stress, no sense of panic because they have a sound mind and a sound minded human being has nothing to fear or panic about or stress about. Simply put : Happiness is achieved when one is free from worries because their mind can comprehend any situation that arises.
[he leadeth me beside the still waters] This comment is relative to Jesus not being afraid in the boat on the rough sea when everyone else in the boat was afraid and is also relative to when Jonah was on the sea in a storm and the others were afraid :

[Jonah 1:4 But the LORD sent out a great wind into the sea, and there was a mighty tempest in the sea, so that the ship was like to be broken.]
[Jonah 1:5 Then the mariners were afraid, and cried every man unto his god, and cast forth the wares that were in the ship into the sea, to lighten it of them. But Jonah was gone down into the sides of the ship; and he lay, and was fast asleep.] = Jonah was not worried in troubles seas but everyone else on the boat was afraid.

And the comment is also relative to the story of Job. Everything imaginable happened to Job but he remained [beside the still waters] mindfully, no panic and no fear no matter what life throws at one because right brain has pattern detection, intuition, complexity, and coupled with left brain a

115

sound human mind can deal with any situation without effort so one is not prone to give away their freedom for a little security if the wind blows, the rains fall, or the surf breaks.

[Psalms 23:3 He restoreth my soul: he leadeth me in the paths of righteousness for his name's sake.]

I detect this Psalm 23 is out of sequence.
[He restoreth my soul] means restores the right brain after the written education veils it and thus restores one to a sound mind.

[me in the paths of righteousness for his name's sake.] Righteousness is right brain and so this is saying, I restore my mind and then I am a right brain influenced beings and I speak for right brain, the Lord, the god image in man. So he is suggesting he is a spokesman or a messenger for the righteous(right brain). When right brain in unveiled its intuition and awareness and thus the entire mind is so powerful one can only accurately describe it as unnamable in power. One way to look at it is right brain is so powerful after you apply the remedy about a month later it will unveil and you will feel like a Mac Truck hit you mentally and you will sit for a month or two just trying to get use to how powerful your new mind is with right brain unveiled. Born again is accurate, going to heaven in a chariot is accurate, raised from the dead is accurate.

3/11/2010 7:51:09 AM -
[He restoreth my soul] This comment means you will apply the remedy and discover how extremely powerful our minds are because it is a fact if you sense time you have no idea how powerful our minds are. There is no machine that can measure how powerful the intuition is. The intuition is like being aware of everything as a concept and then one has to get warmed up to be able to translate those concepts to words, and words are details. It may sound supernatural but right brain is unnamable in power when it is at full power in the conscious state and that is why the beings in these ancient texts were willing to fight to keep the ones that sense time, the scribes, from veiling it in the children via written education. It is along the line of once you unveil it you spend the rest of your life writing

infinite books attempting to explain it with the understanding you never can explain it. Peace and war can be a symptom of fear. As awareness increases fear and hope decreases.

[He restoreth my soul]. What is the soul? Right brain intuition. Why does one have to restore it?
The tree of knowledge veils right brain traits because [reading, writing and arithmetic -- the domain and strength of the left brain].
How does one restore it? [Psalms 23:4 ...walk through the valley of the shadow of death, I will fear no evil:....] Which is a mental self control exercise.

[Psalms 23:5 Thou preparest a table before me in the presence of mine enemies: thou anointest my head with oil; my cup runneth over.]
Who are [mine enemies?] The ones that sense time, [Luke 20:46 Beware of the scribes,..]

[my cup runneth over.] This is a trait of a sound mind or having right brain unveiled. Right brain is a pondering aspect so one can take details and clarify them and see things from many angles. Jesus said something very similar in verse thirteen in the Gospel of Thomas [Jesus said, "I am not your teacher. Because you have drunk, you have become intoxicated from the bubbling spring that I have tended."

[the bubbling spring that I have tended.] = [my cup runneth over.] These of course are attempts to explain how powerful right brain is when it is in the sound mind, fifty percent state in conscious mind.
[thou anointest my head with oil;] This is like saying "I am quick and mentally sharp." Like a well oiled engine so to speak. In case one has not noticed the beings in these ancient texts were wise. These beings were so wise, conscious, civilization even after thousands of years still has not even figured out what they were talking about because civilization is essentially all mentally hindered and thus cannot figure out right brain complexity using simple minded left brain mindset but once one applies the remedy and has right brain traits on their side these texts are like butter and very easy to understand and make perfect sense and are flawless in

117

their explanations. It is logical a mentally hindered being would be able to understand some concepts these conscious beings spoke about but in general the message would not be understood.

[Psalms 23:6 Surely goodness and mercy shall follow me all the days of my life: and I will dwell in the house of the LORD for ever.]

This comment relates to the fact once a person applies the remedy it is permanent and that is a good thing, meaning they will have a sound mind for the rest of their life. The logic is, the mind stops developing, the frontal lobe, at around the age of twenty so after one applies the remedy one can not hinder their mind again. So the remedy is really just a "fix" for the mental hindering caused by learning written education and math and it's a onetime fix and then that is it, no chance to go back to that left brain dominate state with right brain veiled.

[and I will dwell in the house of the LORD for ever.] – House of the Lord is relative to a Master of the house; a being that is of sound mind or a mind in harmony. Forever denotes no sense of time. One has no sense of time in the sound state of mind so one lives forever relative to their perception. The mind no longer does this [Galatians 4:10 Ye observe days, and months, and times, and years.] so one is in infinity relative to their perception.

Relative to this 23 Psalm being in random access, if one takes this psalm and arranges it like this:

[Psalms 23:4 Yea, though I walk through the valley of the shadow of death, I will fear no evil: for thou art with me; thy rod and thy staff they comfort me.] = The remedy.

When one seeks the shadow of death and their hypothalamus says "run like the wind" and one does not run:
They [deny their self] relative to [Luke 9:23 ..., If any man will come after me, let him deny himself]
They [Fear not] relative to [Genesis 15:1 ...the LORD came unto Abram in a vision, saying, Fear not,]

They [Fear no evil] relative to [Psalms 23:4 ... though I walk through the valley of the shadow of death, I will fear no evil]

They [lose their life mindfully] relative to , [Luke 17:33 ...; and whosoever shall lose his life shall preserve it.]

They [Submit} relative to the doctrine of Islam.

So this remedy is interchangeable with all these words and shows this one spirit suggesting the same concept in many different ways but in reality it is saying the same thing over and over, for example:

[though I walk through the valley of the shadow of death, I will fear no evil]

[though I walk through the valley of the shadow of death, I will [fear not]

[though I walk through the valley of the shadow of death, I will [deny myself]

[though I walk through the valley of the shadow of death, I will [lose my life (mindfully) to preserve it]

[though I walk through the valley of the shadow of death, I will [submit]]

[though I walk through the valley of the shadow of death, I will [bow]]

[though I walk through the valley of the shadow of death, I will [yield]]

What are symptoms after one applies the remedy?

[Psalms 23:1 ... I shall not want.] = no desires and cravings; greed, lust, coveting

[Psalms 23:2 He maketh me to lie down in green pastures: he leadeth me beside the still waters.] = No fear or panic when troubled times arise because on has a sound mind and can figure things out swiftly.

[Psalms 23:3 He restoreth my soul: he leadeth me in the paths of righteousness for his name's sake.] = One restores their right brain and thus restores their mind.

[Psalms 23:5 Thou preparest a table before me in the presence of mine enemies: thou anointest my head with oil; my cup runneth over.] =- One becomes very wise in contrast to the ones that sense time, the ones with right brain veiled.

[Psalms 23:6 Surely goodness and mercy shall follow me all the days of my life: and I will dwell in the house of the LORD for ever.] = The remedy once applies is permanent and one knows they applied it the full measure because one will perceive they live forever, will have no sense of time.

So Psalm 23:4 is in the middle of these six verses which denotes in the middle, middle denotes sound mind, in one way, but that is the remedy or the symptom of the other five verses so it should the first verse in Psalm 23 and then other five verses are symptoms after one applies the remedy.

So this Psalm 23 is an exact repeat of this verse among others : [Genesis 15:1 After these things the word of the LORD came unto Abram in a vision, saying, Fear not, Abram: I am thy shield, and thy exceeding great reward.]
[Fear not..] =[Psalms 23:4 Yea, though I walk through the valley of the shadow of death, I will fear no evil]

[I am thy shield, and thy exceeding great reward.] What are the traits or the exceeding great reward for fearing not, applying the remedy?
[Psalms 23:1 ... I shall not want.]
[Psalms 23:2 He maketh me to lie down in green pastures: he leadeth me beside the still waters.]
[Psalms 23:3 He restoreth my soul:]
[Psalms 23:5 ...thou anointest my head with oil; my cup runneth over.]

9:59:25 AM –
Question of a forum:

[MyzTek;]Been seeing your posts for a while, this one caught my interest a little. I'm unaware of any scientific studies that favor your hypothesis about drugs or alcohol effecting one side of the brain more than the other. Can you explain where your theories come from?]

[Can you explain where your theories come from?]

I accidentally applied the fear not remedy and unveiled my right brain or returned it to the middle , so I went subconscious dominate so to speak. Right brain has pattern detection, intuition, lightning fast random access processing, so these understandings I explain are patterns and conclusions I have come up with on my own since the accident of about 15 months ago.

One important thing to be aware of relative to drugs is many artists are known to take drugs to be more creative, creativity is a right brain trait. So an artist may do drugs and then get creative inspiration so that suggests drugs do unveil right brain. The deeper reality is one has to understand all that left brain education [we have been traditionally taught to master the 3 R's: reading, writing and arithmetic -- the domain and strength of the left brain] combined with the fact frontal lobe, the cognitive aspect of the mind/spirit does not even develop fully until the age of 20 [In humans, the frontal lobe reaches full maturity around only after the 20s, marking the cognitive maturity associated with adulthood" - Giedd, Jay N. (october 1999).] means the mind has to be affected, the mental harmony one is born with has to factually be affected by all that education because it is taught to them starting at the age of six or seven.

So, the education favors left brain and starts at the age of seven, so even if the mind, is favored 1% to the left the mind is unsound and so the being is unsound so the being has what is known as a "house(mind) divided" and thus cannot stand(think properly or how it was intended) I am mindful it is more like a 90% left brain bend, but even if it was just 1%, then traditional education hinders the mind of the children. Oral education does not have this same effect so only the written education, the scribe education.

Back to the drugs, one thing relative to nearly all drugs is they either make ones sense of time increase or decrease. For example alcohol and pot are known to alter ones perception of time, well that is relative to right brain paradox.

When right brain is unveiled even for a moment an especially when one applies the remedy the mind asks "How much time has passed?" and the right brain paradox says "Time has passed and no time has passed"(a paradox) and that is it final answer so ones perception of time is altered, So a person that drinks or does pot or does any number of drugs has their a sense of time perception altered because it unveils right brain a bit for the duration the drug lasts. This is why Jesus said {No need to do drugs, just apply the remedy, deny one's self, those who lose their life mindfully will preserve it(unveil right brain after education veils it)

This is not fantasy land though, firstly applying the remedy the full measure is very difficult relative to one who has right brain veiled and secondly, in general the left brain bending one gets as a child is permanent for the vast, vast majority because the remedy means one has to seek a situation where their hypothalamus gives them a death signal, like 'You will die if you do to run from this dark spooky place" and then one has to "fear not, or deny their self or submit" and simply put, the vast majority of beings in the left brain state cannot do that unless they are depressed or suicidal, which is what the 9th circle of hell is, treason.

One has to go through the 9th circle of hell, treason, the left brain state , to get out of hell and very few human beings since written education was invented have ever been able to survive that 9th circle of hell, treason and apply the remedy the full measure because the mental damage is so great after all the left brain favoring education, a person is essentially mentally ruined forever. The remedy is simple mental self control but factor in the facet the person in that left brain state has a hypothalamus that is afraid of words, and music and shadows, it is nearly impossible for them to apply the simple self control remedy the full measure. The ones that sense time are trapped by their own perception, so they are their own worst enemy, so to speak.

10:17:52 AM –
[twopekinguys]See bolded portion of your post.
The Psalm isn't arranged that way, so your analysis is therefor moot.]

I will have to arrange or explain it so ones that sense time, the linear left brain based ones can grasp the random access format.

[Fear not..] =[Psalms 23:4 Yea, though I walk through the valley of the shadow of death, I will fear no evil]

[I am thy shield, and thy exceeding great reward.] What are the traits or the exceeding great reward for fearing not, applying the remedy?
[Psalms 23:1 ... I shall not want.]
[Psalms 23:2 He maketh me to lie down in green pastures: he leadeth me beside the still waters.]
[Psalms 23:3 He restoreth my soul:]
[Psalms 23:5 ...thou anointest my head with oil; my cup runneth over.]

The point of this is. These texts are written by beings who have applied the remedy and so they speak in random access and that proves the authenticity of the texts.
In a linear left brain state one cannot detect that reality.
Psalms 23 is a sign post of authenticity because it is in random access.
For example:
If I said : I had a good time, became alert, found great wealth, drank from a cup.
That is in random access and what Psalms 23 is.
Because "I drank from the cup", i had a good time, became alert, and found great wealth.

So my comment [I had a good time, became alert, found great wealth, drank from a cup.] is in random access.

So Psalms 23 is the exact same way.

[[Psalms 23:4 Yea, though I walk through the valley of the shadow of death, I will fear no evil] = drank from the cup, applied the remedy

What happened after he drank from that cup?
[Psalms 23:1 ... I shall not want.]
[Psalms 23:2 He maketh me to lie down in green pastures: he leadeth me beside the still waters.]
[Psalms 23:3 He restoreth my soul:]
[Psalms 23:5 ...thou anointest my head with oil; my cup runneth over.]

So the author is writing he drank from the cup but that is in the middle of the verse [Psalms 23:4] so the verses are out of sequence, sequence is a left brain trait, and instead is in random access , a right brain trait, so that proves its authenticity. So that means whomever wrote this psalm certainly applied the remedy to the tree of knowledge, education, and restored right brain and the proof is he is speaking in tongues, random access. A person who has not applied the remedy could not ever possibly detect that pattern,a right brain trait is pattern detection, intuition and random access, so its along the lines of "takes one to know one"

Simply put there is perhaps no other human being alive on this planet that can understand these texts as well as I can but only because I went the full measure with applying the remedy, and I did it by accident, so It is not me, it is just I unveiled right brain very well so I have lots of pattern detection, intuition, random access fast processing and all that combined means I can breaks the codes in these texts, but I am accident so it's not my genes or intelligence it is just I unveiled right brain well, by accident. This means any human being that applies the remedy well can break the codes in these texts but because the education does so much mental damage, that kind of a person only comes along once in a while. It's not me, it's right brain, the god image in man, traits in my conscious state of mind that allows me to understand these texts.

Patterns are the concepts details overlook.

"Nothing in life is to be feared, only understood." - Marie Curie

This comment is saying "Nothing to fear but fear itself.". This comment is also saying "Fear not". This comment is also saying "Fear no evil." Another way to look at it is, one gets the education and their hypothalamus as a side effects starts sending many false positives relative to fear. These false fear signals may be perceived to be shame, embarrassment, jealousy, greed, lust, envy, hate, anger, wrath, and many other emotions. So the remedy is one seeks openly to get into a situation they get that hypothalamus to give them the strongest possible signal it can give, and that is a death signal, and then they ignore that signal and the amygdala remembers that, it remembers what you fear and what you don't fear, and then the mind is cleared from all those false positive fear signals and in that situation right brain traits can be restored or right brain unveils about a month later and then the ride relative to getting use to consciousness begins.

So this comment "Nothing in life is to be feared, only understood." Is saying, once one gets all the fear out of their mind they can understand, they can think clearly, they can "see" again. Another way to look at it is once one gets the eventuality of life out of the way, out of their mind, they think clearly and are not bound by this stone around their neck any longer, the fear of death aspect.

3/12/2010 12:48:26 AM – This is relative to Aleister Crowley. Most of these observations are simply detecting patterns and right brain is the aspect that detects patterns. He was expelled from Cambridge and then decided to write poetry. So this means he got plenty of the left brain favoring education. Poetry is relative to concepts and concepts are a right brain trait so this poetry we wrote was favoring right brain but clearly his right brain was veiled so he was subconsciously attempting to find the path to God so to speak. Relative to a person that senses time Crowley appears very "evil" but relative to reality he was denying himself on a world stage. For example he wrote a book called "The book of the Law" and this book essentially explained how one should be free to do as they wish and he believed if everyone did as they wished no one would do bad and that is relative to the concept "if it harm no one do as you wish" and that is essentially what "life liberty and the pursuit of happiness" is. Another way to look at it is no person knows what the pursuit of happiness is relative to an absolute and also there are many paths to God which means there are infinite ways to unveil right brain after education has veiled it and one perhaps can never tell what will unveil it. Some of these interesting patterns relative to Crowley for example is, he started a new religion and in this religion he had a few followers or disciples and one of the rules was if anyone said the word "I" they had to cut their self and the premise was so one would deny their ego. The Latin word for "I" is EGO in all caps. Young children do not have an ego but all that left brain favoring education makes one have an ego which is simply pride so although these words "ego" and "pride" sound inviting they are actually psychological symptoms caused by the mind being bent to the left from the years of education. The thing about Crowley saying he was the beast is the beast would never say he is the beast so in reality Crowley was humiliating or prostrating or denying his ego by suggesting he was the beast and [Luke 9:23 And he said to them all, If any man will come after me, let him deny himself,...]. There is this aspect relative to the reverse thing and it goes something like, a person who is always trying to do good and appear righteous and good in their deeds is simply a very egotistical person which means they have right brain veiled a great deal because they are trying to give off this impression of being good and doing that is a symptom of ego and pride. This is relative to the comment in the ancient texts about the ones that pray in the streets so everyone can see them.

[Matthew 6:5 And when thou prayest, thou shalt not be as the hypocrites are: for they love to pray standing in the synagogues and in the corners of the streets, that they may be seen of men. Verily I say unto you, They have their reward.] = they have a reward of ego and pride.

So relative to the above comment if one wishes to deny their self, they won't pray in public and they may not even pray at all because the reality is if one senses time, their right brain is veiled from the education so the last thing a person in that state of mind wants to do, is what they want to do, which means they want to do the reverse of what they want to do. For example if they want to pray in public and they want to look wise and good, they should avoid that because that only encourages their ego and pride. They should perhaps consider going around and telling people they are the devil and the beast and when people avoid them and insult them for saying that it will assist them in taking their pride and ego down a notch, so they will in fact be denying their self. If a person that senses time is compelled to suggest they are the beast and the devil they should not do that but instead suggest they are a saint, and when people mock them and insult them for saying that it will take their pride and ego down a notch so they in turn will be denying their self.

[1 Corinthians 3:18 Let no man deceive himself. If any man among you seemeth to be wise in this world, let him become a fool, that he may be wise]

This comment is saying, do not kid yourself, you got the education and so your only purpose in life until you remedy that is to be a fool and that is what deny yourself is all about. When one that senses time does something they perceive is wise, their pride swells and their ego swells, so the reverse of that is to be a fool and so that pride dies and that ego dies. Of course applying the full measure remedy means one unveils right brain and then they have no ego or pride at all. Pride and ego is relative to memory so when right brain is unveiled one is in the now or the machine state so they have no concept or pride or ego. One pattern I notice about Crowley is he used drugs and that is certain proof he was attempting to unveil or get in touch with right brain, the god image in man and it essentially killed him or harmed him and that is typical after one has their right brain veiled. After the education one has their right brain veiled and so they do drugs to escape reality and their reality is the place of suffering, the left brain state of mind and they escape that and unveil right brain and return to somewhat sound mind for the duration the drug lasts. Of course this comment is saying you do not have to kill yourself with drugs to feel right brain you can just apply the remedy which takes one second in the right situation and then you will never need drugs to escape sense of time pseudo reality because you will return to reality.

[Ephesians 5:18 And be not drunk with wine, wherein is excess; but be filled with the Spirit(right brain);]

Simply put in real reality, sound mind reality, it is pleasing and you are this cerebral being and nothing in the world is a task or even a challenge and concepts and ideas and creativity are your drugs. Thinking is your drug so literal drugs cannot add anything to that so they become irrelevant completely. The thing about right brain when unveiled is it's so fast in processing and its thought patterns are random access so this concept of having an addiction to drugs or anything for that matter is not even possible to mindfully maintain. Crowley was like many people that get this written education, they spend their whole life looking for the light and the vast majority never find it and that is an indication of how damaging the written education is on the mind of a child considering the mind of that child does not even develop until they are 20 or so, the frontal lobe. The mind of a child is in perfect harmony both left and right brain traits are equal in signal strength and that is how the mind will stay unless that child is around someone who has a sense of time and has their right brain veiled or that child gets the education or both and then the mind starts to bend and favor left brain and so the mind slowly goes off on this left brain tangent and by the time the child is twelve or so the damage is done and the remedy has to be applied to restore right brain traits. So Crowley was like billions of other people showing obvious symptoms of trying to restore their right brain after getting the education and it is no easy task relative to the ones that sense times perception. Crowley was not to crazy about rules and control and neither were the founding fathers of America in fact they downright hated tyranny and Jefferson even hated tyranny over the mind and right brain hates rules because it likes to figure it out on its own and its powerful intuition and ambiguity aspects are a big reason why. Society tries to live everyone's life for them and society is always trying to "save" people. Saving people and helping people is a nice way to say controlling people. Society does not even know what the tree of knowledge is so I assure you they are not capable of saving or helping anyone but they are capable of controlling people, and control is a left brain trait and it's known as coveting. That is why focus on the log in your eye is saying "Do not try to save me because you will not be able to save yourself if you are focused on anyone but yourself." Another way to look at that is after one gets the education they only have about 10% full mental capacity working so they need all 10% to apply the fear not remedy but most do not make it but there are always some wheat, seekers seeking the kingdom (right brain), in the gargantuan pile of chaff.

[Luke 9:23 ... let him deny himself,...] If one does not understand what this deny himself concept is about, then they factually have no chance to unveil right brain unless they have a good accident. Crowley was into many rituals but he overlook this fear not, deny one's self ritual which is sacrifice but he also showed many symptoms of deny himself so he was attempting to wake himself up the hard way, with no assistance, and it just never worked out. Perhaps one of the darkest aspects to the neurosis is at the end of the day one has to deny their self to the full measure and that is an absolute reality if one wishes to fully restore right brain and that simply is too harsh for the majority so this written education and math being taught to children at such a young age is simply to damaging to the majority and that is perhaps far beyond any ones understanding of tragedy. As a species we kill ourselves because of the way we teach the "wisdom" education and that is one fact beyond all facts. There are no other facts that even matter beyond that one. Our greatest accomplishment as a species will be the day we question if all that left brain favoring written education and math may have unintended mental side effects on the mind of children whose minds do not even develop until they are twenty and until we reach that level as a species we are nothing but sand. No matter what inventions we come up with at the end of the day as a species we mentally hinder all the children with our methods of traditional education so all those inventions are nothing but stupidity. As a species we have not progressed one millimeter in 5400 years and in fact we keep digging the pit we are in deeper and deeper. I am not concerned about what any human being on this planet that senses time says contrary to that because my purpose is to convince that being that senses time to mindfully kill their self. Crowley was a human being attempting to restore the kingdom knowingly or unknowingly and in this narrow that seldom works out as planned.

3/12/2010 11:22:58 AM – The hypothalamus is one of the main aspects of the brain affected by the left brain favoring education and not only because it is relative to ones inhibitions such as a fear but because it also affects hunger and sex drive and if one thinks about these sin aspects hunger is relative to gluttony and sex is relative to lust, not on an absolute scale but on a general scale. One can look at the society as being slightly on the obese side and understand the education affects the hypothalamus and thus ones craving or desire to eat and so we have obesity problems or over eating problems and in the same respect we also have people who do not like to eat or have issues with eating such as bulimics'. Another way to look at it is when a person that is of sound mind, has right brain unveiled, eats, it is because they are aware food is required to live and so they are not really

129

eating because they desire or crave or lust after food. For example some of the tribes, the ones that never get the education may eat grub worms. The reality is they are not eating grub worms because that is the only kind of food they can eat they are eating grub worms because that is as good of food as anything else. They are not "picky" or judgmental about what food they eat and this is because their right brain traits are not veiled so that means their paradox aspect is saying "That grub is good for food so it is good food." The ones that sense time may be repulsed by that but that is only because their right brain traits are veiled so they are very judgmental. For example the ones that sense time may say "Shrimp is delicious, lobster is delicious but grub worms are horrible and probably evil", so they are seeing parts. They see some things as good and something as evil or bad but in reality food is food. Another way to look at it is the fact their right brain is veiled means their palette is limited relative to what they eat, what music they like, what pictures they like and what sounds and what words they like or are pleased with. It is kind of like being displeased with some oxygen but liking other kinds of oxygen. That is not very logical to be pleased with one word and then displeased with another word when both are words, so something relative to their perception is a miss. It is not logical to be pleased with some music and to be displeased with other music to the point one "hates" that music because both are music but this is exactly what is happening. A person that senses time may say "I only listen to religious music." The reality is all music is created using right brain creativity and right brain is the god image in man so all music is religious music but that being does not perceive that because they have right brain veiled. All of civilization is based on seeing parts because all of civilization gets the education so they have their right brain traits veiled so they have these contests and judgment contests based on seeing parts about what music is better, what art is better, what country is better, what gender is better, what religion is better, what student is smartest, what profession is best, who has the highest IQ. It is all just vanity because the reality is none of those things or people are the best. I can invent a contest relative to who can write a book in random access, using very few commas and very few paragraph breaks and essentially breaks all known grammar rules known to mankind, and I would always win that contest because I do not perceive any flaws with what I write so I am not a good judge I am just putting my thought into words and as long as I can understand them I am pleased. The deeper reality is I am not writing my thoughts down and at the same time anticipating whether other people will understand them so I am not censoring my thoughts. The right brain ambiguity and paradox aspects no longer allow my mind to determine what "civilization" is. For example many people will write a speech and labor over that speech because they are attempting to reach a certain target audience so they mindfully are aware others are going to listen to what they say. There is a concept about , once a person says something they can never take it back so they should be careful about what they say, but in reality that is a symptom of ego because only a person that has an ego and strong pride would assume what they say is of value to begin with and once they assume what they say is of value they start to censor what they say to try an achieve this "My words have value so I must be careful about what sequence I say words" is a delusion to protect their ego and pride. It all comes back to fear and the ill functioning hypothalamus in the ones that sense time. It all comes down to a very simple logic tree relative to what the ones that sense time say.

If I say something and people do not like it that means people do not like me, so I am not a good person if people do not like me, so I will try to never say anything I perceive people will not like. That simple logic tree is a symptom of ego and pride caused by being conditioned into an extreme left brain state of perception by the written education. Pride and ego are symptoms of fear. One has to first determine they are capable of saying something of value before they can become afraid of not saying something of value. Once a person understands they are not capable of saying something of value in this lifetime they will not be surprised if they don't say something of value. If people were capable of saying something of value they would have said it by now. The point is, why would you ever censor your thoughts and thus your words when you are not going to be saying anything of value anyway. Who exactly are you trying to impress by censoring your thoughts? Perhaps some illusion in your head you perceive is watching your every move? Do you have such a huge ego you believe anything you say ever makes a dam bit of difference? You perceive you may say something and it may hurt someone's feelings so you censor your thoughts because you are such a saint and so caring and so concerned and so righteous. Your mind is telling you that the universe is waiting for the next words that come out of your mouth so it can determine if it should continue to exist or not. In your sense of time state of mind you have a voice in your head that says "What you say matters." and that is your greatest delusion. I hear people on television apologizing for saying words they will say "I am sorry I misspoke" or "I did not mean to say that." and I am pondering if that person understands I only see them as an illusion and I do not require illusions to apologize for their words because their words are of no value to begin with. If words had any value one could say a word and break the curse or neurosis caused by written education and restore their mind in short order but that is not the case so words have no value. Do you think censoring your words and succumbing to fear of saying words is going to get you into heaven or simply ensure you stay in hell? Since the remedy is fear not one has to start doing things they fear to do because sound minded beings are not afraid to say words and are not afraid to speak their mind even if it costs them their life because they understand their life is just a life and nothing worth censoring their thoughts over. Perhaps some are trying to live forever by hiding in a hole of fear in their mind.

[2 Timothy 1:7 For God hath not given us the spirit of fear; but ... a sound mind.]

Spirit of fear = unsound mind = hypothalamus not working properly because of all that left brain favoring education and math. Is anything I have said in the last million words clicking yet?

There is a concept about cultural differences but that is not what is really happening, these cultural differences are symptoms people are seeing parts. Humans do stuff. That comment encompasses all cultural differences.

The ones that sense time see dollar signs but few other signs

3/13/2010 2:11:17 AM – Thousands of years ago mankind invented written language and math. These inventions required creativity and complexity, right brain traits, to invent. At first the only people even considered to be taught these new inventions were the adult males. These beings were known as scribes and they were somewhat of a cult at first. They were valuable because at that time written education was like a new fad and a "magical" invention. As this fad caught on many people could see anyone that learned how to be a scribe was treated very well and the scribes were looked up to so much wealth and assumptions of wisdom surrounded the scribes who wielded this "magical" script. This eventually led people to want their children, at first their first born male children, to be schooled in these inventions written language and math. It was expensive to have a child taught these then new inventions so much pressure was put on the first born males to do well at these inventions so the family would have what is known today as a bread winner. Educating the children is where the trouble started though because at the time is was not known the child's mind developed all the way until they were twenty so teaching these left brain favoring inventions at such a young age had extreme unwanted mental side effects on the children. Soon some of the people that were taught this education became aware of these unwanted mental side effects and they began to speak out against the written education and math being taught to children. This is what became known as the holy war. The complexity of this holy war was only the people that got the education and then negated the mental effects caused by being taught the education were fully aware of the damaging mental effects of the education. Simply put, one had to get the education and thus get the mental damage caused by the education and then in one way or another apply the remedy to the mental damage and restore their mind to be able to fully understand how great the mental damage was. These beings who escaped the mental damage were known as prophets, messiah's, buddha, philosophers, wise men, messengers, oracles and saints just to name a few. The main problem with these beings argument is society by that time already looked at written education as a means to make money and thus a means to put food on the table. The deeper reality is the vast majority that got the education were so mentally hindered they were damaged beyond repair and so this meant they would have children and then ensure their own children were taught the education also and thus perpetuate the neurosis with the understanding the education gave their children a means to make money and thus put food on the table because society had already based its existence around the education. So as the "wise men" spoke out against the scribes they appeared very backwards because the scribes were in the neurosis and could not fully understand how devastating the education was on the mind because the scribes were still in the neurosis caused by the education. So these "wise men" were known as members of the tribes and they were at war with the scribes and the prize of the war was the children. The wise men wanted to protect the children from getting the education at such a young age or at least suggest the remedy with the education and the scribes believed the younger they taught the education to the children the more wise the children would become and the more money the children would make. This created a classic rock and a hard place conflict. On one hand the wise men were saying "If you go down the road of teaching written script and math eventually the whole species would be thrown into this alterative perception neurosis and the whole species would show fruits of that decision". On the other hand the scribes were not fully aware of the mental effects so they perceived they were making a proper decision by teaching the children the written education and math. So this meant both side perceive they had a valid and proper argument so there was no give or take at all in the conflict and this is what led to war known as the Holy war, the scribes versus the tribes. The argument for this war has not changed at all since the war started thousands of years ago. The war is simply over the protection of the children, the offspring, and a battle for their minds. So civilization appeared backwards to the tribes and the tribes appeared backwards to the civilization, the scribes. This was caused because of the opposing perceptions. The scribes had their perception altered by the written education and math teachings so they saw things in a complete opposite light and because they had their right brain veiled they could not fully grasp that the war was even going on in some respects. Relative to the scribes the Holy war appeared to be many unrelated battles and relative to the tribes the Holy war appeared to only be one war and thus one battle. Because of the neurosis the scribes became very afraid and thus they had many advanced weapons to protect their self from the tribes. The scribes created large fortress cities to protect them from what they called barbarians, the tribes. This great fear caused by the neurosis lead the scribes to focus on making stronger and stronger weapons to fend off the tribes. Soon all the scribes had were many weapons to protect them from all the things they feared. The inability of the tribes to keep up with the weapon advancements of the scribes lead to the tribes being soundly defeated on the literal battle field. - 2:58:54 AM

Sedition: actions or words intended to provoke or incite rebellion against government authority, or actual rebellion against government authority.

This is the definition of sedition but one has to understand the words "government authority" is really the ones that sense time because a left brain dominate container is a control freak or simply put left brain is all about coveting so it is a control freak and it may also mean you. So civilization in general is a control freak because they all got the education and did not apply the remedy so they are all left brain influenced containers and thus are prone to controlling deed's and aspects. So once one separates their self from the person aspect everything is reduced down to what influence they are driven by. So the ones that sense time are not as much human beings as they are left brain influenced containers and a left brain influenced container is not possible in a true vacuum so they are left brain influenced containers because they were conditioned into the left brain dominate state of mind by the education and thus by other left brain influenced containers who also were conditioned as a result of getting the education. So in that respect [provoke or incite rebellion against government authority] really means provoke or incite rebellion against the ones that sense time, yourself, the left brain influenced containers and relative to focus on the log in your eye that means rebel against yourself, self being that sense of time state one is after the education. On a species level in doing this sedition the left brain containers are going to suggest words in order to resist losing control or power and that means you. The left brain containers will never suggest anything that will hinder their control and will always say things that will insult any aspect that attempts to negate their control. This of course is not done on a conscious level this is simply the fruits or nature of a left brain. One cannot exhibit right brain traits, tendencies to not control, if they have right brain traits veiled, is another way to look at it. So a left brain container will perceive this controlling and coveting aspect is natural or normal. This coveting aspect means the left brain containers are pleased to control and are pleased to be controlled. Contrary to that a right brain influenced container is not pleased to be controlled, told what to do, given

135

directions and is also not pleased to control or give directions. So for a left brain container to not be controlling they have to use self control to achieve freedom and for the right brain container they have to let go of freedom and use self control to be controlling. Another way to look at it is a left brain container has left brain aspects in the conscious state and have right brain aspects in the subconscious state so they are essentially prone to control and prone to be controlled and right brain containers have left and right brain traits in the conscious state but in mental harmony right brain traits rule so they have to use some self control to think along the left brain controlling thought patterns. A left brain container is ruthless in their quest for control but not always relative to their perception because they are in neurosis. Essentially what the left brain container perceives is common sense is in fact insanity and lacking reason but they do not perceive that. So the rule of thumb relative to sedition is to encourage them to break every single rule they subscribe to and this is in line with denying their self. One has to let go of this delusion about saving people. The vast majority of the beings that sense time are mentally ruined for good so they are mentally done and cannot ever be recovered and so this leaves a small fraction that can be recovered and they are known as the wheat or the seekers and the meek. These seekers or the wheat are willing to listen and are willing to experiment and willing to listen to ideas they perhaps have never heard of before. This experimental mental state is a right brain aspect so the fact they are willing to listen and experiment shows they are at least in a position to possibility be mentally salvaged. So this sedition aspect relative to rebellion against control structure would be perceived to be anarchy. So anarchy : the absence of any formal system of government in a society; is simply the hindering of the control structure. This anarchy is not relative to physically breaking the law it is simply a mental state one is in where they go about their life and appear to be following the rules of the control structure but in their mind they have nothing but contempt for the control structure. The point is right brain deals in paradox and a paradox is two contradictions that equal one truth so this mental anarchy state in turn negates absolutes, and rules and laws suggest absolutes. This avoidance of absolutes is relative to the concept of "there is a time for war and a time for peace". That comment suggests no absolutes. Simply put you absolutely got mentally hindered into a mental state of suffering by the education pushed on your before your mind was even near developed but it is not an absolute your mind has to stay that way. Another way to look at it is, the unveiling right brain is your only purpose and so anyone that attempts to make you avoid this "denying yourself" exercise to restore your right brain aspect should be looked at like nothing but an illusion whose sole purpose is to make sure you never restore your right brain, and that way you can just ignore what they say or suggest or ignore their attempts to advise you because your mind is your mind and yours alone. Literal physical war is not going to apply the remedy for you so the war must always remain in the mental stage. This means you are going to have to wage a mental war on yourself that makes physical war look like folly for lightweights. Physical war is folly for idiots compared to this mental war you are going to have to fight to restore your right brain traits. This remedy is sedition against yourself. How are you going to ever defeat the shadow of death if you are afraid of words and music and food? Simply put you never will, so you start detaching from all these stupid unfounded control freak rules. Keep in mind you are seeking to restore your mind so you must be willing to say and listen to anything you have to, in order to let go of some of these rules that have been conditioned into your mind. This is why Moses took the commandment rules and threw them on the rocks because right brain does not deal with absolutes it deals with paradox and complexity. Avoid getting into a position where you seek to avoid talking to the ones that sense time because they are tools to assist you to condition yourself. Simply put if you just hang around ones that have applied the remedy you will not better yourself because they have no problems with you breaking all of these delusional rules of society but the ones that sense time, the ones in neurosis pretty much have heart attacks and insult you and mock you when you break their delusional rules and that's is what will excite your emotions and upset you and make you angry and then you can block those emotions and thus further purge the emotions and then concentrate even better. As emotions decrease mental clarity increases and because of that reality, you want to seek situations that will excite your emotions just so you can block them and this is what humiliation and prostration and denying yourself is all about.

The only way you can restore your mind to a laser sharp lightening fast instrument is to test it and put it to the test. If you attempt to keep the sheep mentality and herd mentality you will fail at restoring your mind. So in the physical world you are pleasing and go along with the herd but in your mind you are an anarchist to the core. You will say anything at any time just for the chance you may be humiliated so you can block your emotions that suggest you should physically lash out. What this means is you are going to be your only teacher and you are not even going to consider teaching anyone but yourself because in all reality the vast majority of the ones that sense time cannot be salvaged no matter what. All of your friends mentally raped you into hell as a child so you let go of that delusion you are here to make friends. For example I find when I suggest this :

"In humans, the frontal lobe reaches full maturity around only after the 20s, marking the cognitive maturity associated with adulthood"

Combined with this:

"" If you reflect back upon our own educational training, we have been traditionally taught to master the 3 R's: reading, writing and arithmetic -- the domain and strength of the left brain"

Means that education could possibly have some unwanted mental side effects many of the ones that sense time suggest "If you would have done better in school you would not be so angry now." This is why the ones that sense time are factually in such deep neurosis they perhaps are no longer are capable of reasoning on any level other than insanity. Simply put their God is the tree of knowledge and they have been conditioned to insult anyone who speaks poorly of their god, the tree of knowledge. In their sense of time state of mind they have been conditioned into they are factually no longer human beings so avoid attempting to assume they are. Do not acknowledge them as human beings in your mind or your attempts to "save them" will destroy you. The kingdom is within and your mind is within so you are allowed to think anything you want no matter how many fear tactics the ones that sense time attempt to manipulate you with. You are seeking to restore your mind so everything is an illusion outside of that reality.

9:29:58 PM – I was watching a documentary about the mind. There were some cases where people died on the operating table but what made the cases extraordinary is they had patients hooked up to many life indicator machines. EEG, brain wave monitors, heart monitors and a host of other machines monitoring the patients and then the patients died and remained dead while still on the monitors and then they came back to life after a period of time relative to a clock. The doctors were not certain about their observations but they discovered the patients while dead were able to recall events that happened in the room after they were dead. What the Doctors suggested is that it is possible the brain itself is not an originator of perception but simply a receiver of perception. So this means it looks like the brain is doing all these things relative to perception but in reality the aspects of the brain we perceive are originating all this perception are simply receivers to allow the perception. For example the hypothalamus is relative to fight or flight signals but in reality based on these Doctors observations it would appear the hypothalamus is simply a receiver for those fight or flight perceptions . So this would suggest without the hypothalamus at all one could still get perceptions of fight or flight. Another example would be memory. These patients were clinically dead so that means there is no possible way they could have any memory yet they did have memories so the memories their self did not originate in the brain they continued even when the brain receiver was turned off completely. This concept the mind itself is not relative to the brain but the brain is just a receiver is very dangerous because of this comment:

[Genesis 3:1 Now the serpent was more subtil than any beast of the field which the LORD God had made. And he said unto the woman, Yea, hath God said, Ye shall not eat of every tree of the garden?]

[Now the serpent was more subtil than any beast of the field] This comment is suggesting written education and math are not written education and math at all, they are just very cleverly disguised , charming, traps to get a being to come under the power of the serpent or possession of the serpent.
So this would mean what we perceive as life and the universe is nothing but a testing ground with very clever traps and relative to our species we have fallen for a trap we perhaps can never get out of. Another way to look at it is we as a species were put in this testing ground and along came this well disguised trap, written education and math and we bought it hook ,line and sinker and we as a species are totally oblivious to it and it is so

ingrained in us now we are in the end stages of destruction of ourselves because of this trap. Another way to look at it is our species ate off this trap and once in a while someone wakes up to the reality of the trap and attempts to explain it but they are fools for doing so because they try to explain to the ones who have the serpent in them that they escaped the trap and the ones who have the serpent in them are not pleased to hear that so they get rid of that being.

Another way to look at it is we are not educating children at all we are just giving them to the serpent, their spirit, and we are all children and all were given to the serpent. If one can just think about that possibility one may be able to understand what this means [Now the serpent was more subtil than any beast of the field]

This would explain why Jesus never wrote any books in the bible and also explain why Mohammad never wrote the Quran he dictated it to scribes, this would also explain why Buddhism is strictly oral traditions. For example all comments that are attributed to Buddha are not really Buddha's words, there is really no recorded writing from Buddha. The story goes, 200 years after he died some beings found his writing and memorized them and burned all his writings because they discovered the written language was the "charm". If one subscribes to this line of thought then all that is happening is one is being tested to see if they will speak out or even more to protect the children from getting the mark of the beast. One can see how war can easily be explained and easily incited if one subscribes to this line of thought. Another way to look at it is existence itself is simply, one is born, they get the mark, the education, they attempt to apply the remedy to remove the mark and once they do they try to stop others from getting the mark and try to assist others from removing the mark with the understanding the ones that are worth their salt end up getting slaughtered eventually. That is perhaps what this line is suggesting.

[John 15:13 Greater love hath no man than this, that a man lay down his life for his friends.]

Another way to look at it is you are either going to apply this fear not remedy the full measure and be fearless or you are going to partially apply this remedy, still have fear in the face of Goliaths vast armies and live

140

out eternity wishing you never heard the words "fear not remedy." You have been conditioned into thinking every problem has as solution, that is linear and simple and one just has to find the solution but you perhaps are not accustomed to situations where there is no solution and there is no beginning and there is no end, so there is no closure. Simply put there is no solution there are only beings attempting solutions in the battle.

3/14/2010 12:20:41 AM – There is one interesting aspect of right brain when it is unveiled that appears very odd to ones that sense time. One way to look at it is left brain wants to know and right brain wants to understand. Wanting to know something means one wants to reach the end and wanting to understand means one wants to reach a conclusion that leads them to seek another understanding. Beings that sense time want to have a clear cut focused plan that ends and thus concludes. Because the education affect's the frontal lobe their dopamine receptors are giving them pleasure for accomplishment and displeasure for lack of accomplishment. So then you have beings that sense time saying "Everything I do I fail at." Or "Everything I do I win at." Society is essentially left brain influenced beings that sense time and thus strive for this accomplishment aspect that is not even real but simply a figment of their perception. If one wants to take it all the way out, human beings started on this planet and they are still on this planet and although we have reached space that is meaningless because we are not going anywhere. We accomplished going to the moon and sending probes to mars but what have we really accomplished? Understandings.

X = a being that senses time "accomplishes" something and they get a euphoric feeling from the dopamine.
Y = A being that senses time "fails" to accomplish something and they get a depressed feeling from the dopamine.
Z = a person with no sense of time so they do not perceive failure or accomplished relative to euphoric feelings or depressed feeling from those events.

A (Y) person is depressed because they have no sense of accomplishment so they tend to isolate their self and appear lazy and they tend to seek things like drugs to enable them to feel the euphoric effects of the dopamine. So instead of "accomplishing" things to get the dopamine euphoric effects they use drugs or food or various other aspects to achieve this euphoric effect's from the dopamine. You will hear someone say "Go accomplish something and you will feel better about yourself." The problem with this dopamine accomplishment aspect is one is reduced to going up and down stairs, other words it is counter productive. Left brain is sloth in contrast to right brain relative to processing speed and thus mental activity so one is lazy or slothful. What this means is one seeks to live in this accomplishment or seeking accomplishment state of mind because after they accomplish something they go back down the stairs and they need to "accomplish" something to go back up in order to get the dopamine euphoric rush.

Think about sports. You will hear a team member of a team that wins and they will say "This is the greatest accomplishment of my life", but what that means is soon they are going to be going down the stairs into the place of failed accomplishment and so in order to avoid the depression they have to accomplish something else. What this means is one is not really accomplishing things as much as they are seeking things they can gain perceived accomplishment from. This aspect is what creates this competition in society. The problem with that is, for every person that accomplishes something another person has to fail at accomplishment. This competition characteristic starts in school. The grading curve is simply competition between the kids in a class. They are pitted against each other. A spelling Bee is a competition. Someone wins and someone loses. The concept of "Don't be a poor loser" is impossible because in this extreme left brain state one is either going to perceive "victory" and feel good from the dopamine or "fail" and feel bad psychologically. This also applies to relationships. If a girl dumps you, you will feel bad because you perceive you "failed" and you "lost". This is relative to left brain seeks closure or accomplishment or beginning and end and these things are parts. Simply put, with right brain traits unveiled one will never perceive they lose and never perceive they win so they will not be going up and down stairs. This aspect is relative to the ambiguity of right brain. Sometimes you will feel like you win when you lost and sometimes you will feel like you lost when you won but the mind will never really rest on either winning or losing so one is in a state of neutral. Dopamine is released from the hypothalamus also. When you are in a spooky situation and your heart starts racing and you feel goose bumps and you are afraid that's the dopamine so it is giving you a rush but it should not be giving you such a rush if your hypothalamus was working properly or not giving so many false signals due to the fact the mind was bent so far to the left by the education. The easiest way to look at it is once the mind is bent to the left or the right the entire brain stops functioning properly so everything goes haywire. There was no left brain favoring invention in all of mankind until the invention of written language and math. Harnessing fire did not favor the left brain. Hunting and gathering did not favor the left brain on the scale written education and math does. Dopamine is relative to the nervous system so in the extreme left brain state it essentially cannot do anything but make one a nervous wreck and that clouds the mental clarity and that hinders one's ability to reason. Another way to look at it is things like words, music, pictures should not be making one nervous or upset but they are because you are a nervous wreck because your dopamine is not working properly or as it should in that extreme left brain state. Beings that sense time cannot wait for the weekend so they can feel they have accomplished something. "Thank God it's Friday, I have truly accomplished something and I feel such a relief." That's the dopamine not working properly.

The D-1 dopamine receptor affects your behavioral responses. A person that senses time will have a "loss" and fall to pieces and that shows their behavior response is seriously hindered. This is relative to the story of Job and relative to how Jesus responded in the boat in the middle of the storm. Their behavioral responses were not panic and nervousness. They did not crumble in the face of uncertainly or in the face of loss but the ones that sense time crumble over spilt milk from a leaking container. Job lost everything a person can lose in life from his family to his home to his wealth to his health and he still did not have a nervous breakdown and that is relative to the D-1 dopamine receptors, and the D-1 dopamine receptors working properly because he had a sound mind. Just you thinking about watching a scary movie alone at night in the dark or just you thinking about going to a spooky abandoned house in the middle of the woods alone at night with no lights or even with flood lights make's you nervous. You may tell yourself it does not scare you or make you nervous but your hypothalamus could care less what you think because it is not functioning as it should and is giving you false positive fight or flight signals even on words.

I should be nervous when I chat with people and tell them about the effects of written education and they respond with:

[16:49] [ecstasy] i am very dissapointed and pretty much depressed
[16:49] [ecstasy] never felt like this in my life
[16:50] [ecstasy] I thougt i was the strong type of guy
[16:50] [ecstasy] but in the end ... we are always wrong

I should feel sad and depressed that I told this person something that made them upset and disappointed and depressed. I should keep my mouth shut so I do not hurt others feeling by telling them the truth but I do not feel nervous and I do not feel like I am going to be shutting up. I am mindful I harmed this being to a great degree by telling them the truth about written education and math before they were mentally able to handle it but I am mindful that is the way it is going to be so I do not feel sad or depressed or nervous. My mind can fully comprehend his reaction is a logical reaction from a being in an unsound state of mind being told the truth. The scribes put theses being in this extreme left brain state of mind and somehow I am going to wake them up faster than the scribes can put them to sleep even if I have to put them all into deep depression by telling them occult truth long before they are ready. I am in indifferent to that prospect and your opinion about it is irrelevant.

[> [ecstasy] but in the end ... we are always wrong]

In the end we are always wrong. "We" are the ones that sense time. He is not talking about me he is talking about you. There are only two responses you are ever going to get from the ones that sense time by telling them the truth.

Either:
[16:49] [ecstasy] i am very dissapointed and pretty much depresed]
Or
[Pacbox: "Still at it Rohrer? It's nonsense. Give it up. You're argument holds no water and never will. It's made up out of thin air."]

The former is what is known as the wheat and the latter is what is known as chaff. The wheat may not apply the remedy but at least they are mentally in a state they can grasp reality when they hear it. That means their mind is not completely ruined by the education but it also does not means they will rush out to mindfully deny their self to the full measure either. So If I had an emotional capacity I would never tell anyone what I tell everyone because there is always the possibility someone will understand me and if they do they will feel like this: [ecstasy] I am very dissapointed and pretty much depresed].

Simply put, anyone who listens to the words I type long enough may become sane and that is extremely dangerous considering the narrow. The world becomes very dark when one becomes sane. Wisdom and awareness are relative to grief. So the comment "Don't hurt others feelings" is stupidity because one should not have an emotional capacity to begin with unless their mind has been bent so far to the left their emotional capacity is infinite and the slow slothful left brain thought patterns will never allow the emotions to escape. Your greatest happiness is shortly followed by your greatest sorrow. You do not even know what the tree of knowledge is and that is a 5000 year old common sense understanding so I have to ponder if you know anything at all. In sixteen months I have gone from attempting to explain the situation relative to the tree of knowledge to the best of my ability to attempting to scare everyone away because it hurts the neurotic's feelings when I explain it flawlessly. At this stage I can only explain it flawlessly and that is infinitely bad news if you sense time. I bet you think your genes are bad because your IQ is not 205. I passed up 205 after the second book. With right brain intuition and pattern detection and lightning fast random access processing human beings have no IQ because it continues to grow and grow and grow and never stops but with right brain traits veiled even slightly an IQ of 205 appears genius. Go ask all your geniuses what the tree of knowledge is and the remedy and you will see what you call genius beings are not at the mental level of common sense understandings. Buddha explained it best when he said "The leaves in my hand are what I have taught you and the leaves in the forest behind me are what I have not taught you." Show me a concept, pattern or ideal and I will explain to you what you never understood about it in real time as I go, is another way to look at it. It all comes back to ground zero, only a complete lunatic would veil right brain traits for any reason ever into infinity yet society does it like it is the wisest thing in the universe with their wisdom education and then they brag about it "No child left behind" = No child gets to have their right brain traits.

Jonah summed it up properly:

[Jonah 4:11 And should not I spare .... persons that cannot discern between their right hand and their left hand(the ones that sense time); ...]

[And should not I spare] Is out of sequence it should be [And should I not spare] So his very last line of testimony is the signature or sign post that indicates he is authentic. Jonah certainly was a big fish. I am compelled to explain there is no being in any ancient texts that perhaps woke up as well as Jonah and if they were lucky they were equal to Jonah. One might suggest a being that determines it is best to kill their self for no real reason is one seriously hardcore seeker.

[Jonah 1:12 And he said unto them, Take me up, and cast me forth into the sea;]

Jonah was essentially saying "Kill me first." That is what denying yourself and submission and fearing not is all about. It's the mindset. Your mindset in applying this remedy is "I have no other purpose in the universe but to seek the shadow of death in a dark spooky situation and when my mind says "Run or the shadow will kill you" your mental response is "Take me up, and cast me forth into the sea;". That is called a meek mindset and self control and that is the remedy in principle. It is a mind exercise that negates the mental damage caused by all that left brain education and although it appears harsh to some perhaps it is really a painless one second self control aspect that is permanent and completely restores ones perception to proper perception. Avoid allowing the words used to describe it convince you it is dangerous. Your mind can handle things you perhaps are not aware of in your current state of mind. Lose that low self esteem mindset you have been conditioned into, if you cannot defeat death no one can and if you are not King no one is. Submit to authority with mindful sedition.

3/14/2010 3:07:44 PM - Amendment 14 - Citizenship Rights. Ratified 7/9/1868

"All persons born or naturalized in the United States, and subject to the jurisdiction thereof, are citizens of the United States and of the State wherein they reside. No State shall make or enforce any law which shall abridge the privileges or immunities of citizens of the United States; nor shall any State deprive any person of life, liberty, or property, without due process of law; nor deny to any person within its jurisdiction the equal protection of the laws."

The 14th Amendment is simply saying if you are born in America or become naturalized you are given the benefit of the doubt that you are able to make your own determinations relative to life, liberty and pursuit of happiness until proven otherwise. This is not what is happening though relative to education. You are determined to be less than equal when you are born so in order to become equal you are forced by law to get the written education and math via compulsory education laws. Some will argue along the lines of "It has been proven those who get the written education and math are better off." What they are really saying is "I got written education and math and look how great I turned out, so clearly everyone should be forced by law to get said "brand" of education." Avoid assuming anything I write is because of my traditional education, that brand of education nearly killed me and I spit on it. Don't you dare ever name a school after me. That spirit of logic "everyone gets a set education" is not what life, liberty and pursuit of happiness is that spirit of logic is what tyranny is. Tyranny is simply an argument to force you to do something and tyrannies greatest weapon are fear induced arguments. "If you do not do this, fearful things will happen." 'If you don't get our brand of education fearful things will happen." You will not get a good paying job. You will have a hard life. You will live in poverty. You will get a slave job." Until there is at minimum a waver a parent and child has to sign to remove any liability from the education system and thus the government if the education has mental effects on the mind of that child, the whole system is just a tyranny and a farce.
A Farce is a ridiculous situation in which everything goes wrong or becomes a sham.
When a person goes to a psychologist and the psychologist says "We have some new medication but in order for me to prescribe it to you, you will have to sign this waiver in case there are some bad side effects from the

medication." That is what has to be done relative to traditional education because it factually hinders the delicate mind of a child so unless that is done the entire system is nothing but tyranny over the mind and negates life liberty and pursuit of happiness so it is unconstitutional and it is not important if a judge or a government says it is not, it still factually is. The education system and thus the government that pushes the education system is simply forcing people by law to have their mind altered and thus their perception is altered and thus their life, liberty and pursuit of happiness is altered and that is factually what a tyranny over the mind is. If the government is aware education alters the mind but they make no mention of that then they should be abolished or altered and that is the right of the people to do that and if the government is not aware of the potential mental damaged caused by the education then they have no business being in a leadership role to begin with so they should be altered or abolished and that is a right of the people.

"That whenever any Form of Government becomes destructive of these ends, it is the Right of the People to alter or to abolish it, and to institute new Government, laying its foundation on such principles and organizing its powers in such form, as to them shall seem most likely to affect their Safety and Happiness.' - Declaration of Independence.

[That whenever any Form of Government becomes destructive of these ends] Infringes on a citizens life, liberty and pursuit of happiness. Compulsory education laws means a child must start the left brain favoring education at six or seven or they are illegal and a criminal but the education pushed on a child at that age factually hinders the mind so it is against the law to not get mentally hindered and to not mentally hinder your child or children so it is a law that harms people.

[it is the Right of the People to alter or to abolish it, and to institute new Government] = Get someone who is competent to be the government and the catch is the citizens are the most competent in the first place because they answer for their own actions because they rely on their self.

[as to them shall seem most likely to effect their Safety and Happiness.] = If the government is pushing education which effects and alters the perception of any being that gets it then that affects ones Safety and happiness.

[Safety and happiness.] = One cannot possibly be happy if one entire hemisphere of the brains traits are veiled and since one entire hemisphere of the brain traits are veiled by the education one cannot think clearly and so they are not safe. Simply put a human being with the full spectrum of their mind in the conscious state and in harmony can fend for their self in any situation and a human being with either aspect of their mind hindered cannot fend for their self at all so then they must rely on others to fend for them, as in the government, so they become helpless sheep or slaves. A human being factually needs both hemisphere aspects working at full power in order to determine their own pursuit of happiness and if that is not the case they have to rely on outside influences to determine for them their pursuit of happiness. The truth is you have never heard one single representative or senator that has ever even mentioned written education may have unwanted mental side effects on the delicate mind of a child so either they are not even at the mental level to grasp elementary cause and effect relationships or they are hiding something from you and the truth is, they got the education, so they know not what they do. Your safety and happiness is relative to the mental abilities of the beings you elect to rule you. You perceive they are well educated so that is why you elect them. They are from high class education institutes so that certainly proves they are wise.

You believe with all your might that the tree of knowledge is a :[Genesis 3:6 ... tree to be desired to make one wise.] Because your cognitive and thus reasoning ability which is relative to right brain intuition has been altered by the education you are making decisions based on a premise that written education and math proves one is wise when in reality if not taught properly it factually mentally hiders a person and if the remedy is not applied one remains mentally hindered, so because you are mistaken in that initial premise all of your other assumptions based on that premise are also in error. You do not know written education hindered your mind but you have never been told that it could hinder your mind by other beings that have lots of that education. You are in a situation that you trust what beings that have lots of that education say about the written education and so they will never suggest it has unwanted side effects because if they do they have to first submit they have been mentally hindered by the education so then if they do that you will not listen to them nor elect them. The deeper reality is they were taught the education as a child and they have no idea it mentally hindered them just like you have no idea it mentally hindered you. The obvious cause and effect relationship is simply, the written education and math favor the left brain and the mind itself and thus the cognitive mental maturity of the mind does not develop until one is twenty so the fact the education starts at the age of seven means there is no possible way the mind could not be hindered at the end of the education. It is not important if every being in the universe says that not possible or true it still is true and factual. A delusional person will deny or ignore obvious cause and effect relationships. It is not really about whether what I suggest about the damaging effects education has on the mind is factually true or not it is more along the lines that you do not want to face starting your entire life over again. Simply put you were mentally hindered as a child and the sooner you apply the remedy to restore your mind the sooner you can start your life because in your current mental state you are not living life you are in some alternative perception world the ancient texts call hell, the place of suffering meaning you were mentally hindered by education into an unsound state of mind or alternate perception reality that is abnormal. I am mindful once the species addresses this education mental hindering reality many problems we face now will fix their self. So this written education neurosis once addressed will solve many problems without the need to even address those problems and until that happens attempts to remedy all the side effects cause by the written education neurosis are simply vain attempts to bail the water out of a leaking boat with teaspoon while gallons of water pours back into the boat. This whole situation is really about understanding as a species we invented something that had some major unintended mental side effects when taught to children whose minds do not develop until they are twenty. Once the mind is restored the fruits of a being are restored and so on a species level once the species comes to grips with the mental hindering caused by written education then the species can start to be restored. As a species we are cerebral giants and that reality is what enabled us to invent written language and math and learning those inventions at such a young age has mentally hindered us to the point of retardation and that retardation or neurosis is what keeps us as a species mentally hindered. This education has turned off the traits of your right hemisphere and reduced them to a subconscious level so if there is any definition of retarded it is a being that has one entire hemisphere of their mind reduced to a subconscious state. Another way to look at it is, if you are not dyslexic relative to your spelling at all, your right brain random access thought patterns are so silenced they are essentially gone from your conscious state and so you perceive the fact you are not dyslexic shows how sane you are or mentally sound when in factually reality it is proof you are mentally hindered and thus mentally retarded as a result of all those years of left brain education. If you show no symptoms of dyslexia that only means you are what is known as a mental fatality to the education and that means your chances of actually applying the remedy are slim to none, the mental damage was too great. The entire point of the land of the free is to show every other nation on the planet what people can be like when they are free, not what people can be like when they are usury focused and thus working at odds with each other. The point of America was to set an example to show all other people of the world that life, liberty and pursuit of happiness can work but we have turned into a dictatorship of control freaks and rule mongers. George Washington would have the heads of the control structure and corporations in this nation on a stake in about eight seconds and that is a fact, you saw what he did to the British who tried to control people with fear tactics. One cannot possibly know what freedom is with the freedom aspect of their mind, right brain veiled, all they can possibly know is how safe they feel when they pass more rules and laws, left brain loves rules and laws and directions because it can't think for itself because it has absolutely no pattern detection or intuition aspects at all. Simply put it is impossible for a human being to make determinations when their pattern detection and intuition has been all but turned off so they become sheep eager to be led. Moses led the people into the promised land, that means he attempted to assist them to restore their right brain traits so they return to consciousness and could thus think for their self again, and being able to make your own determinations means you are free, a free thinker. Moses was attempting to suggest, "When exactly did you determine you are not able to determine your own destiny?" He was attempting to raise the mentally dead.

"But when a long train of abuses and usurpations, pursuing invariably the same Object evinces a design to reduce them under absolute Despotism, it is their right, it is their duty, to throw off such Government, and to provide new Guards for their future security."
Declaration of Independence

Firstly this comment is a repeat exactly in spirit of this comment.
[That whenever any Form of Government becomes destructive of these ends, it is the Right of the People to alter or to abolish it, and to institute new Government] = [But when a long train of abuses and usurpations, pursuing invariably the same Object evinces a design to reduce them under absolute Despotism, it is their right, it is their duty, to throw off such Government,]

The beings who wrote this are saying the exact same thing twice but they simply reworded it. For example:
[That whenever any Form of Government becomes destructive] = [But when a long train of abuses and usurpations,]
[it is the Right of the People to alter or to abolish it,] = [, it is their right, it is their duty, to throw off such Government,]
[alter or to abolish it,] = [to throw off]
What this means is one can rearrange these words and mix them up and come out with the same spirit of what they are saying, For example:

[That whenever any Form of Government becomes destructive of these ends][it is their right, it is their duty, to throw off such Government,]

[But when a long train of abuses and usurpations, pursuing invariably the same Object evinces a design to reduce them under absolute Despotism] [it is the Right of the People to alter or to abolish it, and to institute new Government]

The spirit of these two comments even when intermixed together and rearranged still come out with the same spirit or suggestion. There is no other countries in the world that in their declaration of intent encourages and even give the citizens the right to abolish the government if the government

152

starts infringing on the basic liberties the people are guaranteed. The spirit of these comment is so radical because they are saying "If the government ever gets out of line even slightly demolish it and try a new government and if that one gets out of line even slightly demolish it and it is your duty and right just like it is your duty and right to breathe." Granted it is logical a tyrannical control freak would not agree with that. That's unfortunate relatively speaking. Even I have moments of clarity so to speak, such and such.

[That to secure these rights, Governments are instituted among Men, deriving their just powers from the consent of the governed] This comment in the Declaration is where the concept of "The government serves at the mercy of the people." comes from. Washington said Government is not reason. What this comment above means is the government can never be more powerful than the people or the government is no longer serving at the consent of the people. Simply put, at every election there should be a vote to see if the people wish to keep the government or abolish it and start all over from scratch using only the initial documents that founded the nation as a base starting point.

[and to institute new Government, laying its foundation on such principles..]

The founding documents are the principles. Jefferson said the tree of liberty must be watered from time to time and that means the government must be abolished from time to and everything should be started over from scratch because if one does not do this the government itself becomes an entity more powerful than the people that give it consent to exist. One can look at the government as this entity that started off at the founding of the nation as this weak entity and the people were clearly in control but as time goes by the government starts passing laws and creating amendments that gives it more power and in turn takes away power from the people and then eventually the power balance switches and then the people are serving at the consent of the government and that is not how it is supposed to be so the only remedy to that is to start the government over from scratch using the founding documents are the principle or cornerstone for the new government. The government will always say "No we can't do that we will collapse and fearful things will happen." and that again is just a fear tactic. The deeper reality here is the education favors left brain and left brain cannot adapt to change very well because right brain is the pattern detection aspect and so it loves change because change to it means a challenge, something new to conquer or a challenge to give the mind "daily bread", but since the education makes everyone left brain dominate they hate change so they would resist ever starting the government over even though it is their right and duty to do so, but they don't because they are in that left brain state prone to fear, fear of change. The people would rather live in a tyranny they know than face the unknown which is what freedom is all about. This is not really a conspiracy on the government's side because the government people give their own children the education so a conspiracy is completely out of the question. The bottom line is a being in this extreme left brain state is so afraid they are willing to give up freedom for security because they cannot adapt to change in that extreme left brain state and the unknown is freedom. Another way to look at it is the people have no idea written education and math hinders the mind and the government does not know it either so it is simply the blind leading the blind into a tyranny.

I do not detect a single human being in America in a position of power believes this :
Y = "In humans, the frontal lobe reaches full maturity around only after the 20s, marking the cognitive maturity associated with adulthood"
Z = " If you reflect back upon our own educational training, we have been traditionally taught to master the 3 R's: reading, writing and arithmetic -- the domain and strength of the left brain"

I do not detect a single American in a position of power believes Y + Z = potential mental damage on the mind of the children so they are blind leaders leading the blind people into tyranny, blindly.

["In humans, the frontal lobe reaches full maturity around only after the 20s] What this comment means is a person does not mentally even develops fully until they are twenty so it is impossible they could ever know what being mentally developed is because they get this [reading, writing and arithmetic -- the domain and strength of the left brain] starting at the age of seven so it is impossible their mind ever became fully developed. It really comes down to the fact since the mental development is aborted by the education it is logical the person cannot even tell their mental development was aborted because they are mentally hindered as a result of being mentally aborted. Another way to look at it is the beings were made blind before they were able to even see and so they perceive blindness is normal because they have never experienced or were allowed to see. If this is true - : reading, writing and arithmetic -- the domain and strength of the left brain- then everyone is potentially in neurosis so one has to be able to accept they may be surrounded by lunatics and ego and pride will not allow many to do that and ego and pride are side effects of said neurosis.

X = sound mind at birth
Y = Mind bent to the left starting at the age of seven
Z = Mind fully developed at the age of twenty.

X is aborted by the left brain favoring education so one ends up with a (Y) mind so it is impossible they could ever know what (Z) is like because that development happens long after (Y) occurs. It is like a child that goes blind when they are two years old, and when they are an adult they no longer remember what vision was even like so blindness becomes normal. Another way to look at it is a child is born mentally sound but even then their mind is not fully developed until the age of twenty so it is impossible because of the education they ever experience what it is like to have a fully developed sound mind. The only possible way one can know what a sound mind is like after they get the education is to apply the fear not remedy and restore their mind and then all they will be able to say to the ones that are still of unsound mind, or in the neurosis is "I once was blind but now I see, I once was lost but now am found." and the ones in neurosis will respond with "You are some religious freak shut up." It would make my purpose much easier if I detected ghost and aliens and lizard men because it is much harder to explain elementary cause and effect relationships to being's who are unable to reason because their cognitive ability was aborted starting at the age of seven. It is not important who you see as wise on this planet, if they sense time I assure you they are only mentally hindered into hell and

155

nothing more. They will all say the same thing when I am finished talking to them :

[16:49] [ecstasy] i am very dissapointed and pretty much depresed
[16:49] [ecstasy] never felt like this in my life
[16:50] [ecstasy] I thougt i was the strong type of guy
[16:50] [ecstasy] but in the end ... we are always wrong

Simply put right brain is so powerful when unveiled it will reduce every being that senses time and thus has right brain veiled to their knees in short order. That is not an opinion that is a fact beyond all facts. Right brain with its pattern detection, lightning fast random access processing, intuition, complexity has no equal. One can attempt to use their left brain sequential simple minded logic against right brain but that is simply an act of infinite vanity because that kind of logic is no match for the powerhouse. I am just not use to the fact I still try to reason with the ones that sense time. I am simply unable to dumb myself down enough to use sequential simple minded logic at all at this stage and that is all they are capable of using ever in their big sense of time state of mind. I attempt to tell them it is not me it is simply I unveiled right brain after the education veiled it so all they have to do is apply the remedy and they will unveil right brain and then we are equals and so there is no need to look at me as special or gifted or idolize me in any way shape or form and they take that as me being humble and meek when in reality I am just telling them the facts. I do not even know what meek or humble relative to my perception outside of saying "Thank you" and "Please" oft. I was meek once and that is when I did not try to save myself when my mind said it would be wise to save myself but I am not meek now and I am not humble now because I am not even sure what those concepts really mean relative to my perception. I only know what meek and humble is relative to your sense of time perception not that I ever get off topic. Another way to look at it is a person can be meek once in their life time after they get the education and that is when they are in a position their mind says "run or you will die" in a spooky dark situation and then when they do not run they submit or bow or fear not and after that is achieved one applied "meek" and so one can never be meek again because then they become warriors and are without fear. One has either been meek once or they have not been meek once. If one has not been meek once they are simply in various states of arrogance. One is either fearless or arrogant and the transition from the state of arrogance to the state of fearlessness is the concept meekness.

[Pacbox: "Still at it Rohrer? It's nonsense. Give it up. You're argument holds no water and never will. It's made up out of thin air."]

Perhaps the spirit of fear is normal but not according to the ancient texts. [2 Timothy 1:7 For God hath not given us the spirit of fear; but of... of a sound mind.]
So what gives us this spirit of fear? The tree of knowledge, written education and math because it favors left brain so much is makes the hypothalamus stop working properly as in the hypothalamus starts sending lots of false fear signals. There is much chaff and little wheat.

[<+Tootie> TRohrer : what is your highest level of education? Have you completed high school?]

[If one does not understand a person, one tends to regard him as a fool.] - Carl Jung

The door can be opened with many keys as long as the key fits the lock.

There is a concept called The Devil is in the details. Left brain see's parts or details and right brain is holistic or see's everything as one thing. So a being in sound mind where both aspects are at 50% see's holistically because right brain traits rule the mind when the mind is in harmony. Only a being that got the education and has not applied the remedy has a mindset based on detail or parts. The devil is in the details is just saying the ones that sense time see details, are in extreme left brain state and see parts and they are the devil, the beasts, the vipers, the mental abominations. I won't mention that in my books just my diaries.

10:47:18 PM - As awareness of a situation decreases hope increases. Happiness is achieved when the mind can fully comprehend any situation that arises. A loss is a terrible thing to mind. Wisdom and awareness is relative to grief as sorrow is relative to ignorance. Fear is relative to panic and thus relative to lack of mental clarity. Crying over spilt milk from a leaking container is only required if the mind cannot fully grasp the reality of loss. As fear increases understanding decreases because panic and thus nervousness increase. Being afraid, ashamed, or embarrassed of a word or a sound is a symptom of a delusional disorder because both words and sounds are intangible. Ambiguity is the ability to question everything one has been told is truth. The core of the onion perhaps reveals everything is the reverse of what one believed it to be. Pride and ego separates the wise from the fearful. As logic decreases emotions increase and emotions are relative to fear. Sometimes a tyrant will feel threatened when their control is questioned.

3/15/2010 4:01:03 PM - Depersonalization Disorder is a disorder affecting emotions and behavior. It is characterized by a change in how an affected individual perceives or experiences his or her sense of self.

The education alters ones perception, like sense of time, sense of hunger, sense of fatigue, so it is logical it alters how one perceives their self. This aspect called ego and pride is relative to how one perceives their self and is a symptom of the left brain favoring education conditioning. Low self esteem is a symptom of the pride and ego aspects. This is why the ones that sense time can become very afraid or sad when certain words are said. This is why some children kill their self for being cyber bullied, that is just a symptom of fear of words and also how their self esteem is but the deeper reality is their right brain random access thoughts no longer factor properly into their cognitive abilities. One that senses time can hold a grudge but that is impossible with right brain unveiled because one it like an absent minded professor so one forgets petty comments easily. The reverse thing applies, with right brain veiled, one has a good short term memory but a horrible long term memory and in sound mind one has a bad short term memory but a vast long term memory. Thus the comment: Those who forget the past (poor long term memory; the ones that sense time) are doomed to repeat it. The ones that sense time forgot the ancient texts comments about the tree of knowledge was referring to written language and so they keep harming each other by teaching it improperly. The being that coined the phrase "those who forget the past are doomed to repeat it" was a Spanish philosopher, and the main speaking point Socrates made was no true philosopher fears death. and that is the remedy.

If one goes through the valley of the shadow of death and fears not, they do not fear death. Valley denotes depression, one is never ever going to seek the shadow of death unless they are suicidal mindfully, thus the comment the meek shall inherit the earth, the meek are the depressed and suicidal. They do not believe they have a right to live, and that is the end stage before right brain unveils, but many do not make it from that state of mind, so depression is not depression it is a symptom right brain is attempting to come back to 50%. It is logical the mind seeks harmony, so education veils right brain and then right brain tries to come back to the center and a side effect of that is depression and suicidal thoughts. So the entire concept relative to antidepressants means society is attempting to keep people from unveiling right brain and thus the comment misery loves company. Of course society is in neurosis so they know not what they do. the only kind of being that knows not what they do is a lunatic or an insane person, so Nietzsche said "A causal stroll around the lunatic asylum shows faith proves nothing" The lunatics are the ones that sense time. Simply put even if a person that senses time wants to apply the remedy they first have to be suicidal and depressed and once they are in that area the 9th circle of hell, treason, society will attempt to get them out of there because society, the left brain influence does not want anyone to wake up, unknowingly of course. Nezchez was quite a comedian.

3/15/2010 6:52:20 PM – There is a lot I would like to cover in this poorly disguised thick pamphlet diary but it is just not happening. No being would intentionally harm a child mentally on the scale education harms children mentally, so the only logical conclusion is they got the education and are in neurosis and know not what they do. There is no hope only attempts. Hope is a symptom of inability to comprehend the situation our species is in.

3/17/2010 4:15:25 AM - If we had purpose we would all be going in the same direction. Herding cats into cold water requires a sharp pen.

3/17/2010 2:57:34 PM –

[Luke 1:7 And they had no child, because that Elisabeth was barren, and they both were now well stricken in years.]

This comment suggests a miracle birth because Elisabeth was barren. She was the Mother of John the Baptist and wife of Zacharias.

[Luke 1:13 But the angel said unto him, Fear not, Zacharias: for thy prayer is heard; and thy wife Elisabeth shall bear thee a son, and thou shalt call his name John.]

This is suggesting Zacharias knew and understood the fear not remedy just like Abraham had initially explained so this means Zacharias got the education and applied the remedy and then he figured out what the remedy he applied was, he understood or figured it out = [But the angel said unto him, Fear not, Zacharias] This just means he used the unnamable power of right brain to figure out what happened, what the remedy was.

[Genesis 15:1 After these things the word of the LORD came unto Abram in a vision, saying, Fear not, Abram: I am thy shield, and thy exceeding great reward.]

[Fear not, Zacharias] = [Fear not, Abram] = Both reverse engineered what they did and found out what they did was feared not, to escape the education induced neurosis.

[Luke 1:27 To a virgin espoused to a man whose name was Joseph, of the house of David; and the virgin's name was Mary.]

This is talking about Jesus but in this case Mary was not Barren she was a virgin so this also suggests a miracle birth.

[Luke 1:40 And entered into the house of Zacharias, and saluted Elisabeth.]

This suggests Mary knew Zacharias and Elisabeth so this suggests an association between the two "miracle" birth mothers and families.

[Luke 1:59 And it came to pass, that on the eighth day they came to circumcise the child; and they called him Zacharias, after the name of his father.]

This circumcise aspect suggests sacrifice which means they gave John the education , taught him the written script at a young age , eight in this case, like most children are taught.

[Luke 1:60 And his mother answered and said, Not so; but he shall be called John.]

This is where the female stepped in and made the final determination about what John will be called. This suggests the authority is with the females.

[Luke 1:61 And they said unto her, There is none of thy kindred that is called by this name.]

This comment kindred is referring to those with no sense of time or those that applied the remedy after getting the education or never got the education.

[Luke 1:67 And his father Zacharias was filled with the Holy Ghost, and prophesied, saying,]

[Zacharias was filled with the Holy Ghost] This is suggesting Zacharias had applied the fear not remedy, filled with the spirit means he was under the influence of right brain, the god image in man.

[Luke 2:1 And it came to pass in those days, that there went out a decree from Caesar Augustus, that all the world should be taxed.]

This comment about taxes suggests a control structure. [a decree from Caesar Augustus, that all the world should be taxed.]

This means a taskmaster had determined there self to be ruler over everyone and then started suggesting everyone will pay money to them and if they do not he will punish them. Usurp would be the proper way to look at it. Usurp: to use something without the right to do so. The traditional education forced on people as children by law is also a form of usurpation.

So this is suggesting the adversary. Someone who perceives they have the right to tells other what to do when they do have that right. Since we are all humans there should never be one human or group of humans telling other humans what they should or should not do ever. So this is why armies and threats of fear and violence are required to get people to bow to these control structures because people would not bow to control structures unless they feared they would be punished if they did not bow to control structures. Taxes are just extortion. A control structure will simply say "If you do not pay me taxes then fearful things will happen and the ones that are forced to get the education are infinitely weak minded because they never applied the remedy and they say "How high should I jump oh great taskmaster, knower of all things." Only a mentally hindered human being would be unable to detect the patterns of extortion when it is right in front of their nose.

[that there went out a decree from Caesar Augustus(Governments, control structures), that all the world should be taxed(extorted).]

[Luke 2:21 And when eight days were accomplished for the circumcising of the child, his name was called JESUS, which was so named of the angel before he was conceived in the womb.]

This is suggesting Jesus was also sacrificed as a young age, so this means they gave Jesus the education, the written education. Another way to look at circumcision is it is the mark one gets when they get the education. Other words one gets the written education and math and they have the mark, right brain veiled, so they are circumcised, cut off from right brain traits, and then they have to repent, which is they have to apply the fear not remedy to unveil right brain and return to sound mind and that is a covenant. So this covenant aspect means, get the education but then apply the remedy. It is a tool that requires one to do something after they are taught the tool. The concept is like swimming to great depths in the ocean , one can do that but after they do that they must sit in a decompression chamber and if they do not they die. The deeper reality is it may take one many years and much sorrow to apply the remedy so it is best to get oral education and then get the written education after the mind develops enough so one does not have to apply the remedy because with oral education the right brain aspects are never veiled. Simply put relative to circumcising it is not logical getting ones genitals cut when they are a young child is going to assist them to apply the fear not remedy after they get the written education and math later in life. This is a classic example of beings that have not applied the remedy attempting to understanding these texts and failing miserably and causing greater suffering on their self and others as a result. These are Holy texts and if a being that is separated from God, has their right brain veiled, the god image in man, attempts to translate these texts they will only harm their self because these texts require pattern detection, intuition, and complexity in thoughts to understand.

[Luke 3:2 Annas and Caiaphas being the high priests, the word of God came unto John(he applied the remedy) the son of Zacharias in the wilderness(Tribes, lived in the wild still not in the cities).]

[the word of God] What is the word of God? [Fear not, Zacharias] = [Fear not, Abram] ; so this is where John the Baptist applied the remedy and then he understood what Fear not meant. The complexity is one does not really understand how profound the fear not remedy is until after they apply it and unveil right brain. So this line is explaining after John the Baptist was sacrificed, circumcised (got the education), as a child, he kept the covenant which means he applied the fear not remedy.

[Luke 3:3 And he came into all the country about Jordan, preaching the baptism of repentance for the remission of sins;]

Then John the Baptist started explaining to other people the importance of the fear not remedy after one gets the written education which is what this is suggesting [preaching the baptism of repentance]. John started giving is testimony. He was saying, I got the education and applied the fear not

163

remedy and now I have contrast and can assist you with the remedy by suggesting how it works.

[Luke 3:8 Bring forth therefore fruits worthy of repentance, and begin not to say within yourselves, We have Abraham to our father: for I say unto you, That God is able of these stones to raise up children unto Abraham.]

[Bring forth therefore fruits worthy of repentance] = The meek, the ones that got the education who are depressed because they are ripe fruits that have a chance to apply the remedy, they are showing symptoms right brain is coming back to the conscious state. So essentially the "rich", the arrogant were not even considered for the remedy only the ones in the 9th circle of hell, treason state of mind. So this is suggesting they were aware most were fatalities to the left brain conditioning. Lots of chaff and not much wheat, so to speak.

[Luke 3:16 John answered, saying unto them all, I indeed baptize you with water; but one mightier than I cometh, the latchet of whose shoes I am not worthy to unloose: he shall baptize you with the Holy Ghost and with fire:]

In this comment John is saying "I use the water to get the hypothalamus to give the death signal and then one ignores it" but Jesus has figured out one can just deny their self and that is a much broader explanation in case a person is not near the water they can still apply the remedy, so to speak. So John is not saying his water version of the fear not remedy does not work he is just saying Jesus has a method that anyone can apply even without water, the "those that lose their life (mindfully) will preserve it" Another way to look at it is the "kindred" support each other, the ones with no sense of time, because they are always outnumbered by goliaths vast armies, Goliath being in this case [Caesar Augustus, that all the world should be taxed .] and his minion scribes. Caesar had vast armies and if you did not do as he told you, or paid him money as tribute you faced his armies and that is just like modern day extortion. Pay your taxes or you go to jail and we label you as a criminal and take all your possessions.

Extortion: obtaining something such as money or information from somebody by using force, threats, or other unacceptable methods, and that is what this is suggesting: [Caesar Augustus, that all the world should be taxed.] This is a common theme because Moses had issues with this control aspect as suggested here:
[Exodus 2:14 And he said, Who made thee a prince and a judge over us? intendest thou to kill me, as thou killedst the Egyptian? And Moses feared, and said, Surely this thing is known.]

And the control freak does not like anyone to suggest they do not have the right to be a control freak as suggested in the next comment: [Exodus 2:15 Now when Pharaoh heard this thing, he sought to slay Moses. But Moses fled from the face of Pharaoh, and dwelt in the land of Midian: and he sat down by a well.]

It is as simple as : Give me taxes and money and allow me to rule over you and tell you what to do or I will kill you. That is extortion and that is all civilization is and does. It's very simple, someone is saying "Give me taxes and pay me homage and do as I tell you to do or you die or suffer." And then I suggest "Give me your taxes and give me your homage and do as I tell you to do.", and then the one who wins is the one with a big army of thugs backing them up along the lines of might makes right. Of course once in a while someone comes along who is fearless and stands up to the bully and perhaps defeats the bully or at least gets slaughtered attempting to. I do not detect supernatural I detect a control structure struggling to retain control and beings attempting to deny that control structure. I do not detect ghosts and aliens and lizard men floating around in these texts if you do perhaps you should sit in a cemetery until you feel better. Civilizations control structure is an extortion type situation and it's cornerstone is the education to make people mentally dumb. The control structure in civilization does not care at all about the well being of the people they care about extortion, the common people are looked at as sheep that are a means to an end, money. If the control structure cared at all they would not make you mentally retarded by force of law starting at the age of seven unless they know not what they do and are therefore lunatics. I am saying you are infinitely intelligent and I know how you can restore your mind and the control structure is saying you need to be told what to do and your genes are bad so you need to pay them money so they can tell you what to do or bad things will happen.

[Luke 3:21 Now when all the people were baptized, it came to pass, that Jesus also being baptized, and praying, the heaven was opened,]

This is saying John the Baptist applied the water version of the fear not remedy on many people and Jesus was one of them and they all unveiled right brain and broke the neurosis, curse caused by the written education, the tree of knowledge which is what this comment means : [, the heaven was opened] = their minds were restored, their spirit was restored, they were "raised from the dead"

[Luke 4:1 And Jesus being full of the Holy Ghost returned from Jordan, and was led by the Spirit into the wilderness,]

This is just saying after Jesus applied the remedy in Jordan, where John the Baptist applied his water version of the remedy, Jesus was pondering how he would give his testimony. [was led by the Spirit into the wilderness,] Jesus was compelled to ponder how he would give his testimony and also was pondering new ways to suggest the fear not remedy. Jesus suggested "deny one's self" and also "those that lose their life (mindfully) will preserve it" so his versions suggest a mental self control aspect absent of any material aspect being required such as water.

[Luke 4:2 Being forty days tempted of the devil. And in those days he did eat nothing: and when they were ended, he afterward hungered.]

[Being forty days tempted of the devil.] This is suggesting it takes a while to "warm up" or get use to the no sense of time perception dimension after ones applies the remedy. The remedy is essentially a realignment of one's perception and so one day a person senses time and strong hunger and the next day they do not and this takes some time to adjust to. I would suggest it takes just over a year relative to a calendar to fully adjust to ones new "self".

So the point of this section is: Zacharias was the founder or the center of the revolt against the "control structure" known as the new testaments. Zacharias is the teacher of John the Baptist and indirectly of Jesus and so every being John the Baptist and Jesus assisted with the fear not remedy were also indirect Disciples of Zacharias. Elisabeth and Mary of course play a role in this but Joseph the father of Jesus is not mentioned because Joseph never applied the remedy. Only a person that gets the education and then applies the remedy can give a testimony firstly to the mental or spiritual damage it caused them and then testify about the remedy itself but some do not testify, some don't apply the remedy the full measure. So Zacharias is who started the "new testament" situation, relative to the revolt or uprising against the ruler scribes. Zacharias explained the remedy to his Son John the Baptist and the ruler scribes cut John's head off because he was very good at waking people up using his water version of the fear not remedy and Jesus is proof of that, and Jesus had his own version of the fear not remedy and was effective at convincing people to apply it and the disciples are proof of that.

So this comment is being repeated with John the Baptist and Jesus and the Disciples and many other "kindred", one with no sense of time, ones of sound mind.
[Exodus 2:15 Now when Pharaoh heard this thing, he sought to slay Moses. But Moses fled from the face of Pharaoh]
So this line could be in the new testaments case:
Now when the Control structure heard that John the Baptist, Jesus, the disciples were waking up his slaves he killed them all without mercy because he knew they were putting his taxes (money) , extortion scheme in jeopardy.

So the New Testament was started when Zacharias convinced his son to apply the remedy and his son applied the remedy on Jesus and it worked very well on Jesus and this is what created the testaments of the beings that applied the remedy the disciples so it was like a revival of what Abraham suggested hundreds of years earlier.

[Genesis 15:1 after these things the word of the LORD came unto Abram in a vision, saying, Fear not, Abram: I am thy shield, and thy exceeding great reward.]

Some apply the remedy better or fuller than others and some wake up better than others and it is relative to their mindset when they apply the remedy. The ones who are in the 9th circle, treason longer tend to be the ones who fully mindfully let go of life and that is what is required to fully unveil right brain. The deeper reality is the vast majority of these beings in the new testaments gave their lives testifying and they were killed at the hands of the ones that sense time for doing so, on the commands of the ruler scribes. They all got slaughtered for testifying and so they are all equals, they did not fear Goliath.

[Luke 23:10 and the chief priests (Ruler scribes) and scribes (Minions of the ruler scribes) stood and vehemently accused him (Jesus).] They were saying Jesus was a liar and there was nothing wrong with the written education. They were saying there were no spiritual or mental side effects as a result of teaching all that left brain favoring education to children.

[Luke 22:2 and the chief priests (Ruler scribes) and scribes (Minions of the ruler scribes) sought how they might kill him (Jesus and the ones who had applied the remedy; the ones with no sense of time); for they feared (fear is a symptom one has the neurosis; feared they would lose their control) the people (the common people).]

If the common people ever found out they were being put to sleep and forced by law to mentally harm their own children via written education the control structure on a world scale would have their heads put on platters in about zero seconds. That's unfortunate relatively speaking. The deeper reality is the control structure is in neurosis so they perceive what they do is logical and reasonable and so they perceive it was logical and reasonable to kill John the Baptist and Jesus and the disciples because they were meddling in affairs they should not have been. The control structure was doing the best it could based on its awareness, perception and understanding. An insane person may kill another person and then say

168

"it was righteous to kill that person they were evil." and that person goes to their grave believing that is fact. That is what neurosis is.

[Luke 1:30 And the angel said unto her, Fear not, Mary: for thou hast found favour with God.] Here is a mention of the remedy again.

[Fear not, Mary] This suggests Mary applied the remedy.
There is a hierarchy of control and I will explain it up front. The women are calling the shots relative to attempting to protect the offspring from the mental damaged caused by the written education and they are giving orders to the men to carry out. This is why in these texts the women are not killed but the men are killed because the women are the big bosses so to speak. For example:

[Luke 1:59 And it came to pass, that on the eighth day they came to circumcise the child; and they called him Zacharias, after the name of his father.]

[Luke 1:60 And his mother answered and said, Not so; but he shall be called John.]

This comment is where "they" are attempting to name John the Baptist [Zacharias, after the name of his father] and Elisabeth trumps that suggestion by "they" and calls him John. This demonstrates the women held a great deal of sway. "They" could be referring to the "kindred" priests.

This comment is clearly showing that Elisabeth was the dominate person in this situation.
[Luke 1:39 And Mary arose in those days, and went into the hill country with haste, into a city of Juda;
Luke 1:40 And entered into the house of Zacharias, and saluted Elisabeth.]

This is saying Mary went to the house of Zacharias and instead of saluting Zacharias she saluted Elisabeth. The reason the women are the leaders in this entire situation relative to the education is because the education hinders the mind of the children and the females purpose is to protect the offspring and they do anything they have to including commanding the males to protect the offspring.

This is just a very elementary concept that a female will do anything to protect the offspring and that includes any child. It is the same concept that a female mammal will take care of babies of other mammals even if those mammals are not the same species and sometimes it even goes across the mammal barrier. A female will take care of babies and protect babies is another way to look at it. Just think about a scenario where innocent children are being harmed, who do you think will raise a greater voice to protect children a male or a female? Another way to look at it is, the education taught the way it is harms the children mentally and thus harms the children and the females will not stand for that and so they are incorporating the males to assist them to protect the children from the "scribes", the scribes being males that are teaching the children the education and not suggesting it has harmful mental side effects and also are not suggesting the fear not remedy. The mental damage to the children is not obvious to the scribes because they are mentally hindered by the same education but it none the less is happening and the females are aware of it and that perhaps is all that matters. In a scenario of a house with a man a women and a child, if someone breaks into that house and is a threat to that child the male is the first line of defense then the female is the second line of defense and the male is protecting the female and the child so this means the male is in contrast to the child and the female, expendable.

[Matthew 19:14 But Jesus said, Suffer little children, and forbid them not, to come unto me: for of such is the kingdom of heaven.]

Jesus is saying to the scribes, "Have mercy on the children and at least allow me to suggest the "deny yourself "lose your life mindfully to preserve it" remedy to the children so they do not suffer with their right brain traits veiled after you educate them, scribes." And he is speaking on behalf of Mary and of course Elisabeth. He is saying to the scribes, "If you keep harming all the children with your script education and not suggesting to them the remedy after they get the education the females are going to suggest we butcher you, just like they suggested Saul and David butcher you."

[1 Samuel 18:7 And the women answered one another as they played, and said, Saul hath slain his thousands, and David his ten thousands.]

That did not go over well with the scribes because the scribes are in neurosis and frankly have no idea they are in neurosis because they got the education and no one told them about the remedy so it is impossible they would know they are in neurosis. So the hierarchy relative to the new testament based on actual names mentioned is:

Elisabeth
Zacharias
John the Baptist
Jesus
Disciples

Mary is the heir to Elisabeth.
John the Baptist is the heir to Zacharias.
Jesus is heir to John the Baptist.
James is heir to Jesus as suggested in the Gospel of Thomas:
[12. The disciples said to Jesus, "We know that you are going to leave us. Who will be our leader?" Jesus said to them, "No matter where you are you are to go to James the Just, for whose sake heaven and earth came into being."]

The complexity in all of this is any being that applies the fear not remedy to the full measure alone starts a lineage. For example: Isaac was heir to Abraham and Abraham started that lineage so Abraham woke up on his own.

3/18/2010 2:03:32 AM - The fountain of youth is the no sense of time state of mind caused when right brain paradox traits are restored after left brain favoring education veils them. The mind itself cannot notice time passing so one always perceives they are zero days old and thus the body reacts to what the mind tells it. One still lives 120 years max but relative to their perception they live forever.

Schizophrenia: Characterized by abnormalities in the perception or expression of reality.

The education alters ones perception because it veils right brain traits. One starts sensing time, sensing strong hunger and strong emotions and fatigue so they have abnormalities in the perception or expression of reality.

A person may experience a traumatic event, and then have PTSD, but PTSD is because they recall the memory with strong time stamps and strong emotions attached to it so they relive it over and over but that is only because they are schizophrenic from the education.

When right brain is unveiled all memories are simply concepts with no memory having more value than another one and all time stamps and emotions are absent from them.

3/18/2010 8:36:43 AM – In the year 610 Mohammed said this:

"Proclaim! (or read!) in the name of thy Lord and Cherisher, Who created-Created man, out of a (mere) clot of congealed blood: Proclaim! And thy Lord is Most Bountiful,- He Who taught (the use of) the pen,- Taught man that which he knew not.(Qur'an 96:1-5)

[And thy Lord is Most Bountiful,- He Who taught (the use of) the pen,..]

This aspect of the comment is saying right brain, the Lord, the God image in man, creativity, complexity, intuition is what allowed human beings to create written language and math but the problem was when these inventions were taught to children before their minds even developed there was devastating consequences to their mental development. It is similar to how smoking cigarettes does not do as much harm to an adult as to a child because an adult is already mature. Smoking does not stunt an adult's growth because an adult is already mature relative to growth but when a small child of seven smokes, it does alter their growth. That same principle applies to written education and math except on a mental development level. Simply put one may very well be able to teach written language and math to an adult whose frontal lobe is fully developed, around the age of twenty, and there may not be any unwanted mental side effects but when the exact same inventions are taught to a child starting at the age of seven, whose mind does not develop fully for another thirteen years, the consequences are mentally devastating. It all comes down to one thing. Adults, mentally developed, invented written language and math and everything appeared just fine but then they started teaching those inventions to children and that is where everything went south, so to speak. Written education and math are just like drugs and so one should not give children drugs they should have patience and give the children oral education only until the children mentally mature. If one does not fully understand that concept they should not ever be allowed to be in a position they are able to make determines about children relative to their education. Another way to look at it is when one pushes all the written education and math on a small child they mentally destroy that child and so they in turn destroy that child and there is at least one being in this infinity that does not take kindly to observing small children being destroyed. How much does your vote matter now?

9:45:00 AM - [Matthew 7:13 Enter ye in at the strait gate: for wide is the gate, and broad is the way, that leadeth to destruction, and many there be which go in thereat:]

[Enter ye in at the strait gate] A strait is a narrow. One way to look at this comment is, do the reverse of what society suggests you do. This is a repeat comment of this one : [1 Corinthians 3:18 Let no man deceive himself. If any man among you seemeth to be wise in this world, let him become a fool, that he may be wise.]

[Enter ye in at the strait gate] = [If any man among you seemeth to be wise in this world, let him become a fool.]
Simply put, in the world or civilization ones only goal in life is to get as much written education as one can get so they will make lots of money. That is "wise in this world". Another way to look at the comment is do not follow the crowd, the ones that sense time.

[Matthew 7:14 Because strait is the gate, and narrow is the way, which leadeth unto life, and few there be that find it.]

[narrow is the way, which leadeth unto life] Is a repeat of, it is easier for a camel to do the impossible than for a rich man to enter the kingdom and also a repeat of "the meek shall inherit the earth" Meek being the depressed and suicidal, they do not perceive they even have a right to live at all, that is meek. So this comment is explaining also the parable of Sower, it is saying after one gets all that left brain favoring education chances are slim they will ever restore their mind so it is essentially killing people. It is suggested Matthew was martyred in Ethiopia or Persia so it is a clear indication one could go to any country at that time and find people who needed to apply the remedy because at this time written language, reading and math were in perhaps every country. Martyred means you tell the truth about the mental damage caused by written education and you get butchered. The logic is, if you apply the remedy and tell the truth and give proper testimony without fear the ruler scribes have to kill you or you will wake up everyone. Another way to look at it is a being with right brain unveiled is in a machine state and they learn by speaking or explaining things so if anyone is near them or reads what they say, that person will wake up eventually but from that being in the machine state perspective they are just assisting their self. Another way to look at it is, if I am not assisting anyone that is of no importance because I am certainly helping myself by focusing on the log in my eye. I am becoming a little less ignorant by looking at my own faults or by teaching myself in real time. The concept in the east is "One does good by doing well" and that means focusing on the log in your eye means others may take notice as a result of your focusing on the log in your eye and in turn be assisted and so one assists others by assisting their self. This is also what the concept of life, liberty and pursuit of happiness is. A sound minded being is happy to just work on their own understandings. In the machine state just coming to an understanding is of value yet that is absent of material aspects and is not really taxable so you see it is contrary to the control structures extortion aspects. It is like civilization looks at thinking and coming to understandings as bad or not important but building a tower to heaven is the greatest accomplishment one can ever achieve even if no one lives in that tower and even if they have to level a forest to build that tower. This is the absolute disconnect between the no sense of time cerebral mindset and the material focused sense of time mindset.

3/18/2010 10:04:05 PM - "There is no coming to consciousness without pain. " - Carl Jung : This comment is saying in order to escape the neurosis, extreme left brain state, caused by the education, one has to "let go" when they are in a spooky place at night alone when their mind says "run and save yourself" and simply submit or ignore that signal. That is mindfully painful but required to reach consciousness. That is step one. The next step is going across the river of Styx, the river of anger. You will unveil right brain and soon enough you will become mindful of how intelligent you are and always were and you will become very angry that this mental rape happened to you, and I or no one can assist you with the anger you must go through for many months relative to a calendar to make peace with that aspect. Attempt to be mindful of the comment by Malcolm X - "Anger is a gift." If you look at this anger as a gift it is wise because you are going to have an unlimited supply for quite a few months after right brain unveils and rightly so. Everyone reacts a bit differently but "Crossing the River of Styx (anger)" is very accurate. Try to look at it like as your anger increases you block that anger and your concentration in turn increases so you progress very swiftly on a cerebral level but at first your anger is going to be beyond my ability to explain in words but you will be very angry and so it is perhaps best you stay away from the ones that sense time and speak to yourself for a while because the ones that sense time are afraid of words. You will progress out of that state into extreme cerebral machine state so just go with the flow, the anger will pass. This anger stage is simply your emotions reverting back to a normal state and so you are going along with huge emotions and ego and pride and envy and jealously then right brain unveils and everything is gone and you are struggling to determine where you are at , so to speak. Like the carpet being pulled out from under you. You in fact go from one perception dimension to another in one second and it is quite a shock or transformation. Things that applied in your sense of time dimension do not apply in the no sense of time dimension so you are left with no other alternative than to start all over relative to you are born again. Psychologically you are going to be spitting quite a bit of blood but just be mindful it is expected and a logical reaction to going from an alternate perception back to normal perception dimension. Look at it like you are in hell then you apply the remedy and the river of Styx aspect is you traveling back to heaven or grace.

- "There is no coming to consciousness without pain. " - Carl Jung = There is no coming to consciousness without anger and grief.

3/19/2010 9:25:56 AM -

Post on Forum:

Firstly, the ones that sense time assume because of the "the first man was 5400 years old" delusion that the planet is only 5400 years old.

"The researchers, using a process called optically stimulated luminescence, were stunned by preliminary estimates that the oldest artifacts may date back 40,000 years, more than twice as old as expected."
http://www.aolnews.com/world/article/archaeologists-find-40000-year-old-tools-at-tasmanian-construction-site/19391927

Aborigines are thought to go back as far as 60,000 years, The Hindu people or people of that area of the world are thought to go back as far as 50,000 years and a tribe that lived on an Island near India the BO, are thought to go back as far as 50,000 years.

[Genesis 11:5 And the LORD came down to see the city and the tower, which the children of men builded.]

The Lord is this comment are beings that negated the neurosis caused by written education the tree of knowledge using the fear not, deny yourself remedy. They are Lords or masters of the house, they have sound minds. The education favors left brain and thus veiled right brain traits, the god image in man, so one is called relative to these texts in this comment "men". "Men" are also called, adversary, Antichrist, scribes, Satan, donkeys etc.

For example:
[Mark 1:22 And they were astonished at his doctrine: for he taught them as one that had authority, and not as the scribes.]

[And they were astonished at his doctrine} who is they? The common people, the readers of script or scribes who were reduced to slave jobs because they did not take to "education" very well. Simply put if education and math makes one so wise how come we are not all wise? There one's that sense time, the scribes will say, it has to do with genes or genetics, and that just shows they are not even at the level of reasoning any longer to understand what the tree of knowledge literally is.

[for he(Jesus) taught them as one that had authority, and not as the scribes(the ones who got the education and did not keep the covenant, which is to deny one's self , apply the remedy to the tree of knowledge to restore right brain, the god image in man).]

Why would they say Jesus taught with authority unlike the scribes?

This suggest the scribes were unable to teach with authority because they had their right brain veiled and that is a symptom of learning all that left brain favoring education.
So Jesus applied the remedy and no longer was a scribe. At this time period the women were perhaps not taught the "script" but the men were but even reading favors left brain.

So the reality check is, who started the new testament? Testament simply denotes men who applied the remedy, restored right brain, the god image in man, and testified written education hindered their mind. That is all testament refers to.

[Luke 1:13 But the angel said unto him, Fear not, Zacharias:]
[Genesis 15:1 After these things the word of the LORD came unto Abram in a vision, saying, Fear not,]

Fear not is the remedy because the education hinders the hypothalamus and ones fear is turned way up. So since fear is a symptom of the tree of knowledge, fear not is the remedy.
So Zacharias had a wife called Elisabeth, she was sterile, barren. She had a miracle child called John the Baptist. Mary had a child Jesus and she

was a virgin so she had a miracle child Jesus. So Mary and Elisabeth were kindred or related "spiritually".

So Zacharias knew of the fear not remedy, he told it to John the Baptist is son, John the Baptist created his own version of it called Baptism, one is dunked under water to get the hypothalamus to give the death signal and then they "deny their self" or ignore it and so they fear not. John the Baptist used his version of the fear not remedy on Jesus and so Jesus understood the fear not remedy and he came up with his own version "Those who lose their life (mindfully) preserve it(right brain, restore their spirit, after the eat off the tree of knowledge)" Then Jesus told his version to many people and 12 listened to him and applied the remedy. So the Linage in the new testament is as follows.

Mary was heir to Elisabeth
John the Baptist was heir to Zacharias
Jesus was Heir to John the Baptist
And as suggested in the Gospel of Thomas, James the Just was heir to Jesus

"12 The disciples said to Jesus, "We know that you are going to leave us. Who will be our leader? Jesus said to them, "No matter where you are you are to go to James the Just, for whose sake heaven and earth came into being."

So the remedy from the time of Abraham all the way to the time of Mohammed is the same remedy. One can use Psalm 23:4 as a template to see this.

[Psalms 23:4 Yea, though I walk through the valley of the shadow of death, I will fear no evil:...]
[Psalms 23:4 Yea, though I walk through the valley of the shadow of death, I will FEAR NOT:...]
[Psalms 23:4 Yea, though I walk through the valley of the shadow of death, I will DENY MYSELF:...]

[Psalms 23:4 Yea, though I walk through the valley of the shadow of death, I will LOSE MY LIFE TO PRESERVE IT(mindfully):...]
[Psalms 23:4 Yea, though I walk through the valley of the shadow of death, I will SUBMIT:...]

Simply put if you go to a dark spooky place and your mind says "Run to save yourself or you will die" and you do not run to save yourself you : Deny yourself, submit, fear not, fear not evil, lose your life mindfully to preserve it. So what Jesus suggested was a continuation of the remedy just worded differently but in principle the remedy to the tree of knowledge, written education.

[Luke 17:33 Whosoever shall seek to save his life shall lose it(remains with the god image in man veiled, right brain); and whosoever shall lose his life shall preserve it(restores right brain traits, the god image in man after education veils it).

It's not that education is bad on an absolute scale it is simply one has to apply the remedy after they get the education or they remain mentally hindered and thus mentally and spiritually unsound, the darkness, the serpent.

I do not expect you to believe what I say because you have not applied the remedy so you are a scribe but perhaps it is best you just ponder what I say.
So man did come into being 5400 years ago but "man" is a human being that ate off the tree of knowledge written education and math and did not keep the covenant, applied the fear not remedy, and thus remained with the god image in man, right brain veiled.
So today essentially everyone is forced to get the education, the sinister is proud of its "no child left behind" law and that means its gets all the children and you were one of them so it is not important if you are thinking it did not get you, it factually did get you, you ate off the tree, so now you have to attempt to apply the remedy. You have to attempt to deny your sense of time temple, it's really quite simple. You have to tear down your temple because your temple is built on sand, because the education veiled

179

your right brain traits so your spirit is in the place of suffering. Just be mindful, the battle is within because the kingdom(right brain, the god image in man) is within. You do not have to worry about going to hell when you die because you are factually in the place of suffering right now. Your only purpose in life is to attempt to "lose your life(mindfully) to preserve your life/spirit" If you cult leader does not agree with that he is nothing but a false teacher so avoid him at all costs. No one is going to apply this remedy for you so you have to rely on yourself. You did not put yourself in this situation but only you can get yourself out of this situation. Do not rely on what those around you suggest about the spirit of these words, think for yourself. Very few are even able to apply this remedy to escape the place of sorrow, but it is up to you. No one is forcing you to apply this remedy and no one can stop you from applying this remedy but you. You are your own worst enemy and you are your only chance at the exact same time.

[Matthew 16:24 ...If any man will come after me, let him deny himself,]

10:13:55 AM –
"A woman uses her intelligence to find reasons to support her intuition."
Gilbert K. Chesterton, known for his philosophical and poetic insight among other things. Intuition is a right brain trait. Gilbert was born in the 1870's so perhaps women were not educated as much as they are today so this perhaps explains why he made this observation about women. The trend is all men are educated but at least in his time period women were not educated as much as men were and so it is logical women had a bit more right brain traits at their disposal. Essentially his comment is saying without right brain intuition one can have lots of knowledge but they have no way to determine what is valuable knowledge and what is meaningless knowledge or data, of course right brain pattern detection and intuition is what it used to determine what knowledge is of value. The equation would be.

X = knowledge or data
Y = pattern detection, intuition
Z = intelligence, wisdom
X + Y = Z

So as Y decreases, via written education veiling right brain traits, potential for Z, intelligence decreases.

One can have a universe of data or knowledge but without full power intuition and pattern detection it is just meaningless data. Ignorant men understand women have potential. Less ignorant men understand women have infinite potential. Wise men understand women have infinite wrath potential.

"Action is the real measure of intelligence."
Napoleon Hill

This comment is a repeat of idle hands are the devils workshop or something along those lines. This of course is all relative to sloth. This comment is very vague though and perhaps confusing because it gives the impression if one just goes out and does any action it proves they are intelligent. Intelligence is pretty vague also. Society has determined one's ability to sequence letters in order determines ones intelligence and one's ability to use the left bran favoring number system, math, is also an indicator of one's intelligence which is hardly in the realm of accurate. As fear decreases intelligence increases.

"Be as smart as you can, but remember that it is always better to be wise than to be smart." - Alan Alda

One definition of wise is : knowledgeable about many subjects.
For example here are some subjects certain beings who were considered wise were interested in.

Mohammed : "He was also active as a diplomat, merchant, philosopher, orator, legislator, reformer, military general, and, according to Muslim belief, an agent of divine action."
Alphonse de Lamartine (1854), Historie de la Turquie, Paris, p. 280:

Plato : "philosophy, logic, rhetoric, mathematics, and founder of the Academy in Athens, the first institution of higher learning in the Western world." – Wikipedia.com

One definition of smart is : amusingly clever and possessing a quick wit and showing intelligence and mental alertness.

This is interesting because all of these words are very conflicting and shows the great flaws in written languages absolutism. Word definitions are probabilities not absolutes. Does one want to be clever, witty, intelligent, wise, smart or mentally alert?

There is only one possible way to ensure one is all of those things and that is to have both hemispheres working at full capacity in the conscious state of mind. One problem with being in the extreme left brain state caused by the education is that one see's parts so they are limited in scope relative to what activities they pursue. For example, a person may be an economist but have no other pursuits' and that is because they mindfully perceive oration or military general is out of their scope. Another way to look at it is, if one is a good orator then they may also be a good philosopher, and if one is a good philosopher they may also be a good legislator and if one is a good legislator they may also be a good diplomat, so this is showing one thing leads back to everything. Another way to look at it is if one has a sound mind they can do anything and if one does not have a sound mind they are limited in their scope. The complexity is right brain when unveiled see's holistically so some of these wise beings did not perceive they were good at all of these separate parts, they were labeled at being good at all of these separate parts by beings that only see parts. Is an orator a good philosopher or is a philosopher a good orator? A good merchant is usually a good orator and also a good diplomat relative to selling his wares. The scope of your wisdom is relative to the scope of your understanding and both are relative to the scope of your mind. Simply put, in that extreme left brain state one see's parts so their scope is narrow and in the sound mind state right brain traits rule so one see's holistically so their mental scope is broad.

"Belief is the death of intelligence." - Robert Anton Wilson

There is a bit of humor in this comment. A right brain trait is ambiguity and a belief is when a person "knows" something so they no longer

182

doubt it or have any ambiguity about it and this concept is what can limit intelligence. For example Einstein doubted Newton's law. The belief that written education and math although they favor left brain and even though the frontal lobe does not mature until one is twenty could not possibly have an unwanted mental side effects is the doom of our species and thus that belief limits our intelligence. So the belief that traditional education does not have any unwanted mental side effects has a gargantuan effect on the intelligence of our species. The reason we do not question traditional education is because traditional education has veiled our right brain trait called ambiguity which is a questioning aspect. Simply put we do not question traditional education because the questioning aspect of our minds has been silenced by traditional education. "Knowing" means one stops questioning what they know and so one becomes a slave to what they know and so questions become the enemy.

3/20/2010 7:53:16 PM – The aspect of right brain called holistic is what allows a person to get the spirit of words instead of seeing separate words. This getting the spirit of a sentence is what allows a "poet" to take one comment and rearrange and substitute the words to appear like they are saying something completely new.

As awareness and comprehension of a situation decreases hope increases. The above comment relative to getting the spirit of the sentence is exactly like saying.
Ignorance is bliss. That is exactly like saying: As ignorance decreases grief increases. That is exactly like saying : As awareness and ignorance decreases hope increases. That is exactly like saying : As bliss decreases, awareness and comprehension of a situation increases. This is not a magic trick or a symptom I am so wise. It is a symptom the holistic aspect of right brain when right brain traits are in the conscious state of mind allows one to get the spirit of any sentence and then one can reword the spirit of that comment and make it appear to ones that sense time, who only see parts, in perceiving it is a completely different idea or concept. Another way to look at it is I am simply taking a concept and then explaining it with different words so it appears like a different new idea or concept but not relative to my perception only relative to the perception of beings

that have right brain holistic aspect's veiled. Everything you know what remains the glow. That comment is exactly like saying: Knowledge when arranged properly creates the illusion of wisdom. That's another way of saying: Knowledge is only good if one can make sense of it. One can look at the collective knowledge for the entire species and if they have right brain traits veiled it may appear like we have progressed so far but from a holistic point of view as a species we are still attempting to understand the tree of knowledge when taught improperly to children has some devastating mental side effects. As a species we are still attempting to grasp a reality suggested perhaps 5400 years ago and we still have not grasped that reality at all. Simply put, the moment the species questions if traditional education hinders the mind of a child then education has to stop. The moment it was suspected asbestos had potentially unwanted side effects relative to a person's well being they did not start putting it in more homes they stopped putting it in homes. What this means is traditional education has to just take a time out completely until the species can get a complete understanding relative to what damage it causes on the mind of children then it can slowly start to understand how to educate children properly. Another way to look at it is we are not in any rush to educate the children because with the current brand of education all we are doing is mentally hindering children and thus killing them. A human being cannot function properly if their right brain aspects are veiled even one degree let alone to a degree those traits no longer even figure into their conscious state of mind at all. Is money more important than a child's mind? Money cannot be more important than a child's mind or mental well being ever because when a person has an unsound mind money does not matter. A being is better off with a sound mind because with an unsound mind everything as a result of that is rotten. The complexity here is a child's parents got the education and so they influence that child so they will turn that child into what they are even without education. Simply put if a parent got the education they are a left brain influence and they will turn their child into a left brain influence by default relative to:.

"Children are educated by what the grown-up is and not by his talk." - Carl Jung

What is a parent? A left brain influence because they got this [reading, writing and arithmetic -- the domain and strength of the left brain].

So perhaps one can detect how deep the hole is we are in as a species. A child needs a parent to raise them but if that child associates with left brain influenced adults they become left brain influenced. If a child hangs around an adult that perceives money is the most valuable thing relative to existence then that child will do whatever they have to do to get money regardless. When that child is unable to get money they will perceive they are a loser or dumb because that parent has instilled in them "the value of money." Money is not more important than a child's mind and acceptance is not more important than a child's mind and education is not more important than a child's mind and that concept applies to the parent also but society believes exactly the opposite. Society believes without education you are a loser, without money you are a loser and without acceptance of your peers you are a loser and that is not possible because the moment a human being takes that first breath as an infant they are a winner. So there are many "invented" measures of worth that are based on false assumptions. Does traditional education mean you are wise? No if you get enough of it an nearly everyone does the right brain traits will be hindered so creativity, intuition, pattern detection, complexity in thoughts will be hindered so one will end up unwise. If one is unwise does money matter? No because if one is unwise they need to do something relative to the remedy and the remedy does not require money it requires great self control applied at the proper time and so money will not assist one to regain their mind. So this means one did not get education to become wise they got education to gain acceptance of their peers and to earn money potentially and it cost them their perfectly balanced mind. This means education costs one the only thing that matters, a sound mind, and all they got back was the potential for money and acceptance from peers. Simply put they made a very bad trade off. They did something for acceptance and the promise of material wealth. This of course is the underlying reality, to ones in the neurosis, ones that sense time, they only perceive they did something wise. This is because disharmony perceives disharmony is wise and harmony is unwise. The reality is the longer that child is separated from the traditional education and separated from left brain influenced beings the better off they are but society believes exactly the opposite. Society believes if they can start the education on a child at the age of five that is better than starting it on a child at seven when in reality that is much worse. A mother that is pregnant does more damage to that fetus if she starts doing drugs when that fetus is two months old then if when that fetus is eight months old. Same concept applies to a child, that child's mind factually does not mature until they are twenty so the longer one allows that mind to mature before pushing all the left brain favoring influences on that child the better. This means it is better to not educate your child at all until they are twenty and simply teach the child orally until they are twenty. Simply put when you go to apply the remedy you are going to find it is a bit more difficult to mindfully kill yourself than you ever dreamed and then you will have a contrast that maybe it was best if you never had to apply the remedy to restore your mind in the first place. You are not going to apply the remedy if you are happy or pleased you will only apply the remedy if you are what the ones that sense time call, suicidal. If you are in a dark spooky place and you have one single attachment to life as you know it when your mind says "run a spooky is coming to kill you", you will run like the wind. That is a harsh price to pay just so you can do math and write words on paper. When you were a child if your peers and the adults around you had even an ounce of insight or foresight they would not have put you in the situation you are in. What that means is you are the only one you can count on because the ones you assumed you could count on destroyed you mentally and even at that they will deny it because they perceive they helped you by "educating" you starting at the age of seven. You may perceive anger if you understand that is fact but I assure you once you apply the remedy and feel how powerful right brain is and become mindful what your entire life could have been with that powerhouse cerebral clarity you will be on a vengeance mission. You simply do not know what anger is until you fully unveil right brain and fully understand what you were robbed of. You will say, "You made me blind but I escaped your blindness and now I can see and I want heads on stakes." Then you will swiftly ponder yourself to the next reality "Society is doing to children exactly what it did to you." And then your anger and grief will multiply. You will be in a situation if you do not block that rage and anger you will be destroyed by it at the levels of awareness and intuition you will have when you unveil right brain. You may perceive emotions are so valuable but I assure you at the levels of awareness you are at when right brain is unveiled emotions are a death sentence. The complexity is once right brain is unveiled the random access processing of right brain will not allow that rage to fester but having said that one has to be mindful it takes nearly a year and a half to adjust so it is important not to make any rash decisions in that time frame. One will apply the remedy and about thirty days later right brain unveils and then one is going to be pure rage and anger mentally but keep in mind you are in progression, you are waking up or returning to consciousness, sound mind, so let right brain do its processing and do not get all caught up in what you are experiencing because you are in a progression and it is swift. There is nothing you can do to make others wake up so be pleased you woke up and then do your best to give your testimony. Avoid thinking you can solve this problem on a species scale because you cannot solve this problem. You can do best by learning to concentrate and that will assist you to give a more clear testimony to others because when it all is said and done the remedy is for one to mindfully kill their self and that goes against the grain of society itself. If society is asked the question "When you are in a dark place alone and your instinct says "Run something is coming to kill you", society will always say "It is wise in that situation to run" and that is exactly the opposite of the remedy. Society says "Those who save their life are wise" and the remedy is "Those who lose their life mindfully restore their mental life." You are not going to perceive you are out in a dark place alone at night applying the remedy you will perceive you are crazy and foolish to risk your life and then when your instinct says "run you will die if you do not" and if you ignore that and just allow it, then you are suicidal. You are suicidal to not run in that dark place when your indistinct says to run, so to apply this remedy you have to factually be suicidal. One has to be pleased with the prospects of death and so one has to ask is all the education worth having to go to that mental place just to restore their mind to how it was when they were a small child?

[Jeremiah 8:8 How do ye say, We are wise, and the law of the LORD is with us? Lo, certainly in vain made he it; the pen of the scribes is in vain.]

Vain: failing to have or unlikely to have the intended or desired result.

What is the main goal of traditional education?
[Genesis 3:6 And when the woman saw that the tree was..... a tree to be desired to make one wise,..]

Traditional education veils the right brain because it is all this : [reading, writing and arithmetic -- the domain and strength of the left brain]

So in getting the education one veils their right brain traits so education does not [make one wise] so education is vain because it fails [to have or unlikely to have the intended or desired result.] It is very unlikely you will be wise with your right brain traits veiled because they are the most powerful traits of the two hemispheres so it is factually impossible you could become anything but mentally hindered and mentally hindered is mentally retarded. Simply put someone you trusted decided to hurry up and make you wise as a child and in that rush they instead made you factually mentally retarded and now that is done they want nothing to do with you so only you can negate that mental retardation and when you do apply the remedy and when you feel how powerful right brain is you are going to be seeking heads and the ones in neurosis will tell you it is no big deal if education hindered you so don't worry about it. Simply put by restoring the mind you were born with you are jumping into an ocean with no bottom and you will either become a master at concentration and be the Lord of concentration or you will be looking for the fastest way out of this narrow. You will ponder what Jonah said for the rest of your life :
[Jonah 4:3 Therefore now, O LORD, take, I beseech thee, my life from me; for it is better for me to die than to live.]
I am not a very good judge because I am mindful I went through the progression of waking up very swiftly. Simply put if you apply the remedy to the full measure you wake up fast and if you do not apply it the full measure you may get stuck on the way up the mountain and so you may have to apply it further. The only rule of thumb is when you lose all sense of time mindfully you have applied it the full measure. The complexity is in the full measure state the right brain random access thoughts are so swift you will not be able to fester these thoughts of anger and rage long enough to act on them and so you will slowly purge all emotions. You may perceive this concept of "we can turn it around as a species " but we cannot

so you have to let go of these left brain "closure" aspects because there is no closure. The whole point of focus on the log in your eye after you apply the remedy is to enable you to give your testimony better and better. You may perceive I repeat myself often but that conclusion is based on your assumption I can win and your assumption I am not in infinity. One cannot repeat their self in infinity because everything is one continuous comment, no beginning and no end. I am fully mindful I cannot win or lose so repeating myself means nothing. The logic line is "If I don't repeat myself I will win" and "If I do repeat myself I will lose." But I am already to the stage I am mindful there is no way to win or lose so I go with the flow. My right brain random access processing has sifted through every possible scenario and it comes up with "impossible to win and thus impossible to lose on a species scale." There are far too many left brain influenced beings that got the education and will not be applying the remedy to turn things around and even if they were forced to apply the remedy the vast majority could not, they would just go insane further attempting to apply the remedy. This is an indication of the damage caused by pushing all the left brain favoring education on the mind of a child whose mind does not even develop until they are twenty. If there was a law that said everyone who gets the education has to apply the remedy the vast majority still could never do it. The vast majority is not recoverable, they are mental fatalities. The meek which are the depressed and suicidal have a small chance but that is it. The only hope our species has at all is to attempt to not put the children in neurosis state of mind to begin with and the problem with that is the vast majority is left brain influenced so they are in neurosis and they would see that comment as evil or bad or improper or stupid or foolish. The insane can only see sane advice as insanity.

If a person can be convinced money represents freedom they will become a slave to it. Hell is the inability to detect the inability to detect reason.

3/22/2010 4:43:46 AM
"Character is higher than intellect. A great soul will be strong to live as well as think."
Ralph Waldo Emerson, was a poet and philosopher among other things.

Cognition is relative to reason, perception and intuition.

Intellect is relative to someone's ability to think, reason and understand. So cognitive ability is relative to intellect. The antonym of intellect is stupidity. The definition of stupidity is lack of intelligence, perception, or common sense. This is all just going around in a circle. There is an aspect associated with left brain called rational that is : showing evidence of, clear and sensible thinking and judgment, based on reason rather than emotion or prejudice. This one aspect is why it is assumed left brain is so powerful. In the extreme left brain state caused by the education ones emotions are very powerful and long lasting because right brain random access is veiled so one can maintain a prolonged state of emotions. So this comment, based on reason rather than emotion or prejudice, relative to left brain rational is confusing. If one has a sense of time then their right brain traits are veiled and so their emotions and very pronounced and so it is unlikely they have much rational because rational is relative to reasoning without emotions affecting ones decisions. The concept of giving up your freedom for a little security is relative to not being rational because a perception of loss of security or seeking security is relative to emotions. It is simply making a decision based on emotions. This can all be reduced down to fear of words. Someone says some harsh words to you and then next thing you know you are depressed or angry or bitter or even hostile and that is relative to lack of rational thinking and lack of rational thinking is relative to lack of intellect and lack of intellect is relative to lack of cognitive ability and lack of cognitive ability is relative to stupidity and all of those things are relative to ones perception and intuition and intuition is a right brain trait and the education veils it and on top of that education by veiling right brain traits alters ones perception and that is also relative to cognitive ability. Simply put all the left brain education makes one stupid and stupidity is lack of intelligence, perception, or common sense. So this means common sense is relative to perception and also intuition. So this comment by Ralph, "Character is higher than intellect." does not really make any sense because character is relative to intellect and intellect is relative to cognitive ability. Simply put if you are stupid your character demonstrates that but deeper still stupidity is relative. Any human being with right brain traits veiled even slightly is stupid relative a human being that is of sound mind or in mental harmony. If a person of unsound mind compares their self to a person of unsound mind they may appear to have

190

common sense and a well founded cognitive ability but when compared to a being of sound mind they would appear stupid. So it comes down to this definition of stupidity: extremely rash or thoughtless behavior. Thoughtless behavior is relative to lack of cognitive ability and also relative to lack of intellect which is simply saying lack of common sense. So absolute common sense is a mind that has both left and right brain traits factoring into ones decision making in equal proportions and that means if either hemisphere's traits are veiled even slightly that reflects on ones common sense. Is it rational to force years of left brain favoring education on the mind of a child of seven when it is understood their frontal lobe does not even develop until they are twenty? No it is stupidity to do that yet society as a whole perceives it is rational and thus society as a whole is lacking common sense because they all got the education and thus their cognitive and intellectual ability is greatly hindered.

Cognitive ability and intellect is relative to character and common sense as stupidity is relative of lack of cognitive ability and lack of common sense, and character and stupidity are both relative to perception and intuition. Simply put once right brain intuition is veiled by the left brain favoring education ones perception is altered so ones cognitive ability is reduced to the level of stupidity. Of course this comment in the ancient texts written thousands of years ago is saying that quite clearly.

[Jeremiah 8:8 How do ye say, We are wise, and the law of the LORD is with us? Lo, certainly in vain made he it; the pen of the scribes is in vain.]

[How do ye say, We are wise, and the law of the LORD is with us?] = How is it possible you have the image of god, right brain, factoring into your thoughts processes and thus factoring into you character, common sense, cognitive ability and thus your intellect when in order to learn written education, script and math, you have to veil your right brain traits? It is saying the pen of the scribes is not in vain as long as your goal is to become stupid and mentally hindered. So wisdom is relative to cognitive ability, intellect, common sense and thus perception and intuition and so once traditional education hinders right brain intuition and thus perception is altered only stupidity reins relative to ones cognitive ability. That's a nice way to say the ones that sense time pose no threat to me because they have been systematically conditioned into a mental state of stupidity and thus they lack the common sense to apply the remedy to restore their mind. Right brain suggests there are not more than 6.7 billion beings that sense time so right brain suggests their numbers are manageable. As for me, I go with the flow. This whole situation is coming down to one aspect only. I have no obligation to prove anything to anyone relative to society, in reality society has to disprove this fear not remedy works. Simply put the fear not remedy works every single time it is applied properly. It takes quite a bit of mental self control to apply the remedy the full measure and so one has to be in the proper mindset to apply the remedy but it works every single time it is applied properly, so society as a whole has to attempt to disprove it works. When they attempt the remedy properly it will work and what that means is traditional education will be proven to hinder the mind and so the fear not remedy is the proper solution to the mental altering that happens as a result of written education and so then society is going to have to weight if applying the remedy is worth the benefit gained from teaching children traditional education starting at the age of seven. When it comes down to it the very fact I understand the remedy to the neurosis so well proves I negated that neurosis and it was not because of a physiological traumatic accident it was a one second mental self control exercise relative to being in a meek and humble state of mind, suicidal, at the proper time in the proper situation and that in essence is what the remedy is. I don't detect ghosts, aliens or lizard men. Since this whole situation is just about negating a mental hindering caused by written education, the tree of knowledge, it is not logical to look at this situation on one hand as literal battle simply because the remedy can only be applied on an individual level. For example, a person that has been very depressed and suicidal or a person who is very addicted to drugs, or a person that perceives life sucks and life is not worth living for any reason is a prime candidate to apply the remedy because they have "seen enough" of the extreme left brain state of mind caused by the education. One can even look at this exercise as a complete perception altering alternative to what is known as "normal mental state' because a person never felt their mind at full power when it is at full power at the age of twenty or so relative to the frontal lobe maturity so this "no sense of time" state of mind is an absolute perception altering situation where one will not even be able to relate to their "sense of time" life. I am mindful it is not logical an actual war would solve this situation because it is not even about physical things. There are of course methods one can go part of the way into the perception altering but it takes this ideal "meek" state of mind to apply the full measure fear not remedy. I will tell you I meet some people I knew before the accident and I could tell after a while visiting them they were human beings with their minds turned down and it is not their fault. The ones that sense time may seek to find fault but in absolute reality a person gets this education at the age of seven and so they cannot possibly, logically be found at fault. This also means the adults who put the child in that state of mind were also as children put in that alternate sense of time state of mind so they are doing what is logical relative to their sense of time state of perception. Because the remedy alters ones perception on an absolute scale it is logical beings from either perception reality would perhaps become caught up in their perception world and lose track of the fact there are two separate contrary perception worlds one can live in, or has a choice to live in.

X = sense of time perception dimension
Y = no sense of time perception dimension
Z = how everyone starts out when they are born relative to mental perception
A = written education
B = oral education until the mind develops

$$A + Z = X$$
$$B + Z = Y$$

The very fact I am aware the concepts suggested in the last five hundred words or so are relative to right brain creativity, pattern detection and intuition and left brain "absolute" detection which is contrary to right brain ambiguity shows it is not logical I have such strong ambiguity yet still can make absolute statements shows I am using both hemispheres in equal portion. What is perhaps complex would be the fact I am so aware I can actually detect which part of my mind is working. This is best understood when one is aware it has been nearly sixteen months just to adjust to this no sense of time perception reality. This suggests the change of perception is so great, it takes one mentally a long period to adjust. The reason there has been a war relative to these two alternate perception realities for some long is because of this equation.

$$B + Z = Y$$

If there was only oral education until the mind develops then everyone would perhaps be in no sense of time perception reality. This means beings in the no sense of time perception reality tend to be beings that applied the remedy in one way or another and so they are simply suggesting there is another reality of perception and it is the reality of perception human being are supposed to be in but the traditional education, the tree of knowledge, has placed one in the sense of time perception reality. This whole argument relative to applying the remedy and going to the no sense perception reality is, no sense of time perception reality is where you should be on an absolute scale. This means something unforeseen has entered the equation, written education, and because it is taught to a being at such a young age it determines that beings perception contrary to how their perception should be on an absolute scale.

So there are two parallel universes relative to mental perception and the education taught as it is taught drags one to the alterative perception reality out of absolute normal perception reality, no sense of time reality. Simply put the human species invented something that pushed them into an alternative sense of time perception reality that is abnormal on an absolute scale. Another way to look at it is as a species we were in the normal perception reality "right road", the no sense of time perception reality, and then we invented written education and that threw us into the "left road", sense of time perception reality. If I used the comma's properly in that last sentence, call. I quote "me" or "I" often.

So this means the main argument from the ones that returned to the no sense of time perception reality is they have to make it look attractive of course it is rather attractive so there is no need to sell it much because it is the reality everyone should be in on an absolute scale. Simply put, no sense of time perception , sound mind reality is where everyone should be before the written education induced altered sense of time perception reality came into being as a side effect of learning written education and math. One might suggest because of written language and math we ate off of a rotten fruit and it put us all in this hallucinatory alternate sense of time state of mind, altered our perception. So on a species level we ate off this fruit and it altered our perception and so we can keep the fruit but we have to apply this fear not remedy so the ill effects of eating off the fruit can be negated. The complexity is although that is perfectly logical and reasonable to understand , the ones in abnormal sense of time reality are unable to reason essentially and that is logical because they are in alternate perception reality in contrast to absolute reality perception, how everyone should be. It is illogical everyone should be in an unsound state of mind on an absolute scale because nature weeds out the abnormalities in all species and also on a species level. Simply put, if human beings naturally had their right brain traits veiled we would have died off by now and a deeper reality is because we now have our right brain traits veiled because of the written education and math we are doomed to die out and thus the written education and math will be fatal to our species if the remedy is not applied and / or we completely alter our education methods. This means that certain people who are in sense of time perception reality simply may not be able to return to no sense of time perception reality because it requires a great deal of "being fortitude' to apply the remedy to the full measure. In order to increase the chances there must be many avenues one can take to reach the no sense of time perception reality and this is relative to the concept of all roads lead to one. The "one road" relates to the holistic state of mind a being is in, in the no sense of time perception reality. This creates a situation where the species itself must create a situation to allow for these two distinct perception realties. Simply put these two perception realties are not supposed to be at all on an absolute scale so it is a division or rift created in the species as a result of the written education and math education methods, so the said division is manmade. Because the written education created the rift it is logical beings that return to no sense of time perception reality would not be able to use the written education and math well and this also explains why ones in the no sense of time perception reality have trouble living in the sense of time perception reality influenced "world". Another way to look at it is, the education created a rift in the spices and the beings that were pushed into the sense of time perception reality continue to do the same to the children so they have built up a large majority, "civilization" and it's not a matter of fighting them literally it is a matter of convincing them that it is simply not the perception reality they should be in on an absolute scale. This removes all barriers relative to people because this whole situation comes down to human beings having been thrown into alternate perception reality as the result of a manmade invention. So the solution to convince the ones with sense of time to come back to no sense of time perception reality would be to explain this entire situation on this planet relative to our species and religious wars and the vast majority of the problems mankind is facing from social to economic to mental health issues are symptoms relative to the mental side effects of the written education and math. One thing to note is the ancient texts attempted that and failed. Not one ancient text or one religious belief system but all of them. This means religion itself is simply mankind's argument to return to the no sense of time state of mind everyone should be in. So any being that is associated with any religion anywhere that has a sense of time is not a true advocate for that religion because religions purpose is to convince a human being to apply one of the many fear not remedies to return to no sense of time perception reality and so that is what a false teacher is relative to the texts. Simply put if one is not in the no sense of time "team" they certainly will not be promoting it will they? Another way to look at it is a being with a sense of time certainly cannot promote or speak about what it is like to have no sense of time because they cannot relate to it. This is an aspect of the rift because a person in the no sense of time perception reality would not be in support of the sense of time perception reality and that applies the other way around also. So it all comes back to the "absolute equation" : B + Z = Y

Y = no sense of time perception reality
Z = how everyone starts out when they are born relative to mental perception
B = oral education until the mind develops

Y, no sense of time perception reality is the absolute relative to how human beings perception should be.
Simply put when a person asks what is normal, the answer is : Y = no sense of time perception reality. This means one cannot exhibit behavior

relative to absolute normal behavior if they are not in the no sense of time perception reality. Another way to look at it is a bowl cannot travel upstream against the current. A human being cannot be in sense of time state of mind and behave like a "normal" human being that is in absolute normal state of mind, no sense of time perception reality. The bowl is always going to go with the current and if one has a sense of time their right brain traits are veiled so they are going to behave relative to that, against the current. That's a nice way of saying once a being gets the education they are in an alternate unsound abnormal state of mind and it is illogical they would be able to act like anything but a mentally unsound being in an alternate abnormal mental state of perception. Another way to look at it is disharmony tends to behave like disharmony. Another way to look at it is disharmony has to get very lucky to achieve harmony and that works both ways. One might suggest I went though quite an ordeal to return to no sense of time perception reality but relative to my perception I cannot relate to that very well because it happened in the sense of time perception reality. What happened to me in the sense of time perception reality is more like a concept or a dream relative to my perception and that is logical because the remedy brings one into the no sense of time reality on a scale of an absolute perception reality. This of course is relative to the concept in the ancient texts about resurrection, transformation and born again. Some call it finding the kingdom so the kingdom is the no sense of time normal perception reality. The word kingdom denotes the absolute normal reality perception or how everyone is born, the ideal plane, the middle way. So this means the entire species is born into the no sense of time perception reality but the education takes them out of that and so they have to apply this remedy to return to how they were as a child relative to their perception reality. The complexity is the ones in sense of time perception reality have greatly hindered cognitive and intellectual abilities a result of being in the abnormal perception reality. Because of the rift created in the species it is logical there should be a leader for each perception realities. Since the ones in the no sense of time reality are of sound mind and thus do not have self esteem issues they would always vote for their self as leader because they all have infinite ego's so it is logical I vote myself leader of the ones with no sense of time with the understanding everyone else in no sense of time perception reality votes their self leader also. The complexity is in no sense of time perception reality everyone is a leader but since they have no sense of time they only learn in real time so in helping their self they may also assist someone else as a side effect. This is relative to the comments, one does well by doing good, focus on the log in your eye and the ever popular "mind your own business". The spirit of these comments is suggesting, since a being in the no sense of time perception reality can only learn in real time or operate effectively in real time they tend "influence" ones in sense of time perception reality because they appear to be "fountains of wisdom" when in reality the ones operating in real time get better as they go along because they detect new patterns , a right brain trait that is very instinctive when right brain aspects are at full power, so that combined with lightning fast random access processing they are only able to be in two modes. Either the high concentration state where they are pondering new concepts and ideas and the humor state where they make causal observations using this pattern detection and when they identify the pattern and comment on it the ones in the sense of time reality perception perceive that is a funny observation they did not recognize because they have their normal pattern detection aspects turned way down because the education veils right brain traits. For example Sigmund Freud said "Ambiguity is the inability to tolerate ambiguity."

Relative to my perception I found great humor in that comment because it was a very accurate description of the situation between the ones that sense time perception reality and the no sense of timers. So it was a very obvious observation and that is relative to pattern detection and even the word neurosis is in fact a jab the ones that sense time, so to speak. Simply put, ambiguity is a right brain trait and the ones that sense time have right brain traits veiled, and the fact they sense time proves right brain paradox aspects no longer figure into their perception, so it is logical they would have trouble with ambiguity because their right brain traits are veiled and one of those traits is ambiguity. So this pattern detection is what allows one to have a sense of humor relative to observations and so a person that is a comedian that makes casual observations would indicate they have very strong pattern detection capabilities. This pattern detection is very powerful and the fact the education silenced pattern detection when it silenced right brain may be the fundamental reasons we became very violent as a species relative to wars on each other.

So, this pattern detection is silenced by education and so we become less than what we should be and that means we become mentally hindered to the degree we resort to war against each other because war is not really possible in the no sense of time perception reality simply because war relies on losing. There cannot be a conflict between two beings that get better and better into infinity because they have normal pattern detection relative to absolute normal perception state. Another way to look at it is, two machines that adapt and get better and better as they receive more data would exterminate their self because the purpose is not ever to win or lose the purpose is to seek further patterns and understandings and get better and better into infinity. It is similar to mutually assured destruction on one hand. What this means is our species is so mentally powerful when in sound mind state we would never attack each other over things most wars in civilization are over because no one would ever lose.

If there was an army of one million men in with no sense of time firstly they would think for their self and be their own leader in order to get better and better and that may assist ones in that army around them and the entire army would be in that same mode so no soldier would need to be led. There would be a concept or purpose and everyone would go about solving it their own way but the complexity is they are so intelligent they would rule violence out so they would not be in an army or warring army. This is similar to how mammals operate also, there are no armies of one species seeking to harm their own species and it is not because they are not intelligent, it is because they never got their right brain pattern detection veiled, so essentially they exist in the no sense of time state of mind and they get better and better without any assistance at all as long as their right brain trait, pattern detection is at full power. I detect some patterns about these books as a whole. In the early books I was very angry or emotions based in my words but as each book progressed I stopped using emotions at the end of the comments like I did at first and so as the emotions decreases from volume to volume the concentration increases. This is a very logical concept because it is just elementary that if you do not think with your emotions one can think clearly, relative to the definition of rational : based on reason rather than emotion or prejudice. Prejudice is a symptom of the neurosis caused by favoring the left hemisphere too much which is what written education and math does. Simply put, one cannot be prejudice if they have a holistic perception so this means prejudice is on one hand a symptom of seeing parts, a left brain trait, and so as one favors that left brain more and more by getting more written education they see parts more and more they become prejudice. Prejudice is seeing or hearing a sound or a behavior or an image and determining one is not pleased with it. That is what the seeing parts reality does to one, it makes one prejudice and thus one cannot be prejudice in the machine state, no sense of time state, because they would be in the holistic perception state and that means essentially everything is pleasing relative to:

[Genesis 1:10 And God called the dry land Earth; and the gathering together of the waters called he Seas: and God saw that it was good.]

[Earth] + [Seas] = [saw that it was good.]= holistic perception , the absence of prejudice.

Prejudice is relative to emotions and since prejudice is caused when left brain "see parts" aspect is turned up to high or favored too much, and that prejudice is what causes the emotions but on a neurological level it is just the hypothalamus is not working properly on a mental level, not a physiological level. A being in the sense of time reality may see a color they do not like and say "I am not pleased what that color but I am pleased with this color." This means if they do not get the color they want they may become emotional or if they get a color they are not pleased with they may become very emotional because in that left brain state they see parts far too strongly and it harms them because they have an aversion to them. Their perception is making colors they are displeased with as a result of being in that extreme left brain state seem "evil" so they react in what is known as "emotions" to escape these "parts" their unsound mind is suggesting are "bad" parts because the education favored left brain so much when they were very young they go around suffering because they see parts when in an absolute scale of mental well being one simply does not see so many parts so they have less prejudice but only if you definition of less prejudice is, they are unable to be prejudice perhaps at all when "seeing parts" aspects are at the normal level of power.

X = one that senses time; left brain seeing part state of perception
Y = one that has no sense of time; right brain holistic sound mind state of perception
Z = 10 colors
A = has an aversion to a color or is displeased with a color
B = no aversion to any color
C = Emotional state

$$X + Z + A = C$$
$$Y + Z + B = C$$

If one is attempting to deal with a problem, staying alive, the fewer emotions they have the more concentration they have. An animal's ability to survive and deal with problems is relative to their emotional state. This explains why as emotions increase decision making processes decrease and so chance of physical violence increases and the emotions are increased when left brain is favored so much because one has an unnatural aversion to many things because they see parts far too much and so that makes them violent or prejudiced and that can lead to violence. So this entire concept of war is relative to after written education and math was invented but that also applies to war against each other. Simply put we are of one species, human beings, and this education has bent our minds so far to the left we actually see other human being as not being human beings because the "seeing parts" aspect of perception is turned up way too high. At these levels of "seeing parts" one can actually see their own relatives and children and friends as "not human" which means they have an aversion to another human being because they see parts so strongly in that sense of time perception reality. It is logical as a species we should have an aversion to ourselves because we inadvertently conditioned ourselves into such an extreme left brain state of mind with the written education so we see parts, a left brain trait so strongly we have issues coming to terms with ourselves and members of our own species to the point we have this mental aversion that is abnormal. Some beings that sense time are more prejudice than others but every single being that senses time is very infinitely prejudice to many parts relative to absolute mental harmony. Simply put beings of sound mind have no prejudice, so any prejudice is infinitely too much. It appears

I have prejudice but I perceive I am keeping clear of the ones I detect are prejudice by the nature of the perception state they were conditioned into unknowingly. I detect that is a logical solution to avoid a potential threat but it is not based on emotions or fear it is based on logic. This of course is not absolute because in reality, one with no sense of time has no prejudice and thus no absolute morals because their only purpose is to come to further understandings and thus detect more patterns and thus get better and better. One complexity is money and economics gets in the way of that to a degree or is counter productive to the reality a human being in a sound mind state only get better and better on a level of progression that keeps multiplying. When a being only thinks in concepts and ideas, then they can move swiftly over details, left brain traits relative to seeing parts, and move onto the next idea but if money or economics is an obstacle they have to stop progression and so their understandings are hindered. It would be similar to having this flood gate opened called a sound mind but it is behind a wall called materialism ,money and economic aspects and so only a small portion of that flood of concepts and ideas are going to get through. This perhaps certainly shows it is illogical we did this to ourselves on purpose, put ourselves in the sense of time perception reality, it shows this written education and math had unintended consequences and put us there. It is very strange but people with both hemispheres at full power or in full harmony on a mental level are not even capable of prejudice and so they are also not capable of a very strong emotional capacity because they are in the now, but also because right brain random access processing keeps the thoughts coming in random order. That indicates as a species we are so intelligent in the sound state of mind we do not even detect any idea or concept or point of view is really bad because everything may lead to a pattern detection opportunity and thus a chance to progress further in understandings. The deeper reality is that sound state of mind is exactly why we invented written education and math to begin with, it was the result of a concept or idea that came to fruition. If one thinks about written education and math it is logical it would have spread to essentially the entire species because our nature in the sound mind state is to take anything and adapt to it and use it to come to further understandings with no prejudice. So written education is exactly like a computer virus because our species in the sound state of mind had no prejudice and saw those inventions as good things that would assist us in progression so we were just like children in the sound state of mind relative to we had no prejudice and we accepted these inventions and it turned out to be a bad invention relative to having unwanted mental side effects. Another way to look at it is we were of sound mind and thus "children" of God, God being in that no prejudice no sense of time perception reality.

[Genesis 1:10 .... and God saw that it was good.] = no prejudice

So a small child has no prejudice because they are of sound mind and their "seeing parts" aspect is at normal levels. The very fact we have over 189 separate countries proves we see way too many parts, so to speak. Simply put there is not 189 different sub species of human beings there is only one species of human beings. There is not even ethnicity that is simply a symptom of seeing way too many parts. It is logical man was violent to each other even though they saw holistically because relative to their perspective conflict in a violent nature is really just an opportunity to come to further understandings and not an all out war for land or resources. Human beings before written education certainly might have had a skirmish but never a world war of country against country over land and resources because these skirmishes were used as an experiment to see what could be learned but in general everyone was docile because human beings in sound mind see holistically or without prejudice.

[Genesis 2:25 And they were both naked, the man and his wife, and were not ashamed.] = no prejudice. This comment is relative to pre tree of knowledge perception which is the no sense of time state. This seeing parts aspect is so devastating because it means one has aversion to other concepts and ideas and that alone means their mental progression is hindered. If one has 10 ideas but because their mind is bent so far to the left they see's lots of parts and thus they have aversions to some parts which incites emotions they may ignore some ideas or concepts for no other reason than they have an aversion to that particular idea or concept simply because if one see's parts they have judgment and judgment is relative to prejudice. If a person dislikes a word they have a prejudice. If a person dislikes certain music they have a prejudice. This also applies to food and many other things. Religion for example. The world has these religions that are all suggesting methods to achieve the no sense of time perception reality but the species is all in the left brain state and only see's parts so it will see the different religions and have an aversion to one or more, because they see parts and thus have prejudice. Simply put religions are belief systems and they are all slightly different in detail but are holistically one thing in principle, remedies to the tree of knowledge, and the fact society has issues with one or more religions proves they are seeing parts way too much. One might suggest the paths to the no sense of time perception reality are many because it is difficult to cross back to the no sense of time perception dimension. It is difficult to go from one dimension to another is a proper way to look at it. One can go from sense of time reality to no sense of time reality, but it requires this one second fear not mental technique and it only requires a bit of mental self control at the right moment. So it is easier to look at it like when a person is born they are in no sense of time perception reality and then they associate with beings in the sense of time reality and they are going to incorporate that into their own understandings through contact and eventually they will go to the sense of time reality and then if they want to come back to absolute reality, no sense of time reality, they just apply the remedy and they make the journey back but it takes a while to get warmed up like maybe a year and a half after that journey. This is an indication how powerful going from one dimension to another dimension is. Two separate dimensions in one space at one time. One is going from a dimension where prejudice is strong, see parts is strong, aversion to ideas and concepts and colors and sounds to a dimension with no prejudice and is totally contrary or anti to the prejudice dimension one has no prejudice just like young children but the illusion is, these beings are not children they are sound minded human beings and human beings minds are so strong when it is in harmony they may appear to be hyper intelligent but in reality they are in this machine state and get better and better on a scale of minutes relative to a clock. Simply put if a sound minded human ever became attached to the material world they may destroy the world because they keep getting better and better at whatever they are doing so it is another failsafe relative to human beings are docile in no sense of time , sound mind state because they are so intelligent and so good at pattern detection and processing and come to understandings so swiftly the thought to be violent or be greedy would be pondered out of before it ever materialized. If beings that get better and better at no matter they do very swiftly, any type of large conflict would end in the species killing itself off so that is why wars started after written education and math inventions Another way to look at it is human beings are docile until they become abnormally prejudice because of too much left brain favoring written education and thus start seeing an abnormally high amount of parts in their everyday perception. Another way to look at it is, if I became greedy for money I would find a way to get all the money and in my efforts I would only get better and better until I had all the money because I would never be after the money I would only see the purpose of getting all the money as a challenge to become better. Other words the money is not the purpose, putting myself into a position I have to use this extreme pattern detection and intuition and lightning fast random access is the purpose. Another way to look at it is I am factually not writing books, I am factually detecting patterns and coming to further understandings and it just so happens I am explaining everything relative to the history of mankind in the process but that is not my purpose, my purpose is to test the limits of these right brain traits and in turn teach myself and become better and better. What this means is the more impossible the problem is the better. Another way to look at it is I unveiled right brain so well by accidentally applying this fear not remedy I can solve any problem there is perhaps in this universe in short order but I am also aware that will only serve the left brain carpetbaggers and their money making desires so I will not do that with the understanding that will perhaps piss them off and perhaps they will determine if they want that money they have to apply the remedy so they will have this kind of cerebral power. I am not prejudice I am just simply not going to do anything that is contrary to my ultimate purpose and that is logical. I think you would describe my ultimate purpose as assimilation. I am assuming control. Something along the lines of might makes right. I am pleased with right makes might. That certainly blew it.

Once there was a single dimension existence relative to perception relative to humans. Humans invented something that when taught to especially young children transport the child into an alternate dimension of perception. This happens over a period of years when the children associate with ones in the alternate sense of time dimension and if they eat off the tree of knowledge, written education. What this means is the entire concept of religion is simply methods to get back to the normal dimension. This means we are traveling dimensions so we have progressed to the point in intelligence we played around with dimension travel knowingly or unknowingly and use written education and math to accomplish it. This means the first scribes were perhaps playing with dimension traveling technology and it got out of control. One might suggest the scribes were messing around with sorcery, dimension travel, and perhaps they summoned something from the time dimension or found the time dimension, or the prejudice dimension, knowingly or unknowingly. Be mindful beings in the machine state only seek further understandings. This is logical because the spirit of the scribes is very destructive because they are in an alternate perception world and are reacting to the absolute world and others around them relative to that alternate world perception and they are reacting improperly because they cannot reason well in an alternate reality dimension. Humans can only exist in the dimension they are born into called sound mind or both hemispheres working in exact harmony, the no sense of time perception dimension. So these "scribes" were playing around with dimension or time travel knowingly or unknowingly and they found a way to do it, but once one traveled to the alternative perception dimension they could not longer function in this world or in the normal no sense of time, sound mind perception reality. The scribes were perhaps not evil or bad they were just sound minded humans experimenting in the no sense of time machine state. They went to this alternate perception dimension and then they could do all these strange things like build towers to heaven and create things using math like a pyramids and they appeared magical to the "normal" human beings that were still in no sense of time normal perception dimension. So these scribes did not physically travel to another dimension they mentally traveled to the absolute alternate dimension, the sense of time dimension and they did that by favoring left brain using these left brain favoring inventions to an abnormally great degree.

All human beings must be notified the written language and math are perhaps really just perception dimension travel inventions. In learning these inventions at a young enough age the child is gradually transported to the alternate perception dimension and it is because these ones who invented script and math were really inventing dimension travel methods knowingly or unknowingly. This means perhaps human beings were so intelligent even 5400 years ago when written language, the dimensional travel invention, started to take off they had already reached a level of dimensional travel and perhaps in fact accomplished that task perhaps too well.

I am not talking about theoretical dimensional travel I am explaining human beings perhaps figured out how to travel to new perception dimensions just by favoring one hemisphere of the brain for a period of time yet were still here on earth and the invention they used is what we call written language and math. It is however possible we did not intend to invent a dimensional travel invention but that would mean we are so intelligent we are getting ourselves in trouble with our vast intelligence because or our normal nature to experiment to come to further understandings. So this sense of time dimension the written education takes one to, known as the place of suffering in the ancient texts or hell, is a dimension in this dimension. Simply put we skipped past the concept of space travel and were in the going to alternate dimensions type of travel knowingly or unknowingly. So the logic is the scribes invented this dimension travel tool and relative to the west that would be the Samarians, and other people heard about it and started using it but at first only the older males, they appeared different in their actions relative to the ones that did not use the dimensional travel tool, written script and math. This is relative to the comment demonically possessed. A possessed person reacts to things that are not really there, they are unable to reason with what reality is anymore. Simply put they were transported to an alternative perception dimension by favoring left hemisphere so much and they are acting weird relative to how we as a species acted in the normal no sense of time, sound mind perception dimension. That is logical a person transported to another perception dimension as a child would grow up acting adverse to their environment and to their self and to others because they are in an alternate perception dimension mindfully attempting to deal with reality, the normal no sense of time perception dimension. The ones that sense time are having trouble dealing with reality because as children they were transported via learning the written education to a complete alternate perception reality dimension. So once in a while a child accidentally or by following the fear not remedy gets back to normal no sense of time perception dimension and attempts to explain it to the species and the ones that sense time called them certain names like shepherds. A shepherd is attempting to explain to the species we in one way or another knowingly or unknowingly keep transporting ourselves into an alternate dimension with that tree of knowledge invention but it is very difficult to reach beings that have been transported as children to an alternate perception dimension. Another way to look at it is, you were transported to an alternate perception dimension as a child because some human beings messing around with dimension travel 5400 years ago knowingly or unknowingly let their little invention get out of hand and you would know them as scribes. The scribes were a cult and it was a special society and one might suggest they were quite effective dimension travelers and you inadvertently got caught up in the consequences of that invention but it is time for you to understand that and come back home to the normal dimension. You have had enough of the alternative perception dimension haven't you? I know the way you can get back to normal dimension but you just have to trust that I would not tell you anything but what I understood to be the proper method to get back. I would not tell you I accidentally found a way out of the alternate perception dimension one is rushed into when they learn the written language if I had not accidentally found the method to get back to standard perception reality. I am compelled to repeat it because I perceive the words may not be enough to convince you that you are factually in an alternate perception dimension within the normal perception dimension.

Normal perception dimension = no sense of time, sound minded harmony dimension
Alternative perception dimension = Ones perception is slowly altered to the point they go to a different dimension of perception completely. Sense of time perception dimension.

The way the dimension travel works is, one favors the left hemisphere so much with those inventions they have a complete perception change and that means they are in a different dimension. This means if you go to any person on this planet that was taught written education and math that has not yet applied the remedy to get back to normal dimension they will tell you they sense time and perhaps tell you everyone senses time. I would not tell you sense of time is proof one is in the alternate dimension if it was not proof. The most important thing to focus on is the remedy or the method to get back to normal dimension. I am simply a human being that accidentally escaped the dimensional travel "spell" and I am telling you how I did it so you can return to the normal dimension. I am not your cult leader I am just telling you how I escaped alternative perception dimension reality and although it may sound odd one could consider it perhaps takes a lot of our very powerful minds to travel back to the normal dimension but in fact because it is on a mental level it is physically painless. What this means is after you apply this remedy in about 30 days you travel back to normal dimension reality and you get a big mental "Ah ha " sensation because you returned to reality or normal dimension and you can function quite well in normal perception dimension one might suggest. Simply put everything you have on earth right now will not disappear after you apply the remedy because you are simply traveling back from a dimension you were teleported to inadvertently as a child as a result of learning and adults dimension traveling tool. This means when you were perhaps ten to fourteen you traveled to an alternate perception dimension so one has to ask what does IQ even mean when we were fourteen we were already traveling to a perception dimension using our minds. How much are money and technology valued at on a scale as children we all essentially traveled to an alternate perception dimension with our minds and to a literal alternate dimension? Another way to look at it is I was not depressed and suicidal because I was as a being, it was just I was not doing too well in the alternate perception dimension so I left it in the funniest way and I left it well. Simply put I traveled to the alternate perception dimension as a child and found out how to get back to normal dimension by accident so I am a sort of dimensional travel expert. What that means is, if you want to travel back to normal dimension I have explained the methods used to do it and there is no pressure and there is nothing anyone can do to stop you from traveling back to normal dimension, you can do it. No one is going to harm you if you cannot travel back to the normal dimension but if you wish to travel back it is my purpose to continue to explain methods how you can do it and then you get to decide if you wish to travel back to the normal perception dimension, to home. Your mind is so powerful as a child you traveled to another dimension unknowingly within the normal dimension and so I am just attempting to tell you if you want you can come back to the normal dimension. You went to another dimension as a child via mind travel and you were never told how to get back. My purpose is to tell you how to get back. I do not want any money from you I just want to tell you how to get back to normal dimension because I know you would do the same for me if you escaped the alternative dimension. So this fear not comment is in actuality the ticket home so to speak from the alternate dimension written script takes one to. So although the ones that sense time perceive education lasts 12 years essentially that is not 12 years of education that is twelve years to perform the dimension travel ritual. Sometimes a person does not take well to the ritual or aborts the ritual and they end up trapped between the two dimensions relative to perception. So the complexity to this entire situation is, the ones that sense time are in an alternate dimension and so they are attempting to get out, using material methods because they are no longer at the level of intuition to understand what they are seeking is mental, they traveled to a dimension that made material things very attractive and so they try to find a way out with material things because they are not aware they traveled to that alternate dimension with their minds as children inadvertently by performing this ancient dimensional travel ritual called script and math dimension travel ritual. This means math was perhaps invented as an alternative method of travel but when both are combined one travels very far or perhaps very fast or faster. So one obvious illusion is, mankind invented written education and math and became wise, the reality is mankind perhaps invented dimension traveling tools and mankind did both at once and traveled to a very strange "seeing parts, prejudice, emotions turned up very high , sense of time" dimension via mental travel routes. So the comment "The kingdom is within" means one has to get back to the normal dimension using the mind, the kingdom within, and the "key" or "ritual" to "open the door" back to the normal dimension and that ritual or key is called "fear not."

X = alternate dimension traveled to using "script and math" rituals.

Y = normal dimension, returned to using "fear not" ritual.

So this means we are simply perhaps way to intelligent because we are traveling dimensions and screwing ourselves up unknowingly. We are attempting to travel to the moon and to mars but in reality we are factually at the level of traveling to other perception dimensions so it perhaps would appear quite vain to go to the moon or to mars or to anywhere in the universe at all since we can travel dimensions and never have to leave our homes and we can travel to other dimension even as children so that is how intelligent we are, so someone needs to factor in traveling to other dimensions on their IQ scale. This means every single person that is proficient at written language and math even up to the age of sixteen or even younger has traveled to another dimension and if they sense time they are still in that dimension.

Be mindful. I sensed time less than 2 years ago relative to a calendar and now I do not, so I mentally traveled back from that alternate sense of time dimension and I did it using the ancient "fear not" ritual accidentally.

So you traveled to a dimension and once you got there mental ability is diminished and that alternate perception dimension even negated some of your mental abilities so now you cannot get back. So out of sheer dumb luck I stumbled into the ritual needed to get back to normal perception dimension and so now I am telling you that ritual so you can come back. I am not suggesting you are dumb I am suggesting you are so intelligent you went to another dimension using your mind unknowingly and once you got there it hindered your mental ability and so you could not get back easily. Perhaps it is beyond you ability to understand you not only traveled to another dimension using your mind, you did it as a child and you do not even remember doing it and neither did I until I escaped by sheer dumb luck back to normal dimension. So since we can travel to other dimensions using our minds it perhaps looks rather silly we are fighting over land and resources. Simply put who cares about killing over land or resources or greed or money or material things when you can travel to other dimensions with your mind. You perhaps do not believe you traveled to another dimension with your mind but I am telling you that you are infinitely more mentally powerful than I can explain to you in infinite books. I will not be mushy with you because I do not want to be put on a pedestal because then that will only encourage others to forget they can travel to dimensions with their mind just like I did when they apply the "fear not" ritual concept. This is not a joke. I am not attempting to make you feel ego or pride because those are illusions caused by the alternate dimension you are in. The most important thing to remember is you can only travel back using your mind and using the fear not ritual. Anything relative to material things will not help you get back. One must come back using mind travel and the "fear not" remedy is something of the fuel to make that journey. Another way to look at it is, the fear not ritual excites great emotions "find the shadow of death and fear not" , excites emotions and those emotions are used to travel back to normal dimension. So it works something like this. One seeks out a situation they will perceive they will die, that is the level of emotions required to make the full journey back to normal dimension, so when one achieves those emotions they ignore them and this creates some sort of propulsion system on a mental or thought level and that is what brings one all the way back to normal dimension, and this is all happening on a mental level and has nothing to do with physical travel. Again I am telling you to your face you can travel perception dimensions because your mind is so powerful so you do this fear not ritual to come back to the normal dimension. Simply put I know what I am saying is fact because I dimension traveled twice and you only traveled to another dimension once, and that is not enough travel to detect patterns in the travel so I have detected patterns in the travel only because I made two trips so far, once as a child to alternative dimension and now I traveled back to normal dimension. So simply understand you played around with "sorcery", dimension travel as a child unknowingly and you went to another dimension and it is no big deal perhaps it is some sort of rites of passage for the species and the goal is to try to get back to normal dimension and the ones that make it really stand out but in reality they are just experts at dimension travel only because the made it back and thus have contrast. I am saying I was in your alternative dimension just like you are now and I applied the fear not ritual by accident and came back to normal dimension and that is a fact and that is true and yes we are that mentally powerful, we invented how to travel to other dimensions using our minds 5400 years ago knowingly or unknowingly and well things just got out of hand, so to speak. You and I are on the same planet, but mentally you are in an alternate dimension and your sense of time is the proof you need to detect you are in alternate dimension. Do not worry about the details simply stay focused on the remedy. Your ticket back to normal dimension is that remedy or ritual. - 3/22/2010 6:53:53 PM

3/23/2010 4:06:36 AM – Granted this is getting a little deep so details are needed. No matter what I suggest that will not apply the remedy for you.

"[Demotic (from Greek: δημοτικός dēmotikós, "popular") refers to either the ancient Egyptian script derived from northern forms of hieratic used in the Delta, or the stage of the Egyptian language following Late Egyptian and preceding Coptic. The term was first used by the Greek historian Herodotus to distinguish it from hieratic and hieroglyphic scripts. By convention, the word "Demotic" is capitalized in order to distinguish it from demotic Greek." – WIKIPEDIA.COM

This comment is suggesting the Greeks called Egyptian written language Demotic and that word means "popular".

Imhotep, means "the one that comes in peace".

"In priestly wisdom, in magic, in the formulation of wise proverbs; in medicine and architecture; this remarkable figure of Zoser's reign left so notable a reputation that his name was never forgotten. He was the patron spirit of the later scribes, to whom they regularly poured out a libation from the water-jug of their writing outfit before beginning their work." - James Henry Breasted – archeologist describing Imhotep.

[In priestly wisdom, in magic, in the formulation of wise proverbs] This may be suggesting a cult or the first cult of the "dark arts" namely dimension travel.

[formulation of wise proverbs]

The definition of formulation: to draw something up carefully and in detail.

Details which are parts is a left brain trait. So this comment [draw something up carefully and in detail.] is saying to focus on left brain traits or favor left brain.

[formulation of wise proverbs] So this comment is also saying wise proverbs were used to focus or favor left brain traits. So this means that just reading is the method used in this cult and so that was its worship or that was its god. Simply put they would create all these wise proverbs and people would read them over and over because they were attractive. The spirit of the proverb was attractive. Think about all the wise proverbs you have read in your entire life. Someone writes a wise proverb and then it becomes something that person is quoted from. If the wise proverb is good it is remembered and so in order to keep it in circulation it is written down and so when a person reads they are actually just favoring left brain.
[reading, writing and arithmetic -- the domain and strength of the left brain]

[reading, writing and arithmetic] These aspects are in order of left brain favoring. Reading favors left brain less than math does but both are heavy left brain favoring inventions. So people saw these wise proverbs and they wanted to be able to read them. So people could read but not all of them were scribes so many could read, some were scribes and some went on to the heavy left brain favoring invention math. Math is all parts so it's all left brain. The numerical system is built on sequence. Imhotep in (2650-2600 BC) and this perhaps is very close to the time of Abraham. 2600 BC is very close to the invention of written language in this area of the world. Somewhere around 5400 years ago is when Samarian was invented in 3500 BC. Sumerian is thought to be the oldest written language on earth and it stands out from hieroglyphics because it started using characters instead of pictures to make syllables. Imhotep was the chief priest of the Sun god Ra in Heliopolis. Every time a person reads something they are favoring left brain and that is either just an unintended consequence caused by the invention or an intentional consequence. So reading is a good way to keep track of long term records and information but in order to read you have to favor left brain because reading is made up a letters and they are details and they are arranged in sequence and sequential sentence structure. Another way to look at it is there is no written language or readable language that is in random access relative to spelling and sentence structure. Perhaps I do not need to tell you why a number system would not work if it was in random access. Like counting would be 2,8,5,10 and that would keep changing or never fixed. Every time someone did a math problem or wrote a word down they spelled it differently so sequencing and thus attention to detail are required and both of those traits are left brain traits. If you think about writing and consider when spelling a word you have to pay attention to details relative to its sequence, how you spell the word "correctly". So this spelling the word properly which meant focusing on details was a sort of way to become popular. If you could read you were popular. If you could read and write you were more popular. If you could read and write and do math you were most popular. So popularity was attached to these inventions but the trade off is, to become most popular you had to favor left brain very much and even if you could just read, you wanted to read everything you could find for if nothing else but the "wise proverbs". So think about the present day. If you can read but can't write or do math you are considered quite "unpopular". In society they make sure everyone gets all three including the heavy left brain favoring math for maximum popularity potential and the word Demotic means "popular".

Dimension: a level of consciousness, existence, or reality

So all of these left brain favoring exercises altered our perception and we went to an alternate dimension knowingly or unknowingly on a conscious level and thus we are existing on a mental level in that alternate dimension. Our thoughts were of the alternate dimension but we were still in physical form in normal dimension so we were divided. It appears very much like it was an accident and unintended consequence but much of the comments about this era are all biased and what that means is they are all still using the "popular" scale. They say this being was known to be very wise because he studied medicine and was able to scribe and was an architect and that suggests math.

This is what Imhotep's name meant :Chancellor of the King of Egypt, Doctor, First in line after the King of Upper Egypt, Administrator of the

Great Palace, Hereditary nobleman, High Priest of Heliopolis, Builder, Chief Carpenter, Chief Sculptor, and Maker of Vases in Chief.

Relativity suggests everything is relative to the perception dimension one is in.

Doctor requires numbers, reading and writing. Imhotep wrote some books on medicine. That means people were reading his books. Someone writes a book an another person reads it to "gain wisdom" but in reality they are favoring their left brain and thus "losing wisdom" or veiling their right brain traits by favoring their left brain traits so much because they are being taken to the alternate perception dimension. So the more of these left brain favoring inventions you were proficient at the more popular you were and Imhotep served under the Pharaoh and became very popular. So this popularity that resulted from learning all of these inventions is what created the control structure known as civilization. The most popular person, the person most skilled at reading, writing and math would be highly regarded and be in a position of power. So since Noah had a son Abraham and one of Abrahams' brothers has a son named Lot and Abraham is the first to suggest the fear not remedy so Abraham had to have been alive very far back, perhaps past 2600 BC. So Samarian is invented in 3500 BC so somewhere between the period of 2600 BC to 3500 BC is when Abraham lived and it perhaps was much closer to 3500 BC because the Torah starts off with talking about the tree of knowledge, then Noah comes along and then his son Abraham comes along then Abraham teaches the fear not remedy to his brothers son Lot just as he taught his own son Isaac and Abraham and Lot went to war against the scribes which were perhaps many of the people at that time because many could at least read to get that pride and ego boosting "popularity" recognition. So it is kind of like a good drug but it has a side effect that the better you get at all three inventions eventually you perception changes and you achieve an alternate consciousness dimension, altered reality or altered perception dimension. The very fact we somehow invented something that completely altered our conscious state to an alternative dimension or alternate reality means we either planned it or we accidentally did it. The complexity here is once one applies the remedy they can still use the inventions and I do not perceive one can condition their self back so that means the inventions are not really a completely bad thing they simply have this altered perception or perception dimension transport side effect from learning them initially. This means the fear not remedy was one of the first forms of "medicine" relative to an antidote to treat this altered perception mental state caused as a side effect of learning written language, reading and math and this was known as the covenant in the Torah. The seven deadly "sins" are symptoms or signposts one is in the alternate perception dimension. Deadly would mean if one is exhibiting those symptoms they are in an alternate perception dimension and a human being cannot exist there so they will die if they remain there because they can only function in the no sense of time normal perception dimension, the perception dimension they were born into.

One problem is this name : Imhotep, means "the one that comes in peace".

[the one that comes in peace] This may be an indication he was not exactly what he was claimed to be.
He came in peace and spread his "wise proverbs" all around and when people started reading them they were slowly favoring left brain and then slowly it altered their perception completely. It would be like if I baked 10 cookies that were very sweet and each time you ate a cookie your perception altered a bit but the cookies were so sweet you wanted another one and when you ate the last cookie your perception was completely altered permanently.

[Genesis 3:1 Now the serpent was more subtil (charming) than any beast.....] = Imhotep, means "the one that comes in peace".= [priestly wisdom, in magic, in the formulation of (wise proverbs(charms))]

The first rule is, I am in an alternate perception dimension mentally, I do not perceive time and you do, so we are in alternate conscious states.
[Dimension: a level of consciousness]
It is logical we would not see eye to eye on many things at all.

There is some kind of mental energy or emotional energy that is created when one "faces the shadow of death and then fears not" which is the remedy to the neurosis caused by learning education.

I am not as angry as I was to begin with but the point is, I escaped the neurosis, the sense of time dimension, and I came back to the normal dimension, sound mind, heaven, ideal plane, nirvana, and I am in a mental state of perception alternate to yours.

In my state of perception I have no prejudice, I see holistically on every level. I am attempting to reach ones that sense time and are still in the alternate dimension.

Let's break this dimension aspect down because it is very complex yet quite simple at the same time.

I am attempting to show the ones that sense time the way out of the neurosis, the matrix, hell, alternate dimension. The remedy is harsh relative to the ones that sense time. You are one that senses time..... You are one that senses time..... You are time that senses one.... You are one that senses time..... You are time that senses one.... You are time that senses one..... You are time that senses one....

.

Anyway the point is, one is born with no senses of time, or in mental harmony and all the left brain favoring education, makes one have a sense of time , it veils right brain traits to subconscious level, so one goes accidentally into an alternate perception dimension mentally.

10:42:56 AM - It is perhaps a bit more difficult communicating with beings in other dimensions than the space movies suggest.

6:15:38 PM – The ones that sense time have been thrown into an alternate perception dimension or reality on a mental level and in their attempts to make everything "work" they continue to create more rules and laws and moral codes to make their world of perception make sense but it will never work because they are in an alternate perception dimension attempting to work in a normal perception dimension. Instead of negating that alternate perception state they are in and returning to normal perception dimension they are trying to adjust to living in a false perception dimension and that is not possible to do so they suffer attempting to make it 'work". One way

218

to look at it is human beings are born in the no sense of time perception dimension and in one way or another the left brain favoring education pulled them into a sense of time perception dimension so the show is over because that is an abnormal perception world and human beings are not supposed to be able to live in that sense of time perception dimension ever, they just suffer attempting to live there. The ones that sense time have been attempting to put a square block into a circle hole for over 5000 years and it shows. When a rule is broken a tyrant is reminded control is fleeting. Mankind's great achievement is written language, reading, and math and questioning if those tools have unintended detrimental mental side effects will be mankind's greatest achievement. Happiness is relative to cognition and thus relative to perception and intuition. Once the right brain intuition and pattern detection traits are hindered by the left brain favoring written education and math a beings perception and thus cognitive ability is hindered and in turn they become a mentally non viable being that is a threat to their self and those around them. -3/23/2010 7:38:45 PM